'I will not ask to come in.'

'Please *do* come in, Mr Smith,' Mary said in a pleasant tone. 'I am well enough to be out of bed, if not downstairs, and certainly well enough for a little conversation.'

'Conversation? I'm not very good at that, having lived so much abroad, you know, and in such rough places. I fear I'm more at home in the stable than in the drawing-room.'

'Well, this is neither. And I cannot believe you have never felt at home in a lady's bedchamber!'

Dear Reader

Petra Nash is back in Masquerade with her latest Regency, HEIR APPARENT, where all is not as it seems. You'll love it. And then to India where it seems that the sins of the parents will be visited on the children, the intrepid hero and heroine of Yvonne Purves' latest adventure, SCANDAL IN THE SUN.

Watch for more loving and excitement in the months to come. . .

The Editor

HEIR APPARENT

Petra Nash

Masquerade is a trademark published by Mills & Boon Limited, Eton House, 18–24 Paradise Road, Richmond, Surrey, TW9 1SR.

First published in Great Britain 1992 by Mills & Boon Limited

© Petra Nash 1992

Australian copyright 1992

ISBN 0 263 13297 8

Set in 10 on 12 pt Linotron Times 08-9206-77474

Typeset in Great Britain by Centracet, Cambridge Made and printed in Great Britain

CHAPTER ONE

'I AM afraid it is true. Our poor brother is dead.'

Georgina, Lady Tarrant, touched the corners of her eyes with a wisp of violet-scented cambric, and cast a hopeful look at her sister, who disappointed her by neither fainting, nor falling into strong hysterics. Her heart-shaped face lost no jot of its delicate colour, no tremor shook the head of chestnut-brown hair that was arranged so neatly and smoothly in its simple knot, nor did she raise her brown eyes from her work. Mary Hadfield continued to stitch composedly at the prosaic mending of something that her ladyship recognised as one of her daughter's torn pinafores.

'Surely you must be mistaken, Georgie. Giles was perfectly well only two days since. You know how my father exaggerates.'

'But this letter is not from Papa! It is always the same with you, Mary! I am not clever, I know, but I am nine years older than you, and I think that I should know when a message is to be believed!'

Irritation brought a flush to her plump cheeks, and sent two genuine tears coursing down them. Mary set down her work, and went to her sister. Though taller than her sister, she moved so lightly and gracefully that her greater height gave no suggestion of an awkward tallness, and she was slim as a willow wand. The present fashion for simple, straight-skirted gowns flowing from a high waist suited her to admiration.

'I beg your pardon, Georgie! You are quite right,

and it is too bad of me. Now do not, pray, upset yourself! It is not good for you at such a time, and I should never forgive myself if you should come to any harm.' She took Lady Tarrant's plump hand in her own slender one, and drew her to the sofa, into which she sank, with some care, breathing a little sigh as her heavily pregnant body sank into the cushions.

'I am afraid I was irritable, dearest,' said Lady Tarrant, leaning into the carefully arranged pillows and submitting to having her feet lifted on to the sofa. 'Oh, that is better! I do think that the Almighty might have arranged for some simpler method of producing babies! It is all very well for Tarrant to be so pleased, and say that he would like another four or five, but when I think what I have to endure. . . Eggs, for instance.'

'Eggs?' Mary was arranging a shawl round her sister's shoulders, but looked up in puzzlement. 'I am sure that you need not endure eggs, if you do not want to. You have only to speak to Cook, after all! But they are so light, and nourishing, that it seems a pity.'

'No, I mean eggs, for babies to hatch out of. I should not even mind sitting on them, if I had to. I am sure it could not be so inconvenient and undignified as this.'

'Oh, I am sure Sir Anthony would arrange a broody for you. So much easier than finding a wet-nurse. Not that he does that, of course.'

'No, indeed! I should not at all care to leave such a choice to him! I always make sure to see them myself, and enquire very particularly into their histories.'

Mary, satisfied that her sister was now calm again, ventured to return to the alarming news.

'About Giles, Georgie. . .'

'Oh, what a shocking thing! To think that I had

forgotten, for a moment, the death of my only brother! How I could be so callous, so heartless. . .'

A few more tears were shed, and Mary comforted her.

'Not heartless at all, but very sensible. You must remember what Dr Black said about being calm, and avoiding any upsets. I wonder, would I be wise to send for him?'

'No, no, do not do so. I shall be quite well. But this news is so sudden!'

'It is indeed, and that is why I ventured to doubt it. Are you able to tell me more? Who sent the news; *was* it Papa?'

'No. It was the rector.'

'The rector? Good heavens, I see what you mean.' No more than her sister would Mary have dared to doubt any message sent by the redoubtable churchman who was married to their eldest sister. While they might, on occasion and in the strictest privacy, giggle together at his pompous manner and his banal, if worthy sermons, they would no more doubt his veracity than they would question the evidence of their own eyes.

'Poor Papa! How he must be feeling! I must return to him at once, Georgie.'

'Yes, I know. Of course your place is with him. Only, he is not alone at home, after all, and it does seem hard that you should have to go away just now! I am sure the children mind you far better than they do me, or even Nurse, and I was relying on you!' She spoke with the petulance natural to one who had been indulged all her happily married life, and Mary was in no way put out.

'You know I would not wish to leave you, when I am so happy here. This is quite a holiday for me!'

Even Georgina's complacent selfishness was not proof against this.

'A holiday! I wish I might see you take one! I know full well that when you are not keeping me company you are up in the nursery letting the children romp with you, and tear their clothes, so that you are obliged to mend them. And no one coming to call but a few old tabbies of neighbours! No society! No parties! Nothing!'

Her nervous irritation brought on more tears, and Mary was obliged to administer some of Dr Black's cordial. As she held it to her sister's trembling lips, Mary spoke calmly.

'If the society of my sister and her family were not sufficient to amuse me, then I should not have come. Your children are delightful, and since you are my sister I do not scruple to tell you that even at their naughtiest they are far, far easier to care for than poor Papa.'

Lady Tarrant, though it was many years since marriage had taken her from Hadfield Priory, could not deny the justice of this remark, but confined herself to a speaking look and a sympathetic pressure on the hand that held her own.

'I do not want parties or society,' Mary continued. 'I wish you would believe that I am perfectly content to be here.'

'I do believe it, and that is just the trouble. You should not be content with such a life, as young as you are!'

'Twenty-five is not so very young. I know that you think you should be finding me a husband, but I can assure you I do not require your assistance in that department.'

Georgina's butterfly mind was easily distracted.

'Do you mean. . .? Oh, Mary, is it true? I had heard from my godmother that our cousin danced with you several times, and seemed quite particular in his attentions. Oh, I am so pleased! Nothing could be more suitable, particularly now! Tell me, is he as good-looking as everybody says?'

A faint blush stained the creamy skin of Mary's cheeks.

'Really, Georgie, how you do take one up! It is true that Mr Hadfield danced with me three times, at the Fordcombes' ball last month. But so he did with several others; he is a good dancer and much sought after as a partner. He is pleasant, and friendly, but there is nothing between us that might not be found between one distant cousin and another.'

Mary felt no scruple in thus concealing from her sister that Mr Jason Hadfield had, indeed, been very attentive at the ball, and that his manner had, of recent weeks, assumed that kind of bantering familiarity that implied a particular intimacy. Though he had not, in fact, spoken words of absolute love, yet there had passed between them such innuendoes of looks, and sighs, and half-formed phrases, that she had little doubt that he would soon declare himself.

As to her own feelings, she could not honestly say that she loved him above all others, but certainly to be singled out, at an age when she had begun to fear that she would end her days in spinsterhood, by a man as handsome and charming as Mr Hadfield, was both flattering and exciting. When he was not there she could think of him quite coolly, but in his presence she

found herself fascinated by him, almost mesmerised by
his handsome face and charismatic personality.

'And now, with poor Giles gone, nothing could be
more suitable! Oh, my dearest, it really does seem that
it was meant!'

Mary frowned. This aspect of the case had not
occurred to her.

'You mean—the entail?'

'Of course I mean the entail! You cannot have
forgotten that his father is the next heir! And he, I
believe, is several years older than Papa. Though really
we know so little of them, it is quite ridiculous. Our
own cousins, and complete strangers to us all, until
now. The wonder of it is that Papa permitted you to
meet him at all.'

'I suppose he would not have done, if he had known.
But you know he never goes to parties, though he does
not object if Mrs McLaren takes me with Emily. It was
the purest chance, I suppose, that he should happen to
be staying in the neighbourhood at that time, and that
I should be introduced to him. And that, he told me,
was only because he heard someone mention my name,
and found it to be the same as his, though he is known
as Mr Hallfield locally, except to his particular friends,
who are all sworn to secrecy. In order not to upset
Papa, you know. For as you say, we know so little of
them, and probably they know just as little of us. And
all because of the entail.'

Lady Tarrant sighed.

'The entail! You would not remember it, of course,
for you and Martha were only babies when Giles was
born, but when I was a child I sometimes thought that
Papa never spoke of anything else! It was an obsession
with him. Of course, he did not discuss it with me or

Caroline, but nevertheless we were always aware of it. I can remember, when I was very small, having nightmares and crying out to Nurse that the entail was coming to get me. Heaven knows what I thought it was. I believe I imagined it as some kind of monstrous serpent.'

'Poor little Georgie! But surely, then, they explained it to you?'

'Yes, but I do not know but what that was not even more frightening. All I knew was that we should all be turned out of doors to starve, because of the entail.'

'Hardly to starve—surely there was always poor Mama's money.'

'Yes, but you know Papa! You said only just now how he exaggerates.'

Mary fell silent. It was true that she did not remember those distant days, before Giles was born, but she knew only too well how large a share of her father's heart her brother had occupied, how painfully interested, even obsessed, he was about Giles. She had heard more times than she cared to remember how they had celebrated Giles's birth, how there had been bonfires, and a feast for the tenants.

Such rejoicing was not unnatural. The elder Giles Hadfield, married at twenty-one to the heiress of his choice, had been only slightly disappointed by the birth of Caroline, his eldest child. Of course a boy would have been better, but the child was healthy, and the mother well, and there seemed then no fear that the longed-for heir would not soon make his appearance. A stillborn son the following year was much mourned, but the renewed hopes of the next pregnancy were dashed by the birth of Georgina. Two more daughters followed in quick succession, both dying in infancy,

unmourned by their father, and then it seemed as
though poor Charlotte Hadfield had exhausted her
childbearing capabilities.

This was the time that Georgina so vividly recalled,
when her father could think of nothing but that his
house and his estate would pass on his death into the
hands of a distant cousin. Hadfield Priory was not, as
the name implied, an ancient foundation, and the
family had been settled there for only three gener-
ations. The original Giles Hatfield, newly rich from
sources he preferred not to reveal, and discovering
with disgust that the town which bore his name was
already blessed with a great house, had changed a
letter in his surname and moved to Sussex. There, in
Hadfield, he had built himself a magnificent house,
complete with a brand-new ruin, and settled down to
live the life of a country gentleman. In his anxiety to
do so, he had arranged matters so that the property
must always pass to the nearest male heir, as was
commonly the practice in the great families, and from
his pride had come his great-grandson's fall, in knowing
he must leave the Priory to his cousin.

This gentleman, much the same age as Mr Hadfield,
was descended from a great-uncle, and since the family
resided in Yorkshire there was not even the barest
acquaintanceship between them. Of this man, his heir,
Mr Hadfield knew nothing but that he had a property
of his own, not large, which he farmed himself, and
that he had not just one, but three sons. This last put
the final seal on the hatred and envy that he felt, and
Mr Hadfield never permitted the existence of his
relatives to be acknowledged or mentioned in his
presence.

Then, nearly a decade after the birth of Georgina,

her mother again found herself with child. Great was her joy and relief, and greater still when the midwife declared that her swollen belly bore not one, but two babies in its straining rotundity. Surely, she thought, one of them must this time be a boy! But it was not to be, and with the birth of Mary and Martha it seemed, for a while, that her husband would run mad. For several months he refused even to look at his daughters, nor would he permit them to be baptised though one of them, Martha, had spinal problems and appeared, for a while, unlikely to live.

After so many years of childlessness, and the exhausting pregnancy and birth, Charlotte Hadfield could scarcely believe that she might be pregnant again. When her natural cycle was not renewed she thought no more than that her body was worn out with childbearing, and it was not until the other signs were borne out by the unmistakable feeling of a child quickening within her that she dared to mention her hopes. Even then she said little, and had little hope, but, as if the birth of twin children had opened some hitherto unfound door, it was followed almost exactly a year later by the arrival of Giles the younger. That she herself survived the birth by only a few days seemed a matter of little interest to her bereaved husband, who appeared to mourn her only as the mother of his son. Her daughters wept for her, and comforted one another, but he would not allow the arrangements for celebrating this august occasion to be marred by any thought of his loss.

And now Giles, so long awaited, was dead, and his father was left to mourn the end of his hopes, the end of what he saw as his family dynasty. Mary, his only surviving unmarried daughter, wondered what she

would find, and how she could possibly comfort him
for such a loss. Though naturally shocked by the news
of her brother's sudden death, she could not pretend
to any profound sorrow. Her brother's spiteful ways
had made her childhood miserable, the more so since
he had employed them most against her much loved
twin, who was usually too weak to withstand him. Since
he had reached young manhood he had been little at
home, and when he had returned it was usually because
he was in want of money. On those occasions he had
treated Mary with the careless churlishness that he
habitually used towards the servants.

'Forgive me, Georgie, but I must know. Does the
rector say how Giles died? I suppose it must have been
an accident?'

'It is so very strange, he does not say! You may see
for yourself; his letter is here in my reticule.'

Mary ran her eyes down the rector's firm handwriting, which covered no less than three pages. The
first two, however, she did not bother to read carefully,
since they served merely to prepare the reader's mind
for a coming shock, the rector being the kind of man
who assumed that women were unable to bear any
unpleasant news that was not approached by the most
circumspect route.

'If he would but be brief! It is like a game of
Grandmother's footsteps—every time he gets within
sight of a bare fact, he stops! If I were hearing this,
instead of reading it, I should have gone mad with fear
by now!'

On the third page, however, the rector was obliged
to reveal himself, and to state baldly that Giles was
dead. And there, quite suddenly, he stopped, with
none of the verbiage Mary would have expected, and

finished with no more than a paragraph of pious hopes for his sister Tarrant's continuing good health.

The entrance of Sir Anthony Tarrant put an end to Mary's reading. A genial, hearty man, he had taken care to absent himself during the first shock of disclosure, knowing that in moments of stress whatever he might do or say would annoy his wife.

'Well, my dears,' he said, tiptoeing with elephantine care across the room, as if he feared a heavier tread might break their composure, 'this is a bad business. A very sorry business indeed.'

'And now poor Mary must leave us, and go to Papa! I do not know how it will be,' mourned Georgina.

'Nor I. It is a sad loss for him. He will feel it very greatly.'

'For him, and for the family, Anthony! Our only brother, and so young! And then, he was so gifted!'

'Ah, yes. Indeed.' Sir Anthony spoke with his usual agreeable good humour, though he had always thought of the poetic effusions of his young brother-in-law as something to be pitied rather than admired. A dedicated sportsman, he had regarded with tolerant astonishment a man who not only did not hunt three days a week during the season, or shoot his own birds, but who unashamedly professed a dislike for such pastimes. Mary, who loved to read, had always privately thought that her brother's vaunted genius amounted to little more than a superficial facility, and therefore maintained a discreet silence on the subject.

Having disposed of these tepid eulogies, they were free to plan for Mary's departure. Her father, who could not bear solitude, had reluctantly agreed to stay with his eldest daughter, in the rectorial residence in a village just outside Lewes, while Mary made herself useful with Lady Tarrant. Knowing him as she did, Mary thought that he would be in a frenzy to return to Hadfield Priory, since even in his better moments he found the rector's pompous voice and overbearing manner hard to bear.

'I must be there as quickly as possible, and take Papa home, if he is well enough to travel.'

'Of course you must. You shall take the carriage, and Sam Coachman. I have already sent orders to the stables that you will leave first thing in the morning.'

For the first time Mary felt inclined to shed tears.

'You are too good to me, Anthony! I cannot deprive you of your carriage and coachman, however! I can travel post just as well.'

'Aye, at three times the expense! It is not to be heard of. As if I would let you do so, Mary, or Georgie allow me to! And you must use the carriage to convey Mr Hadfield to the Priory, since it is almost on the way home. I would not, for the world, inconvenience the rector.' Sir Anthony had a simple man's reverence for the cloth, and would not dream of mentioning his relative by marriage's well-known tendency to clutch-fistedness. Mary could only thank him, with genuine affection and gratitude, before she took herself off to see to her packing.

They spent a quiet evening, and in the short time alone after dinner, before Sir Anthony left his solitary table and joined them in the drawing-room, Georgina again reverted to questioning her sister about what she insisted on calling her conquest.

'What age is he? And what does he do? Are they really farmers, as Papa once said?'

'If they are, I saw no sign of it. He neither had straws in his hair, nor muck on his boots, and he certainly did not confine his conversation to turnips. He is twenty-seven, he told me.'

'You asked him his age? That implies a certain degree of intimacy.'

'Not really. It was part of a general discussion.'

'I hope you did not tell him yours?'

'Why should I not? You know I have never cared for that kind of deception. If a man will not like me, because I am twenty-five rather than twenty, then what should I care for him?'

'Never mind that now. Tell me more of him.' Georgina, bored with inactivity, longed for romance.

'There is little to tell. He is a gentleman, I suppose, and that is all that is to be said of him.'

'How provoking you are! Does he still stay in Sussex? Shall you see him, when you return?'

'How should I know? I think he was intending to stay with his friends until April, but men, you know, may change their plans, and flit round the countryside, in a way that we women are never permitted to do.'

'Now, if ever, would be the time for him to declare himself,' mused Georgina. 'Situated as you are, what could be more proper? You might then continue to live at the Priory, and Papa with you, as if nothing had changed!'

'I hardly think Papa would like to hear you say that,' said Mary drily.

'Well, you know what I mean! For though I am sorry he is dead, naturally, I cannot say that I truly loved Giles as a sister should. I expect it was my own fault, but he was so. . . so very. . .'

'Yes, he was, wasn't he?' agreed Mary equably. 'And of course it is not your fault, but his. I did not love him, either. Indeed, it is hard to see how anyone could, except Papa, of course. A more spoiled, selfish, spiteful child never lived, and he grew up to be a spoiled, selfish, spiteful man.'

'Mary!' Georgina was shocked. 'With our brother not yet in his grave!'

'I say no more than I said when he was alive, and to his face, too. You know I have always held him responsible for Martha's accident. The fact that he is dead does not change what he was in life. Of course I am sorry for his death, as I hope I would be for any human creature, but I reserve the main part of my sympathy for poor Papa.' And, she added silently, for herself, who would have the sole care and company of poor Papa.

It was still dark when Mary left the following morning. She had refused to allow either of her relatives to see her off, and in truth was glad to be spared Georgina's lamentations at her departure. She was glad of the company of her maid, a woman who had been nurserymaid in her own childhood and with whom she had a close relationship, for it was a bleak start to an unpleasant journey. The previous winter would long be remembered for its prolonged spell of icy weather, when the Thames actually froze over and a frost fair was held on its rock-hard surface. Mary had not seen it, of course, but she had listened a little wistfully to tales of stalls set up on the ice, of entertainments and amusements that were only an introduction to the festivities later in the year, when the Regent celebrated the visit of the allied heads of state that marked the end of the wars with Napoleon with his usual gusto and vulgarity. Mary had not seen that, either, and when she questioned Giles about the firework displays, and the great fête at Carlton House, he had been able to tell her only that he had been so drunk that he could remember nothing of it, though to be sure he had enjoyed himself.

The Great Frost of 1814 had been followed by a deep fall of snow throughout the country that had persisted for six weeks. Villages and towns had been isolated from one another, and Mary remembered the period as an endless battle to keep the Priory warm, to care for the poor of the village, and to attempt to beguile her father's boredom, and distract him from his restless irritability because he could have no news of his beloved Giles. To venture on even so comparatively short a journey as this, if it should snow like that again, was a risk, but one that she felt that she could not refuse to take.

The roads were frozen hard, but dry, and they made good time to London, arriving before the heat had dissipated from the hot bricks placed at their feet. A hurried meal in a private parlour was as welcome as the fire, but when they went down to the yard Sam Coachman greeted them with a long face.

'I don't like it, miss, and that's a fact,' he said, with the confident familiarity of an old and trusted servant. 'If those clouds don't mean snow, then I'm a Dutchman. Coming to Lunnon, that's bad enough, but at least the roads is getting better, the nearer we come. But going down to Lewes. . .that's different altogether. Meaning no disrespect, miss, but we all do know what the roads be like in Sussex, and that's bad. Come it snows, we'd be benighted sure as eggs, and frozen to death by morning, most like. And what would Master say then?'

'Well, nothing that could bother us, surely,' said Mary impatiently, but repented at the expression on the old man's face. 'I'm sorry, Sam. You are quite right to be worried, and you should not risk yourself, or your master's horses. But you know that I must try to reach the rectory today, and all the more so if it is going to snow, for then who knows when I may be able to set forth? But I will hire a post-chaise, so you may be easy. I shall do very well, you will see.'

Sam chose to be affronted.

'Go off, and leave you to traipse around the country in the post-chaise, me that knew you when you was no more than knee-high? I'd like to see it! Post-chaise, indeed! The very idea! What would Master have to say to that, I'd like to know?'

'You are very good, Sam, but I do not care to put you into danger.'

'Ar, danger'd be what I would be in, if so be as I went home and told Master as I'd let you go off in a post-chaise! Now give over, do, and get in this carriage, and let's be off, if we're going!'

'Very well, but, if there should be any mishap, on my own head be the blame. You must be sure to tell your master that, as I shall.'

Sam's pessimism was soon seen to be justified. The air, which during the morning had been hard and ringing as steel, now turned heavy and damp, though there was no appreciable diminution of the cold. By the time they reached Godstone the snow was falling: fat white flakes that blotted out such a view that was to be had through the steamy windows, and covered the outside world with a rapidity that was both astonishing and alarming.

As they approached East Grinstead the roads took on, for Mary, the familiarity of home, and she was not sorry to break the journey there, where the landlord of

the Dorset Arms greeted her with acclaim that turned
to dismay when he learned the sad reason for her
journey. When he learned that she was not, in fact,
merely going home to the Priory, he was horrified.

'Carry on to Lewes, in this weather, Miss Mary?
Across the Forest, and all? You'd do better to put up
here, and let my good wife give you a meal, and a bed
for the night. With the Priory shut up, you'd not be
wanting to go there alone, and you know you can trust
my girls to have the beds well aired, and everything
just as you'd like it.'

'I know it, and do not think me ungrateful, but I am
so anxious for my father! I fear for his reason, if not
for his life, and even if there were nothing I could do
to help him I must do my best. But I should not say no
to a cup of tea, and some bread and butter.'

He shook his head, but knew that it was no use to be
arguing with her. Sam, having been reluctant to continue the journey, was even more reluctant to abandon
it when the ostlers told him that he should do so. His
pride as a Hertfordshire man would not allow him to
concede that he feared to continue. So, after a break,
they carried on, Mary peering through the window as
they passed down the hill, and through the village of
Forest Row, until the turning to Hadfield was passed.
Then she sat back, and sighed.

'I hope I have not put us all in danger, Sarah,' she
said to her maid, who had preferred not to look.

'So do I, miss,' was the comfortless reply. There
were times, thought Mary wearily, when it was less
than encouraging to be with servants who had known
one in the cradle, and been in a position of authority
over one's nursery days.

The road that wound up the hill out of Forest Row

had never seemed so long, or so steep. Though it was only just after half-past two the gathering clouds had hidden the sun to such a degree that it might almost have been dusk. Mary could hear Sam's voice as he encouraged the horses, and her heart went out to the patient beasts. Through the window of the carriage, heavily obscured now with driving snow, she could dimly see the great beeches that lined the road, their branches already thickly caked, and their height and thickness added to the darkness.

At length the summit of the hill was reached, but though there was an appreciable addition of light this was of little advantage since it served only to show how very much deeper was the snow on the more exposed plateau of the forest. There could be no going back, however: climbing the hill had been bad enough; to attempt to descend it would be suicidal, with the snow already freezing on to the icy ground.

Two or three more miles were passed in silence. Outside the snow deadened even their own sounds like a blanket of wet wool, and it was thus all the more shocking when a great creaking, groaning noise was followed, so quickly that they seemed one, by a tearing crash. Mary had no time to be aware of it happening, for in the same moment the lead horses reared at the sight of the rotten branch of oak that had fallen so close in front of them that it only just missed them. In that moment of shock Sam was helpless to control them, and their movement sent the carriage skidding across the slippery road to end, half on its side, wheels in the ditch and body against a tree.

His shout of alarm was echoed by another shout, and a mounted figure loomed out of the snow. In some relief he heard the accents of authority.

'Get to the horses. I will see to the carriage,' said the newcomer crisply, dismounting in haste and looping his horse's reins over its head. Sam went to his charges, quieter now but shivering and twitching with shock, and ran anxious hands down their legs, watching out of the corner of his eye as the stranger wrenched at the door of the carriage and climbed inside.

Mary opened her eyes. She seemed to be lying very uncomfortably, with some heavy weight across her legs that was causing her great discomfort. It seemed to be rather dark, and very cold, and she was relieved when a face appeared in front of her, though it was that of a man quite unknown to her. She blinked at him, at the white line of scar that ran down a suntanned cheek and gave what some might consider a ruffianly appearance to what was otherwise a handsome, if rugged face.

'What is happening?' she asked. Her head was spinning; she could not remember where she might be.

'There has been an accident to your carriage, Miss. . .?'

'Oh.' She seemed about to drift off, and his eyes were anxious. In this cold it would be fatal to allow her to fall unconscious, and he needed to know if she were injured before he attempted to move her.

'Come now, wake up! What is your name?'

She answered obediently, as if a child, 'Mary.'

'Have you much pain? Can you move your limbs?'

She experimented, and gave a little gasp.

'Yes, but it hurts. My leg hurts. Oh, dear, I must be Martha, then, not Mary at all.'

He did not attempt to unravel this confused statement. With impersonal gentleness he ran his hands down her, finding nothing that indicated serious injury.

'Who are you?' she asked vaguely.

'Well, if you are Martha or Mary, I suppose I must be Lazarus,' he said with grim humour. 'Now, I am going to lift you.' But even as he spoke, he saw that she had fainted once more.

CHAPTER TWO

MARY'S second, and more complete, return to consciousness occurred some little while later, and this time she broke through the dream-state meniscus that had held her submerged, and came right to the surface of reality. The last thing she remembered was that hideous, crackling crash, and she was not altogether surprised to find herself across the knees and saddle of a rider, held firmly in his arms.

'Sam? Sam Coachman?'

'No.' The voice was deep and steady, slightly familiar and yet oddly accented. Instinct told her to struggle, but common sense reasserted itself before she had time to make more than a feeble movement, and she was still again, though watchful, before he spoke.

'Good girl,' he said approvingly. 'I had feared you would go into hysterics, like your maid.'

'Sarah? Oh, is she all right? Where is she?'

'She's well enough. I found her weeping over you, mopping and mowing and screeching that you were dead. I fear I spoke roughly to her, but she was bent on lifting you, and I wanted to be sure you had no broken bones before moving you. You can feel your feet, and your hands, can you not? I know you can move.'

'I can feel that they are very cold,' she said, conscious for the first time of her discomfort. 'Where are we going? And where is Sarah?'

'There was a farm cottage not far from where your

carriage came to grief, but it was not a place fit for
you. They have, however, consented to lend a donkey
cart, and your Sarah is to follow us in that, while the
coachman brings his horses. There is an inn not far
away, about a mile off the road. I have been staying
there myself, the last few days, and it seemed best to
convey you thither. We are nearly there.'

He said no more and she, conscious that she was
aching in every part of her body, was glad to be silent,
biting her lip to keep back the gasp of pain when the
horse stumbled on some unseen obstacle, and sent a
jolt of agony through her head, and set flashing lights
dancing before her eyes. He felt her quiver, and
tightened his grip, wishing with all his heart that he had
not been returning by that road, on that day. A visit to
Brighton, at the light-hearted invitation of a chance
acquaintance, had been no more than a way of filling
in a few days' leisure. Since he must return to London,
the urge to gratify a mild curiosity to see the countryside round Hadfield and perhaps the house itself had
seemed perfectly reasonable. But now what had he
tumbled into? The very last thing that he wanted, now
or ever, was an encounter with the girl he now held
cradled in his arms.

Nevertheless, the harm was done, and the dim glow
from the windows of the inn were doubly welcome
since he had taken off his caped great-coat and
wrapped it around Mary's form. He rode right to the
front door and shouted, until the landlord came burst-
ing out to seek the cause of the commotion.

'Mercy on us, Mr Smith! I never thought you'd be
back with us today, with the weather so fierce! I said
to Missus, I said, "Mr Smith'll be sure to put up

elsewhere, since he's not back by now!" And she said to me. . .'

'Save it for later, Runforth. This young lady has had an accident in her carriage, and has been hurt. We must get her inside at once.'

'To be sure, to be sure, the poor thing! Do you hand her down to me, Mr Smith, and we'll have her adin doors directly.'

The rider was not sorry to relinquish his burden. Mary, protesting weakly that she was quite fit to walk, found herself carried indoors by the talkative landlord, who bellowed for his wife, for fires to be lit in the second-best bedroom, for Jim to take Mr Smith's horse, and for everyone to do everything as soon as possible, if not sooner. Floating on a tide of words, Mary allowed herself to be taken into the landlady's private parlour, where a bright fire promised warmth and comfort, and laid on a couch with as much care as if she were made of blown glass.

'Now, then, Runforth, what are you thinking of, to leave Miss all wrapped in this wet coat? She'll catch hurt for sure, if she's left in it. Help me to undo it.'

Mrs Runforth, who looked to be only half the size of her hearty spouse, spoke in the gentle voice of one who was used to being obeyed without question.

'Quite right, my dear, quite right, as usual. And what of the fire in the bedroom, and airing the bed?'

'Adone-do with your fussing. I've already sent Jenny to see to it. The gentleman told me he would give up the best room for the young lady, so the fire's already set there, and the bed aired, only needing fresh sheets. There, that's better, and I'll just take your bonnet off, miss. Tch, it's nigh ruined with this wet, and so

handsomely trimmed, too! What are you standing
there, for, Job?'

'Shall I sent for Doctor, Missus? Is the young lady
hurt bad? It's a wicked day, out there, but I'll send Jim
on the cob, if you but say the word. I'd not have it said
that Miss didn't have every care we could give her, and
she do look a shade particular, that she do!'

'Give over talking and go away, you great lummox!
How can I find how bad hurt she is, with you standing
there, and your tongue flapping like it was hinged at
both ends?'

'Ah, you've the right of it there, Missus,' he said
admiringly, no whit abashed by her words. 'Runforth
by name, Runforth by nature, that's me, and I knows
as I do run on a bit! Just you call me, come you need
for anything!'

He strode from the room, closing the door behind
him with a crash that made Mary quiver from head to
foot.

'He means well, Miss Hadfield, but he don't know
how to behave with gentlefolk.'

'You know my name?' Mary pressed one cold hand
to her throbbing head, and winced at the swelling she
felt on her temple.

'Yes, indeed, miss, I recognised you at once, soon as
I had your bonnet off. My sister's youngest is in service
at the Priory and my sister pointed you out to me,
many a time, driving through Forest Row. Now, tell
me, miss, where does it hurt? You've had a nasty
knock on the head, that I can see, but is there anything
else?'

'I don't think so.' Once again, Mary moved experi-
mentally. She was stiff and sore all over, but there
were no sudden pains, and now that her own pelisse

had been removed it could plainly be seen that there was no blood on the fine wool of her gown.

'Then I'll get some arnica for your head, and we'll have you in a warm bed in a shake of a lamb's tail.' Mrs Runforth bustled off, and Mary lay back, her eyes fixed bemusedly on the leaping flames of the fire. For the first time since her emergence from the nursery she felt the luxury of having all decisions made for her, and, worried though she was for her father, there was a relief in knowing that for one night, at least, she was to be spared his lamentations and his general apportioning of blame to everyone for his son's shortcomings.

Mrs Runforth returned, with such remedies as seemed good to her, and obliged Mary to swallow a peculiarly disgusting concoction which she assured Mary would make her feel much better. Having choked it down, and successfully kept herself from vomiting it straight back up, Mary was thankful to lie still with her eyes closed, while a soothing pad of dampened linen was tenderly bound round her aching head. She was concentrating on controlling her nausea, and did not hear the door open, or the approach of gentle footsteps.

'I should never have said it,' she murmured to herself. 'On my own head be it! And now, of course, it is!'

There was the sound of a low laugh, and her eyes flew open. Her rescuer, swiftly changed from his wet clothes, stood over her, the light from candles and fire illuminating the white slash of scar that seamed his cheek, and striking sparks in the grey eyes. Now that he was bare-headed, his hair was seen to be dark brown, very thick and unruly, and in need of the attentions of a good barber. Mary's brow furrowed.

'Oh!' she exclaimed. 'You said you were Lazarus! How very odd! I had forgotten it, until this moment.'

'A connection of ideas,' he apologised, 'since I have recently returned to this country from a prolonged absence abroad. Have you decided what your name is yet? You seemed to be in some confusion, before, as to whether you were Mary, or Martha.'

'This is Miss Hadfield, Mr Smith,' said the landlady repressively.

'Yes, I know. That she is Miss Hadfield, I mean. The coachman told me. Is she much hurt? Should I ride for the doctor?'

'No need, sir, and if there were then Jim could go. But I doubt there's worse wrong with Miss than a good night's sleep will cure.'

'But her head? She was unconscious, you know, and quite out of her senses for a while.'

'I wish you would let me speak for myself, and not talk across me like this,' said Mary crossly. 'Of course,' she added in softer tones, 'I am very grateful to you for rescuing me, and I don't know what I should have done if you hadn't happened to come at the right time. . .'

'Well, you wouldn't have done anything, being dead to the world,' he pointed out, 'but there is no need for gratitude. Why, it is a young man's dream come to life, to rescue a beautiful girl in the nick of time. What a pity there was not a highwayman, as well, whom I could have fought single-handed.'

'Yes, indeed, but why stop at one? Why not two, or three?'

'Oh, I would not like to appear greedy. And, to be honest, I think I could not have managed more than two. I am not such a warrior as my appearance might suggest, you know.'

'I beg your pardon,' Mary apologised. 'I am afraid that my tongue never knows when to stop joking. I did not mean to imply——'

'Of course you did not! And in any case, you are in no state to cast aspersions. Unless I am very much mistaken, you are going to have a real shiner tomorrow morning that will put my paltry scar right in the shade!'

'Not if she's let lie quiet, and I put plenty of arnica on it, she won't,' hinted Mrs Runforth. 'That room should be ready by now, and I'll call Runforth to carry Miss upstairs.'

'No need, when I am here, and already in practice,' he said, and, wasting no time, stooped and lifted her once more in his arms. Mary felt her cheeks flame at finding herself so suddenly clasped to his chest, and she stiffened protestingly.

'But I don't even know your name!'

'Of course you do. Lazarus—Lazarus Smith.' He was already through the door that Mrs Runforth, obedient to his masterful nod, had hurried to open.

'But that was no more than a joke, surely?'

'Then would you prefer plain John Smith?'

'I would not! Of all the unimaginative names to choose!'

'Then Lazarus must do. I own I prefer it to John, in any case. And, after all, ours is but a recent acquaintanceship, and doomed to be but a short one, I fear, since I must leave tomorrow morning.'

'And I too! Poor Papa, he will be so upset!'

'Shall I send a message to the Priory, miss?' The helpful Runforth was waiting in the hall to see them upstairs. 'It's not so far, and we might get someone through, if he should leave at once.'

'No, thank you, for there is nobody there. My father is with my sister, at Lewes.'

'At the rector's? Then he'll be well cared for there, miss, and they'll not be worrying. We'll see how things are in the morning. Your maid's arrived, Miss Hadfield, and she's up in your room now, unpacking your bags. I hopes as you will find everything to your satisfaction, miss, and as you'll feel better in the morning.'

Whether from the blow to her head, or general exhaustion, or the effects of Mrs Runforth's potion, Mary slept deeply and long, awakening in the middle of the morning to the news that the snowfall had been so heavy and prolonged that they were, to all intents and purposes, marooned.

'Stay here? But we cannot! What about poor Papa?'

'There's no good to be done by fretting, Miss Mary,' said Sarah sensibly, revelling in a return of nursery tyranny. 'What Master don't know, won't harm him. He'll think you in London, or at least at the Priory, where any person of sense would have stayed.'

'I know, I know,' sighed Mary. 'I am well served for that piece of folly. And at least it will give my face time to settle down.' For Mr Smith's prognostications had proved only too correct, and the glass showed her, this morning, a pale face disfigured, to her way of thinking, by the rich plum shades of a fine black eye.

Refreshed by her long sleep, and by the hot bath that Sarah prepared for her before the fire, Mary found herself ready for the plentiful breakfast carried up by the bashful Jenny, who had never had occasion to serve anyone half so grand as Sarah, let alone Miss Hadfield of Hadfield Priory. A short battle as to whether or not she should dress and go downstairs ended in victory for Sarah, who controlled the wardrobe, but the victor kindly conceded to the extent of allowing her mistress to sit up, in a dressing-gown, in a chair by the fire, instead of returning to bed. Mary had to admit that her knees still felt wobbly, and her head was inclined to throb if she moved it suddenly, or bent over, and she was not unwilling to stay as quiet as she was bid.

A gentle knock at the door sent Sarah bustling to repel boarders.

'Don't worry, I will not ask to come in,' said Mr Smith in a low voice. 'I merely wished to ask how Miss Hadfield is today.'

'A little better, thank you, sir,' said Sarah. Surprisingly, she seemed to bear him no ill will for his brusque treatment the day before, but on the contrary seemed to respect his show of force. Mary, who would have been only too quick to deny him entrance if he should have asked for it, now felt a contrary wish to call him in, since he did not seem to want to.

'Please *do* come in, Mr Smith,' she said in a pleasant tone. 'I am well enough to be out of bed, if not downstairs, and certainly well enough for a little conversation.'

'Conversation? I'm not very good at that, having lived so much abroad, you know, and in such rough places. I fear I'm more at home in the stable than in the drawing-room.'

'Well, this is neither. And I cannot believe you have never felt at home in a lady's bedchamber!'

'Miss Mary!' Sarah was scandalised, but he only laughed, and came in.

'I will neither confirm nor deny your belief. How do

you do, Miss Hadfield? I believe we have not been introduced.'

'Nor we have. How very shocking.' She held out her hand and he shook it with a little bow of great correctness, his eyes fixed in admiration on her face. The admiration was, she feared, not for any beauty he might find there.

'As I had thought—and I don't know that I ever saw a finer one! Not even on Saturday night in the. . .well, never mind about that.'

'The Hadfields pride themselves on never doing anything by halves,' she informed him grandly. 'Did I thank you for helping me? I don't remember.'

'You certainly did, and there is no need to refer to the matter again. It was simply chance that led me to be in the right place at the right time.' He sounded as though chance had much to answer for, as in his opinion it had, and glanced hopefully at the door behind him. Mary, contrary as her name, gestured him to sit and he did so, without enthusiasm but without visible unwillingness.

'Do you make a long stay in Sussex, Mr Smith?' she enquired with stately politeness.

'I have not yet decided. Probably not.'

'You have no acquaintance in these parts, I suppose, since you are staying here. Perhaps you are here on business?'

'I know nobody here, and as to business. . . I do not expect to find anything to concern me over much. I am merely a traveller, who has been so long away from his native land that it is all equally unfamiliar.'

Mary studied him consideringly. His clothes were of good cloth, but poorly cut and in an outmoded style. His face, with its all too visible scar, was bland and uninformative. It crossed her mind that he might well be a smuggler, or worse, and for the first time she felt a shiver of apprehension.

'And what might your business be?' she asked boldly. His grey eyes looked into hers.

'Oh, different things, in different countries,' he said with affable vagueness. 'For instance, I have been a merchant in India—not a very successful one, I fear— and a cattle farmer in America. That was more success- ful, for a while, but I got bored with it. Then I have been a sailor in the Pacific, and an explorer in the Antipodes.' He smiled at her expression. 'Well, you did ask!'

'Is all that really true?' He nodded. 'Goodness, what a chequered career. And now you are come home to the bosom of your family, to settle down and be respectable?'

'Whatever gives you that idea?'

'But surely. . .if you have returned to England, it is to see your relations. . .'

'I have none,' he said, and closed his mouth like a trap. Mary felt rebuffed.

'I am sorry. I did not mean to be vulgarly inquisitive.'

He shook his head, both in a negative and as one shaking off unhappy memories.

'It is I who apologise. I spoke very abruptly. The fact is, Miss Hadfield, that my family washed their hands of me, many years ago. I am dead to them, literally and metaphorically, and so they are to me.'

'Then you do not intend to be Lazarus at all?'

'No. I do not need anything that they might feel obliged, or even willing, to give me.'

'You are fortunate,' she sighed. He raised his eye- brows. 'Oh, not that I should wish to separate myself

from my family! I am very fond of them. But, even did
I wish to, an unmarried woman, you know, cannot
hope to have the kind of independence that you enjoy.'

'It is unfair, of course. Have you always wanted to
be an explorer?'

She laughed. 'Who hasn't? But, seriously, you must
agree that a young woman's life, if she is of gentle
birth, is in general much trammelled and confined.'

'A few escape. Haven't I heard of Lady Hester
Stanhope, for instance?'

'Yes, poor creature, but she was in love with Sir
John Moore, and only went away after he died. No, in
general, the only way for a young woman to enjoy such
excitements is to marry a man as adventurous as
herself.' His assent was guarded, and she laughed. 'Do
not be afraid, this is not a leap year!' Sarah tutted in
the background, where she was sitting in a window-
seat and mending a tear in Mary's gown of the day
before, and he gave a rueful laugh.

'Alas! For a moment, I dared to hope. . .'

'Dared to fear, more like! I can assure you that while
I may speak of adventure I have no great expectations
in that direction. I am not likely to marry such a man.'
Somewhat embarrassed at the levity she had betrayed,
she was almost anxious for him to know that her
affections were on the way to being fixed on another,
so she cast down her eyes modestly, and let a little
smile cross her lips.

'Have you then, perhaps, an idea in mind of the kind
of man you are likely to marry?'

Her smile broadened. 'You should know that a
young woman never speaks of such things, until there
is a formal arrangement.'

'But there is. . .someone?'

Mary nodded. To his surprise he felt, not relief, but a spasm of irritation. He conceived an instant and irrational dislike of the unknown gentleman, deciding in that moment that he was probably some milksop of a dandy, all high starched collars and scented snuff, fit only to strike attitudes in a lady's drawing-room.

'Who is Martha?' he asked, changing the subject abruptly.

'Martha was my sister. My twin sister. She died, oh, six years ago. Why do you ask?'

'I am sorry—perhaps I should not have done. But when you were in the carriage you seemed to think that you were Martha, because your legs hurt.'

'Did I? I don't remember that. Martha was born with a deformity in her spine; we never knew why, unless the midwife damaged her when we were born. She was never strong, and when she was tired she had dreadful pains in her legs. She was always very brave, but I always knew when she was in pain, and then I would rub her back for her, and that helped a little.'

'I have heard that twins can sometimes sense one another's feelings. Was it like that with you?'

'No, I don't think so. Only that we loved one another very much. Our sisters were many years older, and then our mother died when we were only babies, so it was natural that we should be close.'

'You must miss her greatly.'

The firelight sparkled on the tears that came to her eyes.

'Oh, I do, so very much! She was so good, so patient, and always so cheerful. We could always find something to laugh at together. I think that is what I miss the most. None of the rest of my family understands my jokes.'

She fell silent, and he respected her quietness and sat, the only sound coming from the hiss and murmur of the flames in the fireplace. Even the click of Sarah's thimble against her needle was stilled, for Sarah had succumbed to the effects of a night sitting up watching over her mistress, and had fallen asleep with her head pillowed against the thick curtains of the window-seat where she had sat to have the best of the light for her work. She gave a little snore, and Mary exchanged a glance and a smile with her companion. His voice was low when he spoke.

'She was very weak, I suppose, to have died so young?'

Mary's tones matched his, the suppressed anger in them all the more powerful in the murmur she used.

'Not so very weak. We had always thought—hoped—that she would live for many years; for a normal lifespan, in fact. But my brother would insist on her accompanying him, when he had my father's phaeton out to prove that he was able to drive his new pair of horses. Of course, he was not—he was only eighteen, after all—and the horses bolted. They were heading straight for the ha-ha, and Giles, my brother, jumped out into the soft long grass. She tried to turn them, but of course she was not strong enough, and the phaeton rolled right over. She only lived for an hour.'

Mary's voice was bitter, in spite of her care.

'It is not unusual for a boy of that age to panic, and act on impulse like that. Your brother must have felt very badly about it,' he suggested.

'He was very angry,' said Mary drily. 'He blamed her, that she did not jump when he did—as if she could have done, with her back! And he blamed the groom,

that the horses were too high-spirited, and my father,
that he bought them at all. But never himself. He was
brought up, you see, in the belief that he could do no
wrong, that he could do and have whatever he wanted.
Oh, dear, I should not be telling you all this! It is very
wrong of me to do so.'

'You need not fear to speak openly,' he said. 'Have
you not noticed that often it is much easier to talk
about things with complete strangers than those who
are near to us? And situated as we are, isolated in this
inn by a chance encounter that no one could have
foreseen, there can be no harm in it. You may be sure
that I am not likely to repeat anything that you may
choose to tell me, the more so since I know no one, in
Sussex, to whom I might tell them.'

She was a little comforted, but ashamed that she
should so lightly reveal her inmost thoughts to this
strange, rough man. The warm, firelit room, her own
déshabillée, and the conspiratorial nature of their lowered voices, had conspired to create a curious sense of
intimacy between them. She could only hope that he
spoke the truth, when he said that he would be discreet.

He saw the trouble in her face, and sought to dispel
it.

'I, too, have—had—a brother, and I do not scruple
to say that he cared for me as little as I cared for him.
Certainly I have never missed him, since I was cast off
by my family.'

'Cast you off!' She could not but be intrigued. 'That
is a dreadful thing to do. Whatever had you. . .? I beg
your pardon, I should not ask.'

'Whatever had I done? It was not, I now think, so
terrible. I fell in love with one of the maids.'

'But surely. . .many young men do the same! I

remember the housekeeper complaining to Papa. . .'
She stopped, and bit her lip in embarrassed vexation.

'Kissed the maids as well, did he? Well, I did more
than kiss them. At least, it is not what you think! I
truly believed that I loved this girl, and I was quite set
on marrying her. Young fool that I was, for she was at
least five years older than I, and of course nothing
could have been more unsuitable, but she said that she
loved me, and naturally I believed her!'

'How old were you?'

'Seventeen.'

'So young? Poor boy! Your father's anger I can
understand, I suppose, but surely your mama. . .?'

'She was dead, died when I was born. She was my
father's first wife, and I have since come to believe that
he married her only to oblige his family, because she
was rich. Only a few months after her death he married
again, and it is my stepmother who brought me up, and
was mother to the brother I spoke of, and a younger
brother besides. She never cared for me, nor I for her.'
He spoke with cheerful callousness, but Mary shivered
at the thought of that little boy growing up in so
loveless a household. She, at least, had had two older
sisters to care for her as she grew, and Martha to love
and be loved by.

'But I still cannot believe that they would send you
away merely for that! After all, you could not have
married her, young as you were, without your father's
consent, so he had but to dismiss the maid, or pay her
off, and be done with it.'

'So you would suppose. But in my madness I chose
to defy my father, and arranged to elope with her, that
very night. Of course, she had been sent away but I
was to meet her in the road, outside the lodge gates.

God knows what I thought we would do, where we would go, what we would live on! But when I went she was not there, only two of my father's gamekeepers who took hold of me and dragged me back to the house. My father was waiting for me, sitting in his study for me to be brought before him like a prisoner before a judge. There and then he went for me, in front of the servants. That was what hurt me, more than anything—the sight of them grinning to see the young master in trouble, so of course I lost my temper too. My father had the goodness to inform me that he had arranged a marriage for me, that in view of my disgrace I would be lucky if the girl's father still consented to ally his family with ours, and that I was to go, the very next day, to propose to a girl—woman, rather—nearly ten years older than me, whom I scarcely knew!'

'He cannot have expected you to agree? Was he always so high-handed?'

'Always, but our wills had never crossed on anything that mattered before, so it never occurred to him that I would not obey. My prospective bride was rich, and well connected, and in worldly terms I could hardly have expected to have done better for myself. Poor thing! She was very meek, and had buck teeth. I often wondered what became of her.'

'I am sure her wealth and birth were not left to go to waste,' responded Mary drily. 'Was that when your father cast you off?'

'More or less. He told me that if I would not obey him I should no more be his son, that I should be given a sum of money and must take myself away, never to return. I suppose he thought I would be cowed by the threat, and he probably never intended it to happen, but I was so furiously hurt and angry that I told him I would live without his charity, and flung out of the house. It was headstrong, of course, and later when my blood had cooled I wrote to him, apologising for my disobedience and saying that while I could not marry his choice I would in other respects be his dutiful son, and not marry to disoblige him. But he did not reply, and I never wrote again.'

'But. . .that is dreadful! And what of the girl, the maid?'

He shrugged, with a little smile.

'He had offered her money to go, and she took it. Of course, she did not love me, and no doubt I should soon have learned that I did not really love her, if I had had the chance. He was right, at any rate, to forbid our marriage!'

'But you have not forgiven him?'

He looked surprised.

'Forgiven him? I suppose so. The truth is I have enjoyed my life, far more than I would otherwise have done. So I suppose I should be grateful to him, really. During the first few years after I left I wrote two or three times, merely to say that I was alive, and well. My father never answered. I believe that I am no more part of his family, and I cannot say that it grieves me over much.'

'But—your inheritance? You are the eldest son?'

'Yes, but there was no entail. I suppose it was always expected that I should inherit, but my father always preferred my brother, so perhaps I should not have done even had I stayed. I sometimes wonder. . .'

'What?'

'How my father knew of my intentions. My step-mother was away from home with my youngest brother, who was no more than a child at the time. I could have sworn that no one knew, and my father was the last person to notice anything to do with me.'

'You mean it was your brother who betrayed you? How base. And should he now take your inheritance also?'

'Why not, since he cares for it and I do not? It may be that I wrong him. We were not friends, but I was not aware of any enmity between us. If he noticed anything, said anything, it could have been no more than an accident. He was only fourteen. What could I say, after so long a time? Accuse him, with no atom of proof? You, after all, have presumably never denounced your own brother, whose crime is far greater? Yet you could do so, tomorrow, if you chose.'

'No, I couldn't. Not now.'

'Your father would not believe you?'

'No, but even if he did it would make no difference. I suppose I assumed that you knew why I was making this journey, in such weather. My brother is dead.'

'What?' He jumped to his feet, almost shouting the word, his chair toppling backwards with a crash that made Mary wince. 'Your brother is dead? My God, I had no idea!'

CHAPTER THREE

'MR SMITH! Whatever can be the matter?'

The sleeping maid also started awake at the sound, and jumped to her feet, ready to seize the poker, if necessary, and defend her charge. Mary's look and astonished words seemed to recall him to himself. With a muttered apology he righted his chair but did not re-seat himself, remaining on his feet with his hands gripping the chair-back as if for support, or as if it provided a defence.

'I beg your pardon! I scarcely know. . . I had no idea that your brother. . .' He drew a breath. 'I am afraid that I might have spoken in a fashion that would have given you pain. Naturally, if I had known the reason for your journey, I would never have mentioned your brother in the same breath as mine.'

'There is no need to apologise, Mr Smith. I have never pretended that my feelings for my brother were anything more than duty required of me. My sole concern is with my father.'

'Yes, of course. Your father. He will be very unhappy, having been so fond of the young man.'

'Fond is scarcely an adequate word. He doted on him. That was only natural, since he waited for so long to have a son. Why, my oldest sister is more than twelve years his senior, and my father had almost given up hope of an heir.'

With an effort he sat down, and composed himself to behave naturally.

'All men of property want an heir, of course.' His words sounded inane in his own ears, but Mary only nodded.

'Of course, but in my father's case the need was extreme. The house and the estate are entailed.'

'Ah. Entailed. I see.'

'So you may understand how very precious my brother was, and why he was indulged as unwisely as I consider him to have been. My father placed great pride in being Hadfield of Hadfield Priory, and in passing it on to his son. All his disposable income, since Giles was born, has been devoted to the estate, to enlarging and beautifying the house, improving the land, planting trees. And now, of course, it goes for nothing.'

'I can understand your anxiety for your father.'

'Yes. Otherwise, of course, I would not have attempted so imprudent a journey. But for the past few years, ever since my second sister, Lady Tarrant, was married, I have been the mistress of Hadfield, my father's companion. He has recently been subject to fits of melancholy, and now. . . I do not know how he will bear it.'

'He is lucky in his daughter.'

She shook her head with a small smile. Impossible to explain to this stranger that to her parent she was a convenience, a captive audience, a whipping-boy, even. Only her pleasure in caring for a house such as Hadfield, and the boon of pleasant society near by, had made her life even tolerable. Now, when they might no longer entertain and she could not pay any but the most formal of visits to neighbours while she was in mourning, she wondered how she was to bear it, knowing that she had no choice.

'But you—what shall you do? If your father should die, where will you go? To your sisters? Or will the heir permit you to stay at the Priory?'

She wondered at his concern, but answered quite freely.

'Either of my sisters would, I am sure, offer me a home. But I believe. . . I hope. . .it would not be necessary for me to accept, or at least not for very long.'

'Aah.' He breathed out a long sigh, and sat down again. 'I had forgotten. There is someone, is there not. . .?'

'Yes, someone. . .' Again she smiled that small, secret smile. Sarah gave a little indignant snort, indicating that she thought Mary was speaking too freely. Irritated, Mary glared at her, and rather pointedly sent her out of the room to fetch some tea. The maid went with a suspicion of a flounce, and pointedly did not quite close the door. They listened to her retreating footsteps, and Mr Smith continued.

'And then you will have your own home. . .'

This time she laughed out loud.

'Yes, indeed! My own home!' She stilled her mirth, which, truth to tell, was slightly hysterical. The air in the room was so full of tension that it seemed to crackle, like static on a frosty morning. 'Oh, dear, I should not be laughing like this. But the truth is so strange. . .you see, for all of my life my father has hated and resented his cousin, who is now his heir. We have never had anything to do with him or his family. But recently, and quite by chance, I made the acquaintance of his son. . .'

He stared at her, frowning.

'His son?' he repeated stupidly. 'Your cousin's son? What is his name?'

'Why, Hadfield, of course! Jason Hadfield. And he is. . .is someone!'

'You are telling me,' he said slowly and carefully, 'that you are to marry the son of your father's new heir? That you will continue to be mistress of your old home?'

'Yes! Is it not the strangest, most providential thing?'

'Oh, quite. Very providential.' He stood up once again, quietly this time. His face was hard as rock. 'I should not be tiring you with talk, Miss Hadfield. As I said before, I shall be leaving as soon as the snow permits. If I should not have the opportunity to bid you farewell, please accept my congratulations on your good fortune.' With a stiff little bow he turned and left the room, almost colliding with Sarah as she returned from her errand, and closing the door behind him with delicate care.

'Well, really!' said Mary crossly. 'He is a most peculiar man.'

'Handsome is as handsome does,' uttered Sarah.

'Oh, did you think him handsome?' Mary asked.

'Perhaps not, but he's a good, dependable kind of gentleman all the same,' said Sarah with irrational crossness. 'But you've no business to go blabbing your business to him, all the same.'

'Oh, dear, I know it,' admitted Mary. 'But he seemed so interested in the family.'

'Mark my words, no good will come of it. And as for boasting about your conquests, I don't know when I was so shamed! Counting your chickens, that is! Why, he ain't even asked you, that I know of, and who'd know better'n me?'

'But I think he will, Sarah, I truly do. He has hinted,
you know, and I believe that if it had not been that I
went away so soon after we met he would have spoken.'

'That's as may be. But how many times have you
met him? You hardly know him yet. Marry in haste,
repent at leisure. Yes, that makes you laugh, but it's
no less true for that. And you don't want to go a-
marrying him, just because he's a handsome man, and
all the other girls are after him. No sense that I can see
in that.'

Mary wondered what her maid would have said if
she had known the identity of her lover, which she had
not dared to confide to her.

'Beggars can't be choosers,' she said, taking up her
opponent's weapon.

'A beggar you'll never need to be, Miss Mary, with
your poor ma's money and all. You don't want to go
marrying someone you don't care for, that's all.'

'But I do care for him! At least, I think I do. He is
so very handsome, Sarah, and such a good dancer!'

'That's no great thing in a husband, Miss Mary. A
good dancer, indeed! Whatever next?'

'I beg your pardon, Sarah,' said her charge with
feigned meekness. 'But I thought you would like me to
be married.'

'So I would,' said her servant with maddening incon-
sistency, 'if I could be sure it's what you want.'

'Well, I can't be sure of that myself, yet,' said Mary
sensibly. 'And there is poor Papa to consider, after all.
We must try to get away tomorrow, if we possibly can.'

Meanwhile John Smith, as he had named himself to
the Runforths, having closed the bedroom door as if it
were made of eggshells, took himself downstairs at a
speed that brought his host running, in fear that the

house was on fire. Pausing only to snatch up his great-coat, he flung out of the door and out into the snow, which now came up to the height of his top-boots and soon slowed his rapid progress. Nevertheless, he continued doggedly on, trying by dint of exhausting his body to quiet the turmoil of his mind. In this laudable aim he partially succeeded, so that on his return an hour later, in what was now full darkness, he was so far recovered that he was able to reply quite civilly to Job Runforth's remarks and even, with a little pressure, choose the dishes for his dinner.

This meal, over which Mrs Runforth had exercised such anxious care, he ate without so much as tasting a single bite, chewing and swallowing with stubborn perseverance in the lonely state of the downstairs parlour. Miss Hadfield, he learned, had taken some soup, and some fowl with bread sauce, and had returned to her bed. For perhaps the fiftieth time he cursed the fell hand of providence, then sat drinking Runforth's best—smuggled—brandy, and wondering what, if anything, he should do. Neither the brandy, nor the fire into which he stared, provided any answer, and his dreams were nightmares of flight and pursuit, in which he never knew if he was the chaser, or the chased.

The following morning brought no comfort to him. The snow was as impassable as ever, and he had a fierce headache from his over-indulgence the night before. It was scant comfort to learn that Miss Hadfield had passed an excellent night, and that her own headache was so well abated that she proposed to dress, and even come downstairs later in the day. When, during the middle of the morning, he heard a little bustle above stairs, he abandoned the lonely game of cards he had been playing, left hand against right hand, with a greasy pack the landlord had produced, and made his way out to the stable. There he found Sam, who was if possible even more gloomy than he to find himself trapped, so far from home, and with his master's horses to care for in such indifferent surroundings.

From there he took himself on another solitary walk, returning only when he was so cold that he could scarcely feel his feet and hands at all. Since he had been blessed with abundant energy, his life had accustomed him to solving his difficulties by action, whether violent or otherwise, and nothing could be more irksome to him than to be forced to be still and quiet. Coming back to the inn, he tried to creep upstairs, but Runforth called out to him in his genial, roaring voice, and at once Mary's gentler tones summoned him from the private parlour that led off the hall.

'How d'you do, Miss Hadfield? You must excuse me; I am very wet, and must go directly to change my clothes.'

'Of course you must! Why, you are soaked! How very imprudent, Mr Smith. But perhaps, having lived for so long in hot climates, you enjoy the novelty of the snow?'

His room, since he had perforce given up the principal bedroom to Mary, was small and incommodious, with a fireplace that smoked no matter what was done to it, and a piercing draught through the ill-fitting casement window. He bore it as long as he could, but at length the discomfort drove him back downstairs.

'I hope you have not caught a cold, Mr Smith,' Mary said politely, seeing him wipe his watering eyes.

'Not at all, Miss Hadfield. I never catch colds.

Merely, the confounded fire in my room smokes like the devil. Oh, I beg your pardon.'

'There is no need. I have been quite used to language far worse than that! I should think my vocabulary would amaze you.'

He thought it unlikely, but let it pass. There was silence between them for a while. It had been a long time since he had been in the company of a well-bred young lady, and as he was still undecided on his future course of action it seemed to him impossible to start any conversation, however inconsequential, without revealing to her such things as he wished to keep to himself, or displaying a knowledge that he should not, in fact, possess.

'I am afraid that, situated as we are, we have nothing but our own wits to divert us, Mr Smith. If there were a piano, I could play for you, but as it is, will you not play cards with me? I see that you were playing earlier, and I often played with Martha, when she was in pain and had to keep to her sofa.'

He was thankful to agree, and under the influence of a game of picquet his discomfort thawed. They played for imaginary stakes, cheerfully writing out vowels for fabulous sums and signing them with fictitious names, until by the time dinner was announced they were both laughing uproariously.

'I am afraid Mrs Runforth is very shocked,' whispered Mary when the good lady had served them and withdrawn. 'I should not be laughing like this, with my brother so recently dead. The truth is, it seems so unreal to me that I find myself forgetting that he is no more. I do not even know how he died!'

'Your being cheerful cannot harm him, any more than sitting with a long face can bring him back.'

'Very true. And I shall have enough of that, later, to make up for it.' She spoke without complaint, but he found himself moved by her stoic acceptance of the discomforts of home. Over dinner he told her stories of his travels, several of them quite true, and she listened with shining eyes. He found himself no longer noticing the bruising on her face, when her brown eyes were lit up with the pleasure of his tales.

At the end of the evening she gave him her hand with unaffected friendship.

'It has been such a pleasant evening,' she said. 'One of the most pleasant I have ever spent, I think.'

A certain hardness, which she had noticed from time to time in his grey eyes, softened as he looked down at her, his hand still clasping hers.

'If there should ever come a time. . .' he began, and she looked up at him in frank enquiry. 'Miss Hadfield, I know that you have the protection of your family, of your father, and sisters, of wealth and connections. But if there should ever come a time when you need a friend, then I hope that you would call on me.'

She looked at him in perplexity.

'It is unlikely, I know. But I should like you to remember that, for the next few weeks at any rate, I shall probably be here, at this inn, or at least if I go away I shall undoubtedly leave a forwarding address, so that any message sent here would find me.'

She thanked him, with her doubts ill concealed. He found himself wondering whether Jason Hadfield had yet tasted the sweetness of those soft lips, had held that slender form in his arms. He remembered, achingly, the feel of her as she lay against him, how lightly he had lifted her to carry her upstairs, and how perforce her head had lain against his shoulder, her soft hair tickling his chin and smelling faintly of flowers. Abruptly he raised her hand to his lips, and let it go. With a murmured farewell she was gone, and he groaned aloud.

'I must be gone tomorrow, even if I perish in a snowdrift,' he said to himself. 'This is a game too deep for me.'

Mary, for her part, still felt the heat of his lips against her hand as she ran lightly up the stairs. Jason Hadfield, an accomplished drawing-room flirt, had never yet attempted even so chaste a kiss, and she told herself that she should be angry that this man, who might be a gentleman by birth, if his story was to be believed, but was sometimes so uncouth in his manners, should dare to take such a liberty. Anger, however, she could not find within her. There was something refreshing in such directness, and as for his peculiar request. . . Mary could not imagine any circumstance which might induce her to take advantage of it, but nevertheless there was something so frank and manly in his offer of help that she could not help being warmed and cheered by it.

Once again she slept deeply, and in her fire-warmed room was not aware that the temperature was rising, nor did she hear the rush of softened snow as it slithered down the roof, or the dripping of water from twigs and eaves. In the morning she woke late to the sound of water gurgling in the gutters, and knew at once that there was a thaw.

With the entry of Sarah and Jenny, carrying the ewer of hot water, came the news that the snow was indeed half gone, that Jim had been sent to inspect the road and reported that it was slushy, but passable.

'Then we must go at once,' decided Mary. 'There

must be no more time lost in reaching the rector's, and
my father.'

'I've already spoke to Sam, Miss Mary, and the
horses will be put to as soon as you're ready to leave.'
In a fever of haste, Mary dressed in her travelling
clothes and swallowed a quick breakfast. None knew
better than she how difficult the roads of her home
country could become in wet weather. While they were
still half frozen it would be possible to move, but
should the thaw continue even the better cared for toll-
roads were liable to become quagmires of sticky clay.

In all the rush, it was not until she was bidding
farewell to the innkeeper and his wife that she thought
to ask after Mr Smith, to be told that he had been up
early, almost before it was light, and had left long
before she had woken.

'He did ask me to ask your pardon, miss, for not
bidding you farewell. Left his best wishes for your safe
journey, he did.'

'Please thank him for his kindness, if you should see
him again.' Mary was half ashamed of her duplicity,
but she could not bring herself to ask straight out
whether he intended to return to the inn, as he had
said he would.

'Oh, I will, miss!' responded the innocent Runforth.
'He'll be back in a day or two! Left half his luggage
here with us, he has.'

Mrs Runforth insisted on pressing a bottle of her
sovereign cordial into Sarah's hands, 'for fear Miss
should be took swimmy, like, in the carriage', and then
they were moving. Mary was surprised into a pang of
sadness as she watched the disappearance of that small,
ancient building that seemed to huddle close to the
ground in its little clearing in the great forest trees.

Then she straightened her spine, lifted her head, and prepared herself for whatever reception she should meet at the Grange, where her sister Caroline lived in childless state with the rector.

In the event, her coming had not been looked for so soon. Her family, aware that she would have set off immediately on receipt of the message, had assumed that the bad weather would have kept her in London, and that she would not arrive for several hours, if at all. In the hallway of the Grange, with its cold, gloomy air of ecclesiastical grandeur, she was met by Caroline, thinner than ever, who squeaked in horror at the sight of her eye, the purple of which was now streaked with dirty orange.

'Mary! Whatever have you been doing? Are you all right?'

'Yes, of course, merely the carriage met with a small accident on the way. It looks worse than it is. But tell me, how is Papa?'

Caroline glanced round her, as if suspecting that some critical presence lurked in the chilly shadows.

'My poor father has not left his bed since the news came to us. Oh, Mary, I fear for his reason! He will not speak, even to the rector! All he does is moan, and sigh, and hide his face in the pillows!'

Mary was not altogether astonished to hear this, since it was her father's invariable habit to refuse to confront anything that he did not like.

'It was bound to be so, Caroline,' she soothed. 'You know how he is. My father does not easily bear sorrow.'

'The rector has been very good,' said her sister in an even lower voice. 'Very good indeed! He has sought to pray with him, and has often exhorted to bear his trials

like a man, and a Christian, but to no avail! I fear that
he is displeased, very displeased!'

'I shall take Papa home, if he is well enough,'
promised Mary. 'But how was it that Giles came to
die? The last news I had of him, not a week since, he
was in good health. Was there an accident?'

'Oh, hush!' Caroline's slightly protruding eyes filled
with tears. 'I do not know what happened, but it must
be very terrible, for the rector said it was not fit for a
lady's ears!'

'But you are his wife, and Giles's sister! Surely you
must be told how he died?' Even as she spoke, Mary
knew that her sister would never stand up to her
husband's decree. With no children to fill her mind or
her heart she had devoted the whole of her energies to
her husband, whose every pronouncement she
accepted with as much awe as if it had been carried
down from the mountain by Moses himself. In her eyes
he was perfect, and, if at times she was fearful of him,
she expected no less from such a godlike being.

'Well, I shall ask him myself. But first I must see
poor Papa.'

'Yes, I shall take you up directly. But I must warn
you that you will find him sadly, sadly changed.'

Before she could do so, however, the door of the
rector's study opened and the master of the house
appeared.

'My dear sister! I have just this moment been
apprised of your presence. God be thanked, dear sister,
for your safe arrival.' He pressed a moist kiss to her
forehead, eyeing in some horror her disfigured face, to
which he doubtless felt it would be improper to allude.

'Thank you, Rector. I am certainly relieved to be

here, and as you see my journey has not been without mishap.'

'I am sorry to hear of it. Very sorry to hear of it. Later, you shall tell me of it, unburden your soul. But for now——'

'For now I should like to see Papa,' said Mary firmly. It was not unknown for the rector to hold an impromptu prayer meeting to celebrate, if such was the word, an arrival, a departure, or other unusual event.

'To see Mr Hadfield. Ah, yes. Yes. To see your father. I do not know that I would consider that a wise thing. Not a wise thing, no.'

'He is well enough to see his daughter, I trust?'

'As to that, I do not know that it will make a difference either way. Your father. . .does not bear his affliction lightly.'

'He never has,' said Mary.

'Ah, you speak with the quick, thoughtless tongue of youth,' he said pompously, rocking back on his heels and running his fingers lovingly along the heavy gold watch-chain that adorned the curve of his equally heavy stomach. 'But you must see him, doubtless, you must see him. It is your duty, my dear sister. Your duty.'

'Yes, that is why I am here.' Mary suppressed her irritation at these needless repetitions. 'Shall I go up to him now, Caroline? Will you take me?'

Her sister sought permission with a quick glance, and, receiving a portentous nod, led the way up the stairs, glancing back once or twice to check that she was behaving correctly. At the door of the room she paused.

'The housekeeper is sitting with him,' she whispered. 'The rector thought it better that he should not be alone, and she is a very good, sensible sort of woman.'

If it occurred to Mary that the properest person to sit with Mr Hadfield was his eldest daughter, she did not allow herself to show it, merely nodded, and went in.

The room was very dark. The heavy brocade curtains were tightly shut over the windows, excluding any light, and though a small fire burned in the grate the room was not particularly warm, though the air was close and musty. An unlit candle stood beside the dark cavern of the canopied bed, and a small, shaded lamp illuminated one corner of the room, where the housekeeper occupied herself with darning some linen. There was no sound or motion from the bed, and as Mary stepped forward she nodded to the housekeeper, and looked a question.

'I think he's asleep, Miss Mary,' was the whispered reply, 'but it's hard to tell. He don't say nothing, hour after hour, only sighs. Poor old gentleman, I feel that sorry for him. Shall I leave you with him, miss? Maybe he'll talk to you.'

'Yes, thank you.' When the housekeeper had gone Mary crept to the bed. Noting was to be seen but the mound of the bedclothes, and a tousled grey head buried in the pillows. She took the candle, lit it with a spill at the fireplace, and carried it back to the bedside table.

'Papa!' she said gently. 'Papa!'

There was no movement, but the sound of his breathing hesitated, then resumed.

'Papa, it is I, Mary. How are you, Papa?'

Beneath the bedclothes he seemed to shrink into a smaller compass, and even his breathing appeared to stop.

'I am so sorry, Papa. So very, very sorry.' She put out a hand and laid it where his shoulder must be. 'Will you not turn, and look at me, Papa? I should so like to comfort you, if I might.' She felt his body tremble beneath her touch. 'Please, Papa!'

At last, with infinite slowness, he turned. His unshaven face was gaunt as she had never seen it, the flesh fallen from the bones, and she was shocked by the fragility of the hand that came out, wavering as if palsied, from beneath the sheet, and groped for her own. She took it in her warm grasp, and it felt as bony and lifeless as if he had already died. His eyes were still closed, but from beneath the lids two tears trickled down, finding their way through deep furrows that had not been there before. Mary took out her handkerchief, and wiped them away.

At last his eyes opened, and fixed on her. They seemed to regard her with a kind of horror, and he shrank back from her as she leaned to embrace him. Mary, hoping to rouse him, essayed a more cheering tone.

'Do not look so frightened, Papa! Indeed, it is only I, though I am afraid this black eye makes me look quite outlandish! You need not be alarmed. It was merely a slight accident, caused by the bad weather.'

Slowly, he shook his head. Pleased to have even so small a response, Mary sat down on a chair at the bedside, keeping his hand in hers.

'I came as quickly as I could, Papa. Sir Anthony was so kind, and sent me in his own carriage, with his coachman to look after me, so I was quite safe. Georgie would have come with me, of course, if her condition did not forbid it. So you shall have another grandchild soon, to comfort you, Papa!' She knew how much pleasure he had in the Tarrant children, particularly the two little boys, but he only shook his head again in hopeless grief.

'I am afraid you are making yourself very unwell, Papa,' she said. 'Now that I am here, will you not take a little wine? There is some set ready on the table, and a dish of broth keeping warm by the fire. That would do you good.'

Ignoring his negative, she poured a glass of wine, slipping her arm beneath his shoulders to raise him a little, and obliged him to drink some. She was pleased to see a tinge of colour return to his cheeks, and at last he spoke.

'No more,' he said.

'Very well, if you will take some broth later. Oh, Papa, I know what a terrible loss this is to you, but you must not give way to it! Hadfield is still yours, after all! Does that mean nothing to you? You are still Hadfield of Hadfield Priory.'

This appeal to his ancient pride sent his eyes glancing sideways towards her. If she had not thought it impossible, she would have thought that his face betrayed, not just grief, but a look of guilty dismay. He was still reluctant to fix his eyes on her face: they kept sliding away from her, as if he could not bear to have her in view, yet returning as though fascinated as a rabbit by a snake.

'Do you not want to go home, Papa? You must be well, if you want to travel back to Hadfield.'

'Go home!' His voice was no more than a croak. 'Yes! I must go home! I shall be better there, if anywhere. Take me home, Martha!'

'I am Mary,' she reminded him, quite accustomed to his inability to remember which of his twin daughters was which, but hurt none the less that he should make the mistake at such a moment.

'Mary, then!' he replied with a flash of his old irritation. 'What does it matter, so that you take me home?'

'What indeed?' she answered, but low, and went to fetch the broth.

CHAPTER FOUR

AFTER he had swallowed a bowlful of broth, spoonful by spoonful as his daughter fed it to him, Mr Hadfield confessed himself tired.

'Nights without sleep! You cannot imagine how it has been. No one who has not known such misery can possibly understand how I felt. The rector is heartless! Quite heartless!'

'You must try to sleep, if you want to be well enough to go home,' Mary pointed out.

'I think I might manage a few moments' slumber now. But not alone! I cannot abide to be left alone! And do not send servants to sit with me, if you please! Not the rector's servants, at any rate. They are all as heartless as he, I am convinced of it. You shall stay, and watch by my bed. It will not be for long, I can assure you. I never sleep for more than a few minutes together.'

Mary assented, though she was tired from her journey and her head was aching. Her father, still mumbling complaints, sank into a doze, and was soon deeply asleep. After about an hour there the door opened softly, and Sarah looked in.

'I thought as much,' she hissed. 'Now you come away this instant, Miss Mary, and lie down!'

'I cannot leave Papa. He does not like to have the rector's servants with him, and if he should wake, and find himself alone. . .'

'He won't wake for hours! But I will come back and

sit with him myself, as soon as I've seen you settled. It's barely three hours till dinner, and if you don't have an hour or two of rest you'll be knocked up worse than he is. And don't try to tell me you haven't a headache, because I know better!'

Mary owned meekly that it was true, and submitted without much argument to having her forehead bathed with aromatic vinegar, and to lying down in a newly warmed bed. She woke two hours later, somewhat refreshed, and was pleased to learn that her father had showed no signs of waking. This encouraged her to change her dress, and rearrange her hair, a task which she was perfectly capable of managing for herself, though Sarah generally did it for her. Just as she was finishing tying the ribbons of her gown, a demure garment of white muslin, cut high in deference to the rector's frequently expressed views on female apparel, her sister came in.

'Are you all right, Mary? The rector was very shocked by your appearance.'

'Then I beg his pardon, and yours.'

'Oh, he is not angry with you!' Caroline spoke as though this implied a rare virtue. 'But he is very put out. He wishes to know whether Papa has spoken to you.'

'Only to say that he would like to go home,' said Mary diplomatically. 'I do think, you know, that Hadfield is the best place for him just now. If anything can distract him from his grief, it will be his love of the place.'

'But will it not also remind him of what he has lost? That it will no longer pass to his descendants?' said Caroline, with more shrewdness than Mary had given her credit for possessing.

'It is bound to, but he will remember that wherever he is. In any case, he wishes to go, and under the circumstances it is scarcely possible to deny him. I am sure the rector will be relieved!'

Unable to admit that her spouse could have so un-Christian a thought, but unwilling to lie, Caroline took refuge in a few tears. Then she wiped her eyes.

'Are you quite ready to go down, dear?'

'Yes, perfectly ready. But surely we do not dine for some while yet?'

'No, but the rector sent me to ask you to join him. He is in his study.' Mary's heart sank, but she could do no more than acquiesce as gracefully as she might, remembering as she did so that the rector's study, at least, was well warmed. The heavy silk shawl she had put out to protect her from the draughty dining-room would not be needed just yet.

Entering the hallowed room, it was difficult not to think of herself as a naughty child, summoned to receive justice. The rector's well-padded body stood directly in front of the good fire, legs apart, and, since the only other lighting in the room came from branches of candles on the mantelshelf, the effect was to make him seem huge, even threatening. At Mary's entrance, however, he came forward affably enough, and took her hands. She stood with lowered eyelids, suffering him to kiss her forehead once again, a form of salute she particularly disliked. He smelt of singed cloth, and soap, and clean linen, by no means unpleasant except by association. He led her to a chair, then took up his fireside stance again.

At first, the interview followed very much the pattern Mary had expected. After offering up a long prayer, during which Mary was thankful not to be obliged to kneel, he informed his sister-in-law, at great length, how very unhappy she must be feeling, and how her only hope of future happiness lay in doing her duty by her father, devoting herself to his care, and attempting to distract his melancholy. It was no more than Mary had told herself, but it was very dispiriting, all the same.

'Of course, my dear sister, your poor father is not a young man! Not a young man at all! It is scarcely to be expected that he will be spared to us for many more years, particularly after this fearful shock! And in the light of this unhappy event, this sad loss of the heir, I should like you to know, my dear sister, that you must never consider that you have no home, no resting place for your head. When that much to be lamented event occurs, and you are an orphan, you must not hesitate to come to us!'

'You are very kind, Rector,' murmured Mary, 'but I hardly think. . .'

'No, no, it will be no trouble to us! No trouble at all! And as to the expense, you are not to be thinking of it! Of course, with your dear mother's money, you will be quite an heiress—thirty thousand, is it not?—so you might always make some little contribution to the expenses of the household, just to make things feel quite comfortable between us!'

He beamed on her, clearly feeling that he had arranged matters very well, and that she must be grateful. Mary thought privately that not even in the direst penury could she spend the rest of her days living in this house. Polite usage, however, forbade her to say so, and once again she expressed her gratitude with the greatest warmth she could muster, though without committing herself. She could not help wondering how welcome she would be if, instead of bringing with her the income of thirty thousand pounds, she were penniless. That shelter would be offered, she had no doubt, but that she would earn her keep she was similarly certain.

At this point she would have risen to leave, thinking that the interview was over.

'One moment, my dear sister,' said the rector. 'One moment.' Mary sank back into her chair. 'There is something else I am constrained to tell you. Something that, I am afraid, will make you very unhappy. Something. . .in short, something that no young lady should be called upon to know. I think that a brief prayer, asking that strength be granted to you to bear this affliction, and that the purity of your girlish mind should not be sullied by what I have to impart. . .' Obediently Mary folded her hands and bowed her head. Behind her closed eyelids scenes of horror unfolded. What, she wondered, was to be told her?

The prayer finished, the rector seemed at a loss to know where to start. He swayed backwards and forwards on his wide-spread legs, rising to his toes and rocking backwards on to his heels until Mary feared he might actually fall into the fire. She waited with what patience she could muster, and at last he made an attempt at speech.

'What I have to tell you, my dear sister, has to do with the death of your brother. Giles,' he added, presumably in case she might have some confusion as to whom he was referring.

'I am glad to hear it,' she said. 'It has seemed to me that there is some mystery connected with his death, for nobody has been able to tell me why or how he died.'

'I beg your pardon, I did not mean to be so. But truly, sir, it was not in Giles's nature to behave so. You must not forget that we were almost of an age. Martha and I spent the first years of our lives with him, in the nursery. I do not think that I could be so deceived in him.'

He frowned.

'I am afraid you must accept, my dear Mary, that there are many things in which a woman must be guided by her male relatives. In this case I must desire you to submit to my judgement, both as a brother and as a cleric, and accept what I say. You are aware, of course, that your poor, misguided brother had pretensions of a poetical nature?' Mary nodded. It would have been difficult, she thought, for her to have been ignorant of it. 'You, whom I have always regarded as an example of pure-minded young womanhood,' he bowed, and Mary gravely inclined her head in thanks, 'can have no idea, no idea at all, of the way of life such men sometimes lead. Of his abilities I say nothing. I am not fitted to judge. Though I must admit that with his sentiments, however expressed, I found myself frequently out of tune, and on occasion quite disgusted. But I digress. Your poor brother, Giles, thinking that in order to produce great poetry he must experience all the varied excitements and experiences of life, had begun to mix with what I can only describe as a very wild set, a very wild set of people indeed. People whose names I would not soil my lips by repeating. Their manners, their habits, their morals were all of them such as to disgust any right-thinking person, and among these habits was that of taking laudanum.'

'But I have taken that myself, when I had the toothache!'

'Yes, indeed, and so have I. But when I say taking, I should more properly say over-indulging! You know, I suppose, of the extract opium, that gives laudanum its power? In small doses what a boon, what a gift to suffering mankind. But when taken to excess. . .a poison. Your poor brother had acquired this habit, seeking the strange and exotic visions that it is said to bring. And then some misfortune befell him—I know not precisely what. At his age, one may suspect that he was crossed in love. Whatever the cause, he was heard to speak very wildly, very wildly indeed. And the very next morning he was found, dead, with the empty phial of laundanum by his side!'

He paused, in triumph. Clearly he considered that his case was so complete that it would brook no argument.

'Are you saying, Rector, that it is accepted belief that my brother committed suicide? That he may not be buried in hallowed ground?' Mary spoke out bluntly, in her shock.

'Accepted belief? Certainly not. Naturally, his friends saw to it that the death was seen as no more than an accident. But I, having heard the full details, had no doubt, no doubt at all.' Clearly, he expected Mary to share his certainty. She rose to her feet.

'You will excuse me, Rector, if I continue to differ with you. I find it impossible to believe that Giles would kill himself for love of any woman, or indeed for any other reason. It seems to me only too likely that Giles, who had a weak head for drink and probably for this drug also, merely took a second dose by accident, being fuddled with the first. It would be just like him!' she finished bitterly.

'You are, of course, entitled to think as you choose,'

he responded stiffly, clearly without any sincerity. 'You are to be congratulated, I suppose, on your loyalty to your brother.'

He was obviously deeply affronted, and Mary was relieved to hear the sound of the dinner gong. He offered her his arm, as she rose, with much correctness, but the meal was a very silent one, with only as much conversation as was necessary to keep up appearances before the servants. Mary ate little of the food set before her, though the rector was famed for the excellence of his table, and as soon as was possible excused herself, and returned to her father.

Mr Hadfield woke soon afterwards, protesting that he had hardly slept more than a few moments at a stretch, and had merely been lying with his eyes closed, in obedience to his daughter. Too used to this kind of behaviour to remonstrate, Mary persuaded him to eat a light supper, and drink two glasses of wine. He agreed, reluctantly, to her going to her own bed, on the understanding that she was to be called at once if he should need her.

The following day seemed very long. Sitting in her father's room, Mary could not help recalling the cheerful afternoon and evening she had spent with the man she still, in her own mind, called Lazarus. That time in the inn seemed, in retrospect, like an interval in another world, a period of halcyon peace that was all the more unreal since no one but Sarah knew of it. Caroline, informed by the rector that her sister had chosen to disagree with him, naturally displayed a subdued and anxious face on her rare encounters with the recalcitrant one, and Mary found herself longing for the morrow, when she might take her father back to Hadfield.

Once again the carriage left early, and such stilted farewells as were given had taken place the night before. The journey, though slow, was as comfortable as the weather and the time of year would allow, and Mary felt a rise in her spirits as Sam Coachman turned the horses on to the public highway, and headed for Uckfield. When, later on, they passed the place where the track to the inn branched off through the trees, Mary kept her eyes studiously trained forward, and did not permit herself so much as a glance out of the window.

Never had Hadfield Priory looked so imposing to her eyes as it did that day, never so welcoming, so much like home. The knowledge that she might never, on the death of her father, live there again, or that in other circumstances she might find herself its mistress in truth, gave it a kind of luminous aura in her eyes, gilding every familiar stone, every tile and timber and window, with its own radiance.

Mr Hadfield, however, could do no more than weep, and Mary was obliged to use her best efforts to comfort him as they crossed the threshold. He glanced around the well-appointed hall with a depreciating look.

'Alas, alas,' he wailed theatrically. 'The last of the Hadfields looks on his own, but for how long? My dear, I very much fear that my days on this earth are numbered.'

'Come, now, Papa, you are tired, and overwrought. Things will not look so bad tomorrow, I hope.'

'How can one night possibly improve things?' he snapped. 'A thousand nights cannot do that. My son is dead, and. . .' He paused, and once again his eyes met hers with an expression of guilty dread. 'What did the rector say to you?' he asked suddenly, in sharp tones.

'Oh, nothing that you need concern yourself about,' she prevaricated.

'Nothing? You are quite sure?'

'Well, he may not be able to be here for the funeral,' she mentioned carefully. He appeared relieved, but said only,

'Heartless! Quite heartless!' As this was his usual term of opprobrium for anyone who chose to disagree with him, Mary was not particularly worried.

The funeral was held two days later, and fortunately the weather provided quite sufficient reason for the absence of the rest of the family. The tenants, as duty bound, attended, but those of their neighbours who did so came, as Mary knew, to comfort and support the living rather than out of any sorrow or respect for the dead. Giles had not been popular in the area.

'My dearest Mary!' Emily McLaren, Mary's particular friend, embraced her warmly. She and her mother had come to the Priory early in the day, assuming that Mary would not attend the actual ceremony, and intending to bear her company. 'You are surely not meaning to go out?' She gestured to the pelisse and bonnet, complete with thick black veil, that lay ready for use.

'Yes, I think I must. Neither the rector nor Sir Anthony is able to be here, you know, and I cannot leave poor Papa to go through such an ordeal on his own.'

'In the general way of things, I should consider it most improper for a young lady to go to the actual graveside, but under the circumstances, my dear child, I cannot blame you.' Mrs McLaren also kissed Mary. A widow, with no more than a respectable competence to support herself and her only child, she had come to Hadfield many years since. She was a woman of much

good sense, and Mary had frequently been grateful for
her advice in the past. Emily, though two years younger
than she, was her closest friend, and possessed the
same cheerful and practical nature that made her
mother so universally popular in the neighbourhood.

'Can you bear it, Mary? There will be no other
women there, but the tenants, I suppose.'

'I can, because I must. And I need not pretend to
you, I know, that I feel any deep grief.'

'I know, but still. . .it is a solemn thing. Mama, may
I not go with Mary? She should not be alone at such a
time.'

'I would not hear of it, Emily. I shall do very well
with Papa.'

'Emily is right, my dear. Though I should prefer that
she remain here; will you allow me to accompany you?
I shall not do so, if you do not like it, but my age and
situation make me a most suitable person to be with
you, I think.'

Mary was grateful, and said so. In the event she was
very glad of the silent support of her friend's mother,
for even behind the thickness of her veil she felt very
conspicuous at the graveside, though most of her mind
was set on supporting her father. A light drizzle was
falling on ground where the snow still lay in sheltered
pockets, and the small church was thronged with black
cloaks and coats, beneath which it was almost impossible to distinguish individuals.

After the last words had been spoken, the company
began to disperse. Mr Hadfield was led away, but Mary
lingered for a moment. An opulent wreath of flowers
and foliage had been laid on the coffin itself, but she
carried a small posy of sweet violets, picked that
morning in the glass-house.

'I should like to put these on Martha's grave,' she said in low tones to Mrs McLaren. 'Pray do not wait in the cold; I shall not be long.'

'Of course, my dear. I shall wait for you in the carriage.'

Mary was grateful for her companion's sensitivity in allowing her these few moments of solitude and peace. She laid her flowers on the quiet grave, and stood there quietly for some minutes, not in prayer, but simply breathing in the clean, cold air, which seemed so welcome after the heavy atmosphere of home, and the almost overpowering scent of the hothouse flowers that had pervaded the church. Turning, she saw a solitary figure watching her from the far side of the graveyard. As she looked towards him in some surprise and anger, he lifted his hat and she recognised the rugged face and dark hair of her newest acquaintance. Glancing round, she saw that she was screened from sight of the carriages, and walked swiftly towards the waiting figure, raising her damp, clammy veil to see him better.

'Mr Smith! What are you doing here?'

'Paying my respects, I suppose. All the countryside was aware that the funeral was for today. I did not hope to see you here, but, as I do, may I ask how you are?'

She found herself amazingly cheered by the sound of his voice, after the hushed and reverent tones of other visitors to the Priory.

'I am well, thank you. My poor father feels his loss very greatly, I fear. And you? Have you yet found any business in these parts?'

'I think I might have done. I am not yet sure.' His eyes were fixed on her face, noting its pallor, unmarked now except for a faint yellow shadow on her eyelid, and the fact that she was thinner. 'Are you sure you are well? You do not look it.'

'Why, thank you, sir! You are not very gallant!'

'Well, it is the company I keep,' he said with a twinkle.

'Of course. I know I should not ask, but are you a smuggler?'

'A smuggler?' He looked amazed, and flung back his head to laugh, recollecting just in time where he was, and in what circumstances. 'I have been many things, but not a smuggler, as yet. Why on earth should you think so?'

She felt herself grow warm with embarrassment.

'Oh, merely that you are a stranger, yet you have some mysterious business that you will not tell me of. There are many smugglers in Sussex, you know.'

'Should you mind, if I were?' he asked curiously.

'No! At least, I don't know, but I don't think so. I believe that many perfectly respectable people are connected with them. I suppose there is hardly a house of note in the county that does not have a barrel or two of brandy in its cellars that has had no duty paid on it. No one thinks any the worse of it. Of course, if you had had anything to do with that robbery of the Blue Coach at Handcross—but no, that was three years ago. I suppose you were not in England at that time?'

'I was not,' he answered, his repressive tones belied by the twinkle of amusement in his grey eyes. 'Do I really look like a highwayman?'

'Well. . . I have never been acquainted with one, that I knew of. But this was no mere highway robbery, but a coach of the Brighton Union Bank. I believe as much as eight thousand pounds was taken, and they have never recovered it, or caught those responsible. Yet.'

'I see that you still harbour a suspicion that I might be the guilty party. Shall you inform on me?'

'Oh, dear, I suppose I could not do so, when I owe you my safety. But I should inform you, sir, that I am making a considerable sacrifice, for there was a reward of eight hundred pounds offered! But I must not stay here talking, though it is so agreeable to have a conversation that is not connected with my brother.'

'I am glad to be that much of service to you, at any rate. You must not remain here, however. Tell me only that you have not forgotten what I said.'

'I have not, though I cannot imagine—— Oh, there is Mrs McLaren coming to look for me. Goodbye!' She put down her veil, and he bowed, making no attempt to detain her and indeed seeming quite anxious to be gone.

'Who was that, my dear? Some friend of Giles's, I suppose, who knows no better than to keep you talking in the cold and the wet. Come, we must get back to the Priory. Your father will be wanting you.'

Mary was glad that she was not called upon to answer her first question, and meekly followed her friend back to their carriage.

Later, when the visitors had departed and her father had been settled, exhausted with emotion, in his bed, Mary sat with a sigh of relief in the little upstairs sitting-room that had once been the schoolroom, and was now regarded as particularly her own. Emily had begged to stay, and her mother had given permission, seeing that the company of one her own age would be the best comfort for Mary, stipulating only that her daughter should not keep her friend up talking half the night.

'My poor dear! Was it so very dreadful?'

'It seemed very long, certainly. But my father has borne it better than I had feared.'

'Poor Mr Hadfield! I am so sorry for him!'

'Let us not talk of it now. Tell me what has been happening here, since I went away. There must be a great deal of news. Have there been many parties? And has Miss Fordcombe become engaged yet? I was sure there would soon be an announcement.'

Nothing loath, Emily chattered of the numerous small doings of their set, confirming that the gentleman who had showed so marked an interest in Miss Fordcombe had indeed come up to expectations.

'I am so pleased! She is a thoroughly nice girl, and I think it a most suitable match. And, with three daughters to settle, I imagine her parents must be happy?'

'Oh, beyond anything. And, since we are speaking of suitable matches, a certain gentleman has been most assiduous in asking for news of you.'

Mary frowned, blushed, and laughed.

'I cannot think what you are talking about,' she lied.

'Of course you cannot! Perhaps I should remind you of a relative of yours, who may not be in possession of the Golden Fleece of his namesake, but certainly has hair to rival it! Does that give you the clue?'

'I suppose you mean Mr Hadfield,' said Mary. 'You must be careful how you mention his name in this house, Emily. You know how Papa has always felt about that family, and now, in particular. . .'

'Of course! Of course! But he has been most discreet, I can assure you. I do not think that many people are aware of the connection. He is actually calling himself

Hallfield, as you know, so as not to cause any awkwardness.'

'It would never do for word of his presence to reach Papa, at the moment, and you know how people talk. . .'

'If that is to my address, you need have no fear. I am far too careful of your comfort for that. He does not even visit in the village, but keeps to the neighbourhood of the Fordcombes, so I have only seen him there. I believe they have hopes of him for Miss Celia Fordcombe, the second girl, but I have not seen him take any particular notice of her. But in *you* he is always interested.'

'I should not listen to you, when you talk like this.'

'Admit that it is not unpleasant to do so, at any rate! I must say, Mary, that if I thought he liked me at all, other than as your friend, I should not be displeased. He is so *very* good-looking!'

It was true that Mr Jason Hadfield, with his head of golden hair that was so beautifully cut and arranged, his classic features and his sparkling hazel eyes, presented a picture of manly beauty that would gladden the heart of any young woman, and Mary could not say that she was indifferent to his charms. To hear that he had not forgotten her in her absence, that he asked for news of her, was flattering in the extreme, and she allowed herself to fall into a little reverie that her friend, with her mother's sensitivity, did not attempt to interrupt.

CHAPTER FIVE

IF MARY had hoped that the passage of time would
bring about some improvement in her father's state of
mind and body, she was sadly disappointed. The passing of the weeks, instead of dulling the pain of his
misery, only seemed to enhance it. He had always been
inclined to be irritable, querulous and demanding, but
now his spirits were so volatile that Mary sometimes
despaired.

The day after the funeral his man of business, who
had as a matter of course attended the obsequies, was
closeted with Mr Hadfield for several hours. When he
finally left, his face was grim, and Mary was not
surprised, on entering the library, to find her father
livid with emotion. Such was his anger that he could
only rail against her, and against the now departed Mr
Camden. Mary bore it with what patience she could
muster, but when her father turned on her and
informed her, in tones of fury unbridled, that it was all
her fault, she could not forbear to ask why.

'Why? Why? You should have been a boy! What's
the use of girls? I never wanted 'em. Useless things,
always demanding settlements, and dowries, and I
know not what!'

Mary was too used to his ways to feel more than a
momentary pang at this, nor did she think it worth her
while to protest that she could not be held responsible
for her sex.

'Well, I am sorry for it,' she said cheerfully, 'and I

80

shall try not to ask you for a settlement or a dowry, at least for a while.' She spoke lightly, meaning it as a pleasantry, but her father gave her a hunted look, and almost collapsed into a chair.

'I did not mean it!' he said, almost whining. Mary looked at him in astonishment.

'Of course not, Papa! If you think I can be upset by the intemperate things you say when you are angry. . . now, do not be distressed!' She went as if to comfort him, but he shrank from her as if in terror, and she drew back her hand.

'What is it, Papa? Are you ill?'

He was trembling, his hand quivering as he raised it to cover his lips.

'Ill? Ill? Yes, yes, I am ill. That is it, I am ill. God knows, I have enough trouble to make me ill. Who could have foreseen. . .? But he was at fault! He was much at fault!'

'Who, Papa?'

'Why, Camden, of course. Who else should be at fault?'

'I thought—maybe—poor Giles?' She spoke in hesitant accents.

'Giles?' He sounded as though she had uttered the vilest blasphemy. 'Giles, at fault?' Then he fell to weeping, and proclaimed that Camden had behaved like a villain, and poor Giles, poor dear Giles, had been quite deceived.

'Papa?' While he was in this softened mood, Mary thought that she might risk the question. 'The rector hinted that Giles's death was not. . .not altogether natural. Is it true?'

'Natural? How can it be natural for a young man of

twenty-four to die so suddenly? He was murdered! Murdered!'

'Papa! Can it be so? But by whom?'

He looked at her. For a moment the wildness left his eyes, and she beheld a depth of suffering that was terrible to see. When he spoke, it was almost calmly, and it was this quiet certainty that convinced her where his former violent accusations had not.

'I am sure that it is so. Giles would never have destroyed himself by his own hand.' It was what she had said herself to the rector, and she acknowledged the truth of it.

'What can be done? His murderer must be brought to justice!'

'What could I do? I am only a weak old man, fit for nothing but to live out his few remaining days in misery. I tell you, Martha—Mary, I mean, there is no justice in the world. No justice at all. Men are heartless creatures, at the best of times; I have always known it. There is nothing to be done. I cannot speak of it any more.'

'But Papa——'

'Enough!' he almost shouted, all the former excitability of his manner returning. 'I have said I cannot speak of it! Do not torment me with questions! Nothing can bring him back to me!' He snivelled in a welter of self-pity, and Mary stared at him in horror. Up until then, she had not wanted to question him about the rector's allegations, fearing that they might turn out to be only too true, and not wishing to cause any problem about the impending funeral. Now, with Giles safely buried in hallowed ground, she had asked, and her answer had been even worse than she had feared.

That night, when her father had moaned and snuffled

himself into sleep, she paced her room for a while before opening her writing desk, at which she sat, pen in hand, with the ink drying on the nib before finally scribbling the request for help that she had never thought she would need to make. Surely Lazarus, whoever or whatever he might be, would be able to untangle this knot for her? She entrusted her note to Sarah, with instructions that it was to be sent at once, and without any undue fuss being made. Sarah sniffed a little, but made no other complaint, which would have surprised Mary had she bothered to think about it.

A week went by, and she received no reply. She could not help acknowledging to herself that she was disappointed, but as the days passed and no answer came she told herself that he had spoken idly, perhaps meaning what he said at the time but soon forgetting it. Probably he had left Sussex, left England even, without giving her another thought. She should, she knew, be glad of it. What could he be to her, after all? So lacking in polish, almost rough in his ways, really barely a gentleman! And if not the smuggler she had once thought him, then certainly up to no good, and if his name was really Smith she would eat her best bonnet. Lazarus, indeed!

Meanwhile, the house must be run, her father cared for, and somehow an appearance of normality must be kept up. Emily visited her nearly every day, and Mary was thankful for her company, though even to her friend she hesitated to confide her fears for her father. His behaviour was erratic in the extreme. For some of the time he was so sunk in lethargic misery that he could not be brought to leave his bed, lying for days on end in a darkened room, refusing to speak. Then, quite

suddenly, he would become seized with a kind of
frantic activity. With the energy of a man half his age
he would be out on his horse, inspecting every foot of
ground, every tree, every crop and beast and hedge.
The accounts would be checked and counter-checked,
letters fired off to his man of business, even the
household expenditure examined and, where possible,
cut down. Mary would find herself justifying the cost
of employing a second laundry maid, or the size of the
bill for candles and lamp oil.

'Surely, Papa, you need not concern yourself with
such things, when you are not well?'

'But I must, I must!' he answered feverishly. 'I must
do something. . .'

Mary hoped that his busyness signified a return to a
more normal life, but she soon learned that it led only
to exhaustion, to a return to his sickroom habits, which
in their turn restored him only to a further bout of
activity. She herself he regarded with mixture of resent-
ment, dependence, and something that she would, if
she could have seen a reason for it, have called guilt.

The third such episode had just finished, and her
father was lying once more in his bed, with his head
turned away from the closely curtained window, when
Emily made her accustomed visit.

'I do not ask how you are,' she said when she had
kissed her friend and taken off bonnet and pelisse, 'for
I would not like to have your perjury on my conscience.
I can see for myself that you are far from well.'

'Thank you,' murmured Mary drily. 'I knew I could
rely on you to raise my spirits.'

'Do not try to pretend to me that I have hurt your
feelings, for I know you too well for that!'

'Yes, and, besides, I have only to look in the mirror,

have I not? It is only that I am a little tired. And the
time of year, you know, is not one of my favourites.
No one can look their best at the end of winter, when
spring seems so long in arriving.'

'I will admit all of these excuses, but truly I am
worried for your health, Mary. Spending all day and
every day in your father's sickroom, as you do, will
make you ill yourself, and then what will he do?'

'Nonsense! You know I am never ill.'

'Can you look me in the eye, and tell me that your
head does not ache? No, I thought not.'

'I admit it, you are too clever a diagnostician for me.
I am not used to being so much indoors, that is all, but
that is soon cured. Put back your bonnet, and we shall
have a walk in the garden. The clouds are heavy, but it
does not rain or snow yet, and the paths should be
quite dry.'

Emily agreed, and for a while they walked briskly
down the gravel paths that wound so invitingly through
a pretty shrubbery that, even at this time of year, had
the interest of variegated leaves, and a promise of
spring in the apearance of small buds, to please them.
This, however, was far from fulfilling Emily's wishes.

'This is all very well, and better than nothing, but I
wish you would go out more. I believe you have been
no further than to church on Sunday, and to visit in the
village, since you came home.'

'No, I have not. I hardly like to go too far, with Papa
as he is, and besides, how should I go? Papa does not
care for me to use the carriage just at present, and I
cannot be seen riding round the countryside, as I used
to do. It would be quite unseemly, in my situation.'

'Yes, but you might surely ride on your own land?

To go further might cause remark, but within the park and the estate, who would be the wiser?'

For the first time Mary looked embarrassed.

'I am afraid that it would not be possible. My father has. . .our stable is rather depleted, just now.'

'You mean he has sold your lovely mare? Oh, Mary, why should he do such a thing?'

'I don't know. He has sold nearly all the horses, except a pair for the carriage, and his own cob that he uses to ride round the land. When I asked him why, he just. . .well, he is so unhappy, Emily.'

'Yes, much must be allowed, much forgiven to a man in his circumstances. But it does seem hard! I had hoped we might ride together, as we used to. What a pity I have no second mount that I might lend you!'

'Well, I am sure Papa will be better soon, and then perhaps I shall have a new mare. But now tell me all the news! I am starved for it!'

'I am afraid you must go hungry, for I have none. We are all very dull just now, for the Fordcombes have gone to London.' She glanced at Mary, who kept her eyes demurely lowered. 'They did not, however, take all their visitors in their train. Is that what you wanted to know?'

'I cannot imagine what you might mean.'

'No, of course you cannot. So I need not scruple to ask you to visit us tomorrow afternoon, need I? If we should happen to have any callers, they would be of no interest to you at all.'

'Anyone who likes you must be of interest to me, Emily.' Her friend smiled, and said no more, nor did Mary ask any questions, for fear that the answers might not suit her. The following day, having ascertained that her father did not need her, she set off to walk into the village, and was thankful that the lanes, though dirty, were not in such a state as to preclude a journey of more than a mile on foot. She would not admit, even to herself, that she had dressed with more than usual care, nor that she was being particularly fussy about keeping her petticoat and skirt clean, and her hair neatly arranged. Her gown, though of the utmost simplicity of cut, was of the finest muslin, printed with a delicate tracery of leaves and flowers in pale grey, and ornamented with deeper grey ribbons, as befitted her mourning state. Her pelisse, bonnet and mantle, of a green so dark that they were almost black, were in the Russian style made fashionable the previous year, and ornamented with bands of fur that matched the large muff that protected her hands.

Her welcome was a warm one, but to her surprise she found only Emily and her mother present. It was not long before more visitors were announced, bringing with them news from London of the most startling kind.

'Buonaparte—escaped? I cannot believe it!'

'It is no more than the truth, I can assure you. I had it from my sister, whose husband is well acquainted with Creevey.'

'With Creevey? Then you need say no more. I believe you. But how can this be? I had thought him safe on Elba.'

'Nevertheless, he has made his escape, and now I suppose it will all be to do again. God send, at least, that it should not go on for as long as before.'

'And that we can defeat him,' put in Mary. Her companion cried her down.

'The Duke will do that, you may be sure! I have met him you know. He is charming, quite charming, in

spite of that nose. And his eyes! So bright! So
expressive!'

Mary acknowledged that with these attributes he
could not fail to defeat the Monster of Corsica, and
was deep in conversation with another friend when a
small bustle at the door made her look up, and she saw
her cousin in the doorway, his eyes searching the room.
He found her just as she lifted her eyes to him, and
there was no mistaking his pleasure. His manners were
too good, however, to allow him to make his way at
once to her side, and she was able to study him covertly
as he made his greeting to his hostess, and to Emily,
who wore a conscious look and was careful not to
glance in the direction of her friend.

Mary found herself thinking that she had forgotten
how very handsome he was: even more handsome
than memory had painted him. Tall, slimly but strongly
built, he carried himself well and with a kind of
presence, so that he appeared larger than he actually
was. His hair was of a gold that any society beauty
might have given her eyes for, curling a little, and
beautifully cut so that it always looked well arranged
but not over carefully. It was the same with his clothes,
so well tailored that they verged on dandyism, and yet
worn with an air of unconcern that could only enhance
the beautiful arrangement of the snowy necktie, the
height of the starched collar, the glowing shine of the
top-boots.

As if this were not enough, his face, particularly in
profile, could almost have stood as a model for a Greek
God, Apollo perhaps. He was fortunate that the eyebrows and lashes above his fine hazel eyes were of a
darker shade than his hair, and his only flaw, if such a
thing could be admitted, was in a certain lack of

animation in the features, as if too wide a smile might mar the smoothness of the carefully shaved cheeks, or break the symmetry of the face. Nevertheless, he was generally admitted by men to be a dashed good fellow, since he rode well and had a couple of good hunters, while in the eyes of the ladies he was a paragon.

With easy assurance he made his way to Mary's side, and her erstwhile companion melted away, leaving the seat next to her empty for him to take. As he approached she felt a tingle run through her entire body, as if at some physical shock. She could hardly keep her eyes from his face—he seemed almost ringed with light, with a kind of supernatural radiance that held her spellbound. She held out her hand to him, and, if he kept it in his own for longer than a mere greeting necessitated, it could be seen as no more than an accompaniment to the words that naturally were the first that came to his lips.

'Miss Hadfield, you must allow me to express my deep sympathy at your recent sad loss.'

His words were formal, but his voice was warmer and while his lips framed her surname his eyes called her Mary.

'Thank you, sir. It was naturally a shock, particularly to my poor father.'

'Of course.' Again, his look expressed to a nicety what his words could not acknowledge, which was the peculiarly awkward situation in which they were both placed. As the son of the next heir, the death of her brother could do him nothing but good. While he had never, perhaps, expected to be in such a position, it could not be denied that the future, for him, had taken a turn for the better as dramatically as her father's had done for the worse.

'What an impossible thing this is!' he exclaimed. 'I cannot express my sorrow, without sounding completely insincere!'

'It is awkward,' she admitted, pleased with his openness, 'but less so than if we were meeting for the first time. That, indeed, would have been uncomfortable. But since we are already acquainted——'

'Acquainted!' His look spoke of a kind of playful hurt. 'Acquainted! That is a very cold word, a very distant kind of word to use. I had hoped. . .'

He paused, looking at her warmly. Mary felt a pleasurable heat suffuse her face, an agreeable flutter of her spirits, and dropped her eyes.

'We have known each other for so short a time, Mr. . . Hallfield. What had you hoped?'

He glanced around, and spoke with a lowered voice.

'I had hoped that there was something warmer between us, than a mere acquaintanceship.'

'Well, we are cousins, of course. . .though you do not choose to acknowledge it just now.'

'Do you blame me for that? It is true that I feared to let the relationship be generally known, for your father has always been so very. . .but it is only natural that he should dislike me and my father, of course. I cannot blame him for that. I should not, perhaps, have come here at all. If it were not for one thing, I should say that I regret having done so. It was whim that led me here, and dare I say a certain curiosity? And now I am punished for it.'

'Because you find yourself in an embarrassing position?'

'Because I have lost something, something very necessary to my happiness. Shall I tell you what I have lost, M. . . Miss Hadfield?'

This was moving rather more quickly than Mary had expected. She glanced round the room, to see if anyone marked them, and he was quick to interpret her look.

'I beg your pardon. I spoke more warmly than is allowable in an acquaintance.' He gave her a quick sidelong glance, and she could not help smiling.

'How you do harp on that word! Of course, if we had been brought up knowing one another, as cousins, I should think of you as such, but, since we were not, it is difficult to know what our relationship is.'

'Yet I am not the less your cousin, because our fathers were not friends. Indeed, one could say that it is our duty to heal the breach between them. There is, after all, a goodly precedent. What do you say to that?'

His manner was half playful, half serious. Mary hardly knew how to reply. If she should take up his allusion, as perhaps he intended, then she would be acknowledging that there might be, between them, a love that was more than cousinly. A few weeks ago she would not have hesitated, but would laughingly have hoped that she would come to a happier end than Shakespeare's star-crossed pair. Now, with the death of her brother having so unexpectedly changed their situations, she would do nothing that might appear to encourage him, to lead him into an outright declaration. If he had been merely an unknown and very attractive cousin, she might have done so. But as he was the next heir, after his father, to her own father's estate, her pride would not allow it.

'I would say that I hope I should always be ready to do my duty, sir,' she said sedately, and as they were then interrupted he had perforce to be satisfied.

Though the days were beginning to draw out, the winter afternoons were still short, and Mary rose to take her leave not much more than twenty minutes later. Her father's strange behaviour regarding the sale of most of their horses had meant that she was very reluctant to ask for the carriage to be put to merely to bring her home, and she was resolved on walking. Since she was known to be an energetic person this occasioned little surprise to her hostess, and she was able to slip from the room without any fuss. She knew that her sisters, and their husbands, would frown to know that she intended to walk such a distance in the dusk, unattended, but comforted herself that nobody would know, and that she could hardly be in any danger in a place where every stone, almost, was a familiar friend.

Nevertheless, she walked briskly, a little concerned to find that the sky was less light than she had thought, and that a young moon was already clearly visible in the lucent blue. When she heard footsteps coming behind her, quite fast and heavy, she was a little alarmed, but determined not to show it. Without looking round she quickened her own pace, her anxious ears straining, and finding to her dismay that the other was also hurrying, and gaining on her. She cast a glance to either side. The road, no more than a small country lane, was quite deserted, and she knew only too well that she would pass no human habitation for at least half a mile, when she would come to the lodge gates of the Priory. She had no riding crop or stick with which to protect herself, and she doubted whether she had time to find anything by the roadside that would be strong enough to be a weapon.

She could feel her heart pounding in her throat. She found herself thinking of her new acquaintance, Lazarus Smith. How happy she would be to see his tall, broad-shouldered figure appear through the trees. How she would welcome the sound of his voice, uncouth though it might have appeared in a lady's drawing-room. The footsteps behind her were very close. She drew her breath to scream, determined at least that she would not give in quietly to her assailant, but before she could utter a sound heard her name called, urgently.

'Miss Hadfield! Cousin Mary! Do not be alarmed!'

She whirled around, the indrawn breath leaving her with a rush that made her head swim, for a moment. She gripped her hands together, waiting as he came up to her.

'Did I frighten you? I beg your pardon. I had no idea you would walk so fast! I wanted to accompany you home, at least to the gates. Surely you do not usually walk through the dark like this, alone?'

'Not as a general rule. I must admit I did not think it was as late or as dark as this. I—I did not wish to ask for the carriage, for Papa has sold most of the horses and I have nothing to ride or drive, just at present. But I often walk into the village on my own. I think nothing of it.'

'It is hardly right, but I do not complain, since it gives me a chance to speak to you.' He stood beside her, head elegantly bent, neither his dress nor his hair at all disturbed by his haste, and offered his arm with a courtly gesture. She laid the tips of her gloved fingers on it, and could have laughed at the difference from the protector she had been imagining. Mr Smith, if that was indeed his name, would have been more likely to scoop her up on to his horse, she thought, or grasp her under his arm.

Her cousin Jason, however, did neither, but paced

decorously beside her. She cast a sideways glance at
him. His handsome profile, seen to great advantage
against the glowing sky, was thoughtful.

'I beg your pardon if I frightened you just now,' he
repeated.

'Oh, I was not very much alarmed,' she prevaricated.
'It was merely the surprise. If I had known you
intended to walk with me, I should have waited.'

'I thought it better,' he said confidentially. 'I thought
you would prefer not to make any kind of talk. I know
how these country villages are: the slightest rumour
flies round like the wind.'

'Thank you,' she responded dubiously. 'Though I
think my credit is good enough for me not to be
compromised by walking with the guest of my sister's
godmother, for so short a time.'

'Of course, of course!' he hastened to say. 'Of your
reputation there can be no doubt! But your situation,
and indeed mine, is one of such peculiar delicacy. And
nothing, to me, can be more important than your
happiness and peace of mind!' He gave her a glowing
look, and just pressed the fingers that lay on his arm
with his other hand. If the look in his eyes was a shade
calculating, Mary was not aware of it. Her eyes were
bedazzled, her spirit englamoured by his presence.

'You are very kind,' she said. 'My fear is not of talk
among my friends, who I am sure would say no harm
of me, but of my father coming to hear of it. I know
you are only too well aware of his unfortunate preju-
dice against your family. He is so—unwell at present
that I should not wish to cause him further distress.'

He looked serious.

'Ah, yes, your father. Not for the world would I
want to give him cause to be vexed with you! If I

thought that I might be the instrument of harming you, through him, I should leave here immediately, at whatever cost to my own feelings!'

She was bewildered.

'My father would be angry, certainly, but he would not harm me! I am past the age for nursery punishments, Cousin, and poor Papa would not think of lifting his hand against me!'

'Of course, of course, but you misunderstand me, Cousin Mary. I was referring to your future prospects!'

Mary was at a loss to comprehend him.

'My future prospects? What can you mean, Mr Hadfield?'

He gave a little laugh.

'You are so delightfully innocent, my dear cousin! I mean, with regard to money! I know that you should receive a not inconsiderable sum, on your father's death. If he should be so angry with you as to deny you this security, I should never forgive myself. Never!'

Mary, who seldom gave much thought to such matters, laughed back to him.

'Then you may be easy! It is quite beyond his power to punish me in that way, even if he wanted to. The sum you refer to is settled on me by my mother's will. No, my fear is on his behalf, that I do not wish to add to his present misery.'

He pressed her hand again, more warmly.

'My dear cousin,' he sighed. 'You are too good, too noble! Your duty to your father, of course, transcends all other duties, but can it be right to blight, perhaps for ever, the happiness of another? You must be aware—it cannot have escaped your notice—that my feelings towards you are very warm, very warm indeed?

And I have dared to hope that you are not indifferent
to me?'

Quite suddenly the conversation, which though per-
sonal had before seemed rather circumspect, had taken
a direction that could lead to but one end. Mary knew
that she should be flustered, that her heart should be
thumping and full of joyful anticipation, and she was a
little disappointed to find that she could listen quite
calmly, and respond in an even voice. It was as if she
were living a fairy-tale, and her life of late had been so
prosaic that magic and romance seemed far removed
from it.

'I could not be indifferent to my newly found cousin.'

'Oh, Mary!' He stopped, and stood facing her. 'If I
could think that I might be more than a cousin to you!
I can be silent no longer! Will you not make me the
happiest of men, by saying that you will be mine?'

Mary looked up at him. The handsome face
expressed everything that was proper to the moment:
ardent affection, and hope, and perhaps a kind of
certainty that her answer would be in the affirmative.
Though this was not unexpected, and she had no
grounds for maidenly dismay even had she been given
to such coy behaviour, she felt a sudden reluctance to
appear over-eager, as if the spell he cast over her might
be broken by too close a contact.

'I do not wish to upset my father,' she temporised.
'Perhaps in a while. . .'

'In a while! My dearest Mary, can you find nothing
kinder to say to me than that? Your father cannot
harm you, and why should this news make him
unhappy? Is it not the best thing that could have
happened? His daughter, at least, will live in his
ancestral home, his grandchildren will continue the

Hadfield line! Surely, when his first shock is over, he will gain comfort from this?'

'You would think so, but Papa does not always see things as others do.'

'Forget Papa. You have not yet given me your answer. Will you be my wife?'

Her pride made her wish to refuse him, the fear of looking as though she married him so that she would not lose her home, but the glamour of his presence was stronger than pride, and she could not say no. She nodded her assent.

'My dearest!' He raised her hand to his lips, but through her kid glove she felt only the pressure of his lips, not their warmth. She gave a little shiver, and he was all contrition.

'You are cold! I am much at fault, keeping you standing here in the dark! God forbid that you should take any harm from it! Come, we will walk on. I can hardly find words to tell you how happy I am! Of course, we can scarcely be married for some months yet. Such a wedding as this will need careful planning, and there is your father to placate. Besides your mourning, of course. You would not wish to be married while you are in mourning.'

Mary thought that her groom was not in a hurry to claim her, but reflected that it was just as well. It would give her time, at least, to try to teach her father to accept her marriage.

As they reached the lodge gates, he stopped again.

'It is better, perhaps, that I should not come to the house just yet. You are not afraid to go alone, from here?' He kissed her hand again and, when she raised her face, her brow, a chaste salute that she accepted with meekness.

'Farewell, dearest Mary. You have made me the happiest of men, and I know that I shall be the happiest of husbands. I shall call, the day after tomorrow, to speak to your father, unless you send word that you do not think it advisable. Farewell!'

He was gone, his footsteps hurrying away down the darkening lane. Mary stood watching him for a moment, then turned to walk down the long drive. She was, she told herself, very happy. Her future was settled in the best, the most appropriate way possible. Her betrothed had expressed himself becomingly, had been fond without attempting to take advantage of their solitude, which showed that he was truly the gentleman, she decided firmly. And if, in his raptures, he had referred only to his own present and future happiness, and made no mention of hers, it was merely an oversight. The building was in view now, bulking huge and dark against the sky. Her home, past, present, and future. And it was merely because she was cold, and tired, that it assumed for a moment the appearance of a prison.

CHAPTER SIX

THE elderly butler was on the watch for her, and the front door was opened before Mary had so much as raised her hand to it. She would have given anything she possessed to have been able to creep in unseen through a side-door, to have made her way quietly to her own room and spend a solitary hour there, putting her thoughts in order. But she knew that Hampton would have been mortally offended had she done such a thing. It was his job, and his pride, to let her in, to exchange the sedate words that his exalted position in the household permitted, and she could not deprive him of this, particularly now when there were so few visitors to the house. She had been in charge of running the Priory for many years, and since her brother's death it seemed that the servants turned to her for orders and advice more, rather than less.

Now she laid aside bonnet and pelisse, and went straight to her father's room. As usual he lay curled up, turned away from the door, either asleep or feigning it. She tiptoed to the bedside.

'Papa? Are you awake, Papa?' She spoke low, in a voice that could not have disturbed him had he been truly asleep, and he gave a little moan.

'Now you have woken me! If you knew how I lay, night after night, never closing my eyes, you would not treat me so! But it is always the same. The young and healthy have no idea, no idea at all, of the sufferings that such a one as I must endure!'

'I beg your pardon, Papa. I did not mean to disturb you. Shall I go away?'

'And leave me all alone again? No one to talk to all afternoon, and now you cannot even spend a few minutes with your poor old father? Well, you must do as you please.'

'So I shall,' she said with an assumption of calm cheerfulness. 'And what pleases me most is to sit here with you, and tell you all the village news, if you would like to hear it? And there is still some while before dinner, so perhaps we might drink a cup of tea together? It is so cold outside.'

He grumbled a little at this, but when she had poured his tea just as he liked it, and plumped his pillows comfortably so that he might sit up to drink, he was a little less fractious. Mary told him such items of local news as she hoped might interest him, exerting herself to make them amusing. He would not laugh, but once or twice she thought he almost smiled, though he quickly hid behind his cup.

'Hmph. Servants' gossip,' was all he said, but he did not stop her when she continued. The news of Buonaparte's escape interested him little. The wars, to him, had meant almost nothing, since they had never been a family with connections in the military or naval world, and his only worry was whether the price of corn would be affected. Mary knew an insane desire to blurt out the only piece of real news she had. What, she wondered, would be his reaction if she were boldly to announce that she had betrothed herself, not half an hour since, to the son of the man he hated most in the world? She looked at his face, which had grown so pale and bony, and thought that the shock might actually kill him. And yet he had to be told. He, of all people, must know of this change in her fortune. But how, and when? In which of his alternating states of mind would he best be able to hear her? The thought was so impossible that she half smiled to herself and shook her head a little.

'You're looking very cheerful, very pleased with yourself,' her father grumbled. 'Glad to have got away from me, to go out and enjoy yourself, I suppose.'

As she protested against these unfair words, Mary thought how typical it was of him, who so rarely noticed anything about her state of mind or appearance at all that she could have grown a second head without exciting much remark from him, that he should see that little smile.

'I suppose I do feel more cheerful tonight, Papa,' she admitted carefully. 'Not that I want to be away from you, but it is pleasant to visit, and meet other people.'

'Old tabbies in the village, and pert young chits! If that's your idea of visiting. . .'

'And gentlemen too, Papa,' she said carefully. He looked at her sharply.

'Gentlemen? The vicar, I suppose. And the general, perhaps? Pair of old fools.'

She persevered.

'Younger gentlemen as well, Papa. Visitors, you know, from the houses.'

He went white, and his voice was almost a scream.

'Young gentlemen? What do you mean, young gentlemen? Flirting, I suppose? Whispering and giggling and pressing hands! I won't have it! I won't have it, hear me? Hear me?'

'I do, Papa. Probably, the servants do. And possibly the village does, also.'

'Don't be pert with me, miss. There's your poor brother, your poor dear brother, hardly cold in his grave, and you're carrying on like a. . . Well. . .' He paused, a little deterred by the flashing look she gave him. 'Well, I do not find it proper, that is all.'

'No, indeed, and nor should I, if I had in truth been behaving as you imply. But surely, Papa, you do not think I would be so lost to all sense of my position, as to be a vulgar flirt, now, or at any other time?'

'But you have just told me there were gentlemen there, have you not?'

'I certainly have, but I hope I am old enough, and sensible enough, to be able to carry on a rational conversation with any person, female or otherwise, without flirting.'

He was soothed, and while it was not in him to apologise his anger subsided.

'Perhaps so. Perhaps so. You are not in your first season, after all,' he murmured to himself.

'But not quite at my last prayers I hope, Papa,' she teased him, hoping to cheer him. He scowled at her. 'Come, Papa,' she said coaxingly. 'You would wish to see me suitably married, would you not? I thought that was every parent's wish?'

He looked at her in horror, as if she had proposed some vile act.

'Married? No. It cannot be. I will not permit it.'

'But Papa——'

'Not another word.' He was gabbling, almost cowering against the pillows. 'I am ill,' he gasped. 'You have made me ill, with all this talk of marriage. I shall die, and yours will be the blame! Selfish, heartless girl!'

He did indeed look ill, his lips blue and trembling, his face livid. Mary started towards him.

'Keep back! Keep back!' he almost screeched, lifting the sheet to his face as if seeking its frail protection.

'But Papa, your cordial! Let me give you some of your cordial! Pray, Papa, do not look at me so! I do not want to hurt you!'

He was breathing in tearing, ragged gasps.

'No, no! Get away! Where is that man of mine? He will see to it. Ring the bell, and go!'

Puzzled and dismayed, Mary did as she was bidden. She waited outside his door, and was comforted when her father's servant came out a few minutes later to tell her that he had taken the cordial, was calmer, and a better colour.

'Leave him to me, Miss Mary,' he said gently. 'He'll soon be right, come you leave him be.'

It was with relief that she approached the door of her apartment. It was, in fact, a self-contained suite of rooms at one end of the old wing, with an antechamber leading to two large rooms, connected by a smaller. In the past she and Martha had slept in the two bedrooms, for Martha's frequent attacks of pain had made her a restless sleeper, and she had been resolute in refusing to allow Mary's sleep to be broken by sharing a bed, or even a room. When Martha had died her sister had, at first, been unable to bring herself to alter her room, but after some months her habitual common sense had asserted itself, with the thought of how much Martha would have disliked to have her chamber kept as a shrine to her memory.

With some tears Mary had caused the bed to be removed, and with the addition of a small piano and a good-sized work table to the existing furniture had made herself a little sitting-room, where their books sat side by side on a broad bookshelf, some of their better attempts at water-colour sketching enlivened the walls, and their old dolls sat in a friendly row on the window-sill. It was in this peaceful haven that she was in the habit of passing her quiet hours, and now she breathed a little sigh of relief as she opened the door and saw the firelight gleaming on the familiar, if battered furniture.

Then a tall figure unfolded itself from the fireside chair, and the sigh caught in her throat as she stifled an involuntary scream. Never before had any man, even her brother or her father, made himself at home in this private sanctuary, and for half a minute she thought she had surprised a burglar. Then the figure turned his head, and she saw the silvery gleam of his scarred cheek. The relief was so great that her knees trembled, and she felt sharp needles of burning cold shoot up her back, and down her limbs so that she gave a shudder. At once he was beside her, one warm hand grasping hers and the other slipping round her waist to support her.

'I beg your pardon! I have startled you!'

'Well, yes, a little!' she admitted. 'I had no idea. . . so few people ever come up here. I suppose Sarah brought you up? Where is she?'

'Looking for you, I imagine, to warn you of my presence. She must have missed you, and it is not difficult to see why. I never was in such a rabbit warren!'

'Yes, I know, it is a little—overweening.' Mary became aware that her hand was still clasped in his, and that he held her in a warm, if passionless embrace. In confusion she almost snatched herself away, then tried to cover her abruptness by going to light the candles. She hoped that the warmth of the fire as she stooped to light a spill would account for the burning of her cheeks. 'I cannot understand why she should have done so—brought you here, I mean. What was to stop you from calling, in the usual fashion, and having yourself announced?' Her voice sounded peevish to her own ears, and she was not altogether surprised when he replied with wry irony.

'Surely you have not forgotten that I have picked up the habit, abroad, of visiting ladies in their bedrooms? It was you yourself remarked on it, I believe. Of course, this is not quite your bedroom, but I do retain some vestige of correct behaviour, whatever you might think!'

Mary had been moving towards a chair, about to sit and to invite him to do likewise, but this unwise speech brought her upright and bristling.

'How very unfair of you to throw my ill-considered words back at me! I think my brains must have been addled when I asked for your help!'

He saw that he had overstepped the mark, and was instantly contrite.

'Forgive me—I am afraid that I have lived too long out of civilised society and am become quite boorish. I meant no more than a jest, and I hope very much that you will still permit me to help you. It is my earnest wish to do so, if I may.'

So handsome an apology made her ashamed, in her turn.

'No, no, it is you who must forgive me, for I knew very well that you were only joking. The truth is that I have had rather a difficult day.' She suppressed a hysterical giggle at this choice of words. 'Pray sit down, and let me ring for some refreshment.'

He did as she asked, but lifted his hand in firm
refusal of anything to drink.

'No, do not ring. Only your maid knows that I am
here, and it might occasion some comment were the
other servants to find out. For reasons which I cannot,
at the moment, divulge, I feel that your father would
not welcome me under his roof.'

'My father keeps to his room, and would not have
been aware of your presence if you had been admitted
and asked to speak to me.'

'I know, and for that reason I could not do so. I
could not take advantage of his state of health by being
accepted as an accredited visitor to this house.'

It seemed odd, to Mary, that his scruples did not
appear to include his surreptitious entry into her private sitting-room, but long experience of the ways of
gentlemen enabled her to be silent. It was, she
reflected, one of those mysterious matters of honour,
like duelling, or the sacred necessity to honour gaming
debts, however dubious, that seemed to most women
more akin to the barbaric superstitions of prehistoric
tribes.

At that moment Sarah burst into the room, panting.

'Oh, Miss Mary! And to think I've been seeking you
all over the house, and you in here already!'

'As you see, Sarah. I gather I have you to thank for
Mr Smith's presence in here?'

Her maid flushed a little, and bridled indignantly.

'Well, miss, I knew as you'd been worrying, the last
few days, when you didn't get no answer to that letter
you sent, so when he sent me in a message, private
like, I thought it were for the best to bring him up
here. For you'd not be wanting to go out in the dark

and cold to talk to him, nor you wouldn't expect a gentleman to wait outside till morning, would you?'

'I wasn't worried, exactly,' began Mary. 'But never mind that now,' she added hastily, seeing that Sarah was ready to argue the point, and noticing the gleam of amusement in her companion's eye. 'Since he is here, it is better that no one should know. Will you make sure we are not interrupted?'

'Don't you worry, miss,' was the hearty rejoinder. 'I'll be in your room, and I'll keep the door open, so I'll hear if anyone comes. Or if you should need me,' she added, with an admonishing glance at the gentleman that Mary, for one, thought rather belated.

'She makes a splendid conspirator, doesn't she?' he said as the door closed. 'You are most fortunate in your maid.'

'Yes.' Now that he was here, lounging at his ease by her fireside, she hardly knew how to frame her request, and she wondered at her own temerity in writing to him. Of course, if she had known that her cousin was about to propose to her, she would not have done so. She could have asked Jason instead; after all, to whom should she turn if not to her intended husband? From him, at least, she should have no secrets, and he who would one day promise to love and to cherish her was surely the most proper person to help her now. And yet the thought of talking to him of her brother and his death was somehow distasteful, almost unthinkable, and she knew that she could never have asked him to find out the truth. The man now with her, uncouth though he might appear, whose true name she did not even know, still gave her a feeling of safety, of a security that was not stifling or over-protective, but made her feel at peace with the world.

She saw that he was smiling at her, with a warm look of kindly amusement and something else that made her blush and lower her eyes with the awareness that he had a tolerably good idea of what she was thinking.

'I should not have written to you,' she murmured.

'Perhaps. But you did, and here I am. So you might as well tell me what is troubling you, and see if I can do anything about it. I make no promises, mind, but you know I'll do my best.'

She knew that it was true. Haltingly at first, then with greater ease as her narrative progressed and he displayed neither surprise nor disgust, she recounted what she had been told of her brother's life and death, both by the rector and by her father. He listened intently, without interruption or exclamation.

'And so, you see, it seems possible, even likely, that his death was not natural. I never pretended to love him, any more than he did me, but he was my brother, after all, and his death has caused so much misery to my father! If it is true that he died by his own hand, I would rather know the truth than not, and if he were murdered. . .'

'Yes, what then? You wish the murderer brought to justice?'

'Yes, I suppose so,' she said dubiously. 'That is, of course such a person should not go unpunished. But there would have to be a trial, and I do not know if my poor father could bear it. I. . .oh, dear, I just don't know. But I want the truth.'

'The truth can be an uncomfortable bedfellow,' he said gently. 'Your brother is in his grave, and no amount of knowledge of the manner of his death will bring him back. Would it not be easier and pleasanter to leave things as they are?'

'Yes, it would be. But I cannot do it, you see. Could you?'

'I think you know I could not, just as I knew you could not. But I had to ask, to be sure.'

'Yes.' There was a companionable silence, as the fire hissed and murmured in the grate. Presently he stirred.

'Well, if I am to find anything out I will not do it by sitting here. I had best be going.'

'Just like that? Do you not want to know where he was living, who were his friends, those sort of things?'

'Do you know them?'

'Where he was living, of course. And some of his friends, although I think he only brought the more respectable of them here.'

'Give me the address, then. The rest I can find for myself.' He spoke with careless certainty, and Mary looked at him in wonder.

'You make it seem so easy. Have you, perhaps, done this kind of thing before?'

'Not precisely. But there have been times when I have needed to learn things, find things out, look for people. . .'

'And you will tell me what you discover? Whatever it might be?'

'You have my word on it,' he promised soberly, rising to his feet. She followed suit, looking up at him in some embarrassment.

'You may be put to some considerable expense. Will you allow me——?'

'No, I will not,' he broke in roughly. 'My dear girl,' he continued in gentler tones, 'there is no need. I am not a poor man. Many would say that I am rich. I dress like this, and stay at Runforth's inn, because it suits me to do so, not because I cannot afford anything better.

And before you ask,' he added with rough good humour, 'it was *not* by stealing the Brighton bank's eight thousand pounds that I made my fortune!'

Scarlet in the face, Mary muttered an apology.

'No need to look so upset,' he rallied her. 'It takes more than that to offend me. Yet another example of the deplorable effect of living in the wilds, I'm afraid. Talking of money does not embarrass me at all these days.'

'Well, why should it? I ought to be accustomed to it also, for my father speaks of scarcely anything else, on the days when he is well and gets up. He is for ever quizzing me over the household accounts.'

His unorthodox entry into the house had given him a glimpse of the stables, empty and cold, and of rooms shrouded in holland covers, and tell-tale marks where pictures had vanished from the walls.

'Turned a shade miserly, has he?' he asked easily.

'I'm afraid he has. I think it is the shock of losing Giles.'

'Very likely,' he agreed, keeping his own counsel.

She held out her hand and he took it, drawing her nearer. In the dim light his eyes examined her face.

'You are very pale,' he said abruptly, 'and I believe that if I were to lift you up now there would be no weight to you at all, you are so thin. Have you been ill?'

He released her hand, and showed signs of intending to test his theory by putting it into practice, and Mary stepped back and took hold of his hands to prevent him.

'No! Yes!' she said disjointedly. 'That is, no, I have not been ill, but, yes, I am thinner. I do not seem to have much appetite just now, and I have been worried about Papa.'

'You should get out more, take more exercise.'

'Yes, Doctor,' she murmured meekly.

'I am not joking. It can be of no possible help to your father if you yourself fall ill. You must take more care of yourself.' He spoke roughly, for he had been alarmed by what he had seen in her face. A little frown, more of perplexity than annoyance, creased her brow, and he put out gentle fingers and smoothed it away. Her lips trembled until she firmed them resolutely, and her eyes glistened with tears, but she would not lower her gaze. She blinked a few times, then gave a little smile.

'Good girl,' he said encouragingly. It seemed only natural, then, to kiss her, and since she neither screamed nor repulsed him he bent and touched her lips with his own. It was a quick, passionless embrace such as he might have given to a child, but her lips were sweet and soft so he kissed her again, more firmly, and would have continued if her eyes had not suddenly flown open, while the hands that had, he was sure, been creeping up to his neck, turned and pushed him away.

'Oh!' Her eyes were round with horror. 'How dreadful!'

'Was it? Not to me, I assure you.'

'No, no, I mean how dreadful of me!'

'I don't think so. I should say the fault was entirely mine. I'm afraid I was carried away.'

'Yes, that's the trouble, so was I. I have never been kissed before, and it was very. . .that is to say, I was taken by surprise!'

His eyes danced at this artless admission, but he

managed to keep his expression becomingly sober, even contrite.

'Of course you were! Think no more about it. And if I should ever be inclined to do it again, I promise to warn you first.'

'But you must not! Oh, you don't understand. I have behaved so very wrongly!'

He frowned.

'Surely you are being unnecessarily missish. What harm is there in so brief an embrace? Who has been hurt by it?'

'My—my betrothed!'

He looked at her, thunderstruck.

'Your betrothed? You are engaged, then? I had no idea.'

She was annoyed by his surprise.

'Well, how should you? I have not seen you for more than a few minutes since I left the inn.'

'I mean, it is not generally known? I think I must have heard of it otherwise. The marriage of Miss Hadfield of Hadfield Priory would be a fine piece of news round here. When did this happen?'

'This afternoon. And nobody knows, not even Papa. I should not really have told you, and I would not have done, if you had not kissed me.'

'But you were with your father just now.'

'Yes, I should have told him,' she admitted. 'But he finds the thought of my marriage very distressing. When I only said that I hoped to marry one day, he was so angry and upset that I was quite worried for him.'

'Well, you have been his only remaining daughter for some while now. It is natural that he should wish to keep you with him.' He spoke absently, not really

thinking much of it, and Mary kept to herself the
thought that her father's behaviour was far from that
of a possessive, fond parent. 'So, who is the fortunate
man?'

'Why, the one of whom I spoke to you. My cousin,
Jason Hadfield.'

He had known it must be so, but his mind had not
wished to draw the inference. Somehow, he had hoped
that she had managed to meet some other eligible man,
or even a wildly ineligible one, come to that. Anyone,
rather than the man she meant.

'Yet you still ask me to run your errands for you? I
suppose he is too fine for such work. Mr Hadfield of
Hadfield must not go grubbing around after the skele-
ton in the family closet.' He spoke bitterly, out of a
hurt that he scarcely comprehended.

'No, no! How can you say such a thing? It is only
that when I wrote to you I had not seen him, did not
know he was near or that I should ever even see him
again. Then, when you were actually here, it seemed
silly not to ask you.'

'No wonder you wanted to pay me.'

She only stared at him, astonished by his attack.

'You said. . . I thought you were my friend,' she said
at last, in a low, shaking voice that pierced through his
anger and pain.

'Yes, I am. I am. Forgive me, I spoke harshly. Of
course you were right to ask me. I had no right to
question your actions or motives, no right at all. And
it is much better that he should not know of it, if there
should be any scandal. You may rely on me to hush it
up.'

'But. . .if it should prove to be murder?'

'You may safely leave me to deal with the murderer.'

He gave a wolfish grin, and she shivered. He looked at
her, unsure whether he wanted to throttle the life out
of her or snatch her up and carry her off with him by
force. With an effort he made a formal bow.

'I will take my leave of you, madam. Accept my
congratulations on your good fortune. You will have to
change neither your name, nor your abode, I presume.
A happy outcome, indeed.'

His voice was cold and distant. Like a puppet whose
strings had been suddenly relaxed, Mary bobbed an
automatic curtsy in response to his bow.

'Thank you, Mr Smith. I am very grateful for your
help. You are angry with me, I know, but I turned to
you as the one person who had offered to assist me. If
I had had another brother——'

'Do not,' he said between gritted teeth, 'say that you
will be a sister to me. A sister! Hah!' And with that he
turned on his heel and left the room. While Sarah took
him out of the building, Mary locked herself in her
room, and celebrated the happy event of her engagement with a hearty burst of tears.

John 'Lazarus' Smith rode off into the darkness of
the winter night at a reckless speed which took no
account of his own neck, or his horse's legs. He was
furiously angry with Mary, and still more angry with
himself, but he reserved the bitterest of his feelings for
Jason Hadfield, the man who had once called him his
brother. In his mind's eye he saw him as he had known
him: a golden-haired child, so beautiful that it had
been scarcely surprising that few people noticed the
calculating look in those clear hazel eyes. The little
events of their nursery days came back to him: spiteful,
secret words and deeds that were never noticed or

discovered. And this was the man to whom she had given her heart and hand.

Or had she? As his blood cooled, he reined in the horse and set his mind to work. That she would marry out of pure self-interest he could not believe, but it had to be admitted that, since the opportunity had presented itself, it was a most appropriate match. That she might be dazzled by his looks, as people had always been, was only too likely, and who should know better than his half-brother how much charm Jason Hadfield could put forth?

At the same time, it was unlikely that their relationship had progressed beyond the superficial level possible when all their meetings must, of necessity, be conducted beneath the public eye. That Jason had not kissed her she had herself confessed, and surely that was strange in a newly affianced couple? Nor had she discussed her problems with her lover, or asked for his help.

A little smile crossed his lips, and his anger drained away like dry sand through the fingers of a child. He acknowledged to himself, for the first time, that he had fallen irrevocably in love with his little cousin, and now he allowed himself to believe that she was not altogether lost to him. Whether he should follow his biblical precedent, and return from the dead to claim his undoubted rights as the inheritor of Hadfield Priory, or whether he should keep to his original intention of allowing his family to think him dead, he had no idea. But come what might, he would do his best to win the daughter, if not the house.

CHAPTER SEVEN

MARY ate her dinner in solitary state. She was thankful for the dim lighting in the gloomy dining-room, where the gleam of the candles seemed all but extinguished by the dark, heavy curtains against the dark panelling. Her eyes felt hot and prickly, her nose swollen and tender, and she pushed the food round her plate without interest, making no more than a show of eating. Her father, she was told, had refused all offers of food with loathing, and when she went to his room afterwards she found him fallen into a restless doze, which she thought a good thing. She sat with him for a while, but since he did not wake she went thankfully to her own bed.

Once there, however, tired though she felt, sleep evaded her. Her whole body ached and that, coupled with the continuing congestion in her head brought on by weeping, made her fear she might be coming down with a cold. In vain she tried to fix her thoughts on cheerful subjects. Her wedding day, which any young woman might be permitted to dream of as a happy and exciting prospect, could scarcely be envisaged without a pang. How could she picture herself floating up the aisle to a waiting Jason Hadfield, when custom decreed that she be accompanied on that triumphant walk by her father? And, looking further ahead, the idea of spending the rest of her life as the chatelaine of the Priory seemed, that night at least, like a sentence of penal servitude.

Then she tried to take her mind back to that happy moment when Jason Hadfield had proposed to her, but somehow the memory was overlaid by her more recent interview with Mr Smith, and its shocking conclusion. Try as she might, she could not summon up her beloved's face, and, though she could recall individual features such as hair, eyes, nose and mouth, she knew that were she to attempt a sketch of his face, as a heroine was required to do, she would be unable to produce any kind of recognisable likeness. Instead, Mr Smith's sardonic face, cold and distant as she had seen it last, kept obtruding itself in her mind's eye, and the memory of his kiss, which should have been hateful, brought instead a kind of delightful shiver that made her feel that even her own body was betraying her.

At last she fell into a heavy, dreamless sleep, from which she dragged herself the following morning with as much difficulty as if it had been quicksand. The morning was grey, damp, and cold, and Sarah greeted her with a sniff and the unwelcome news that the kitchen range, always temperamental when the wind was in the east, had this morning refused to do more than smoulder, with the result that her washing water was tepid, and her breakfast very late. She paused outside her father's room, and his manservant came out to her, his pale face worried.

'He's passed a bad night, I fear,' he said in response to her enquiry. 'I'm not happy about him, Miss Mary.'

'Should I send for the doctor?'

He frowned. 'I don't know as it would help. He's not been eating or sleeping properly, but though that weakens him it's not really the problem, to my way of thinking. It seems to me he's something on his mind, something bothering him.'

'Oh, dear, yes. Shall I come in and sit with him?'
He looked doubtful.

'I suppose so, miss. He's in a strange sort of mood, though. Not like usual, not at all, and that's what worries me.'

'I shall send for the doctor, then,' said Mary decisively. 'He may at least be able to prescribe something to quiet him. Then I'll come and see him.' She correctly interpreted the servant's look. 'Don't worry, I shall do my best not to upset him, and if it worries him to have me there I shall go.'

She found her father, as often before, huddled in his bed with his face firmly turned away, as if denying the reality of the world around him.

'Papa?' she whispered. 'How are you today, Papa? I hope you are better?'

'I shall never be better,' he muttered. 'Never, in this world.' The fact that he did not rail, or complain, or shout at her, was worrying and made her thankful that she had sent for the doctor.

'Come now, Papa,' she said in rallying tones, 'you must not speak like this. If you will only take some nourishment, and perhaps let the doctor give you something to soothe you, so that you can sleep. . .'

'Nothing can soothe an unquiet mind,' he said, so low that she had to strain to hear him.

'I know,' she said sadly. She stroked his hand where it lay on the sheet, but he took it away, as if her touch was painful to him.

'I have not been a good father to you,' he said at last, after a long silence. Mary looked at him in amazement. Never, in all her years, had she known her father to blame himself for anything. Other people, often. His wife, his children—not including Giles, of course—the servants, the King and his court, everybody she knew had at some time or other been held responsible for some ill or slight, real or imaginary. But that he himself—and his son—was without fault was the *sine qua non* of his existence.

'Papa, how can you say so? I have always had every comfort, every luxury, even! My friends have often envied your liberality.' And she had envied them, too, for the affection their parents showed them, though she never blamed him for that. She had had her sisters, and especially Martha, and though she had missed a mother's love she had never expected to be loved by her father, who had never shown more than tepid approval for any of his daughters. It was useless, however, to blame him for a lack that he was constitutionally unable to remedy, and, though she had often been saddened by it, it had not embittered her.

'Not a good father,' he repeated dismally, shaking his head.

'But we all understood, Papa,' she said earnestly. 'My sisters and I, we knew that you could not love us as well as Giles. Perhaps, if he had been born first. . . but you must not blame yourself.'

He looked at her blankly, as if she spoke in some unfamiliar language that had no meaning for him. Then he turned away from her, with a gesture of dismissal. She waited for a while in silence, but he had closed his eyes and was either asleep or wishing to be thought so. Worried and distressed, she left the room.

Outside, on the landing, she found the butler hovering. If she had not had so much on her mind she would have wondered why he had come himself, instead of sending a footman, but as it was she even failed to notice his air of scarcely veiled excitement.

'A gentleman to see you, Miss Mary. A Mr Smith. I've put him in the morning-room, as there's no fire lit in the library.'

'Mr Smith? How very odd, I thought that he. . .that is, thank you, Hampton. I shall be down directly.'

'Shall I bring the Madeira, miss?'

He was, she saw, delighted by this small return to the old days when the house was often full of visitors.

'Oh, yes. Thank you, Hampton.'

'I shall bring it myself, miss,' he said with a conspiratorial smile. It seemed strange, for not only had Mr Smith declared that he would not call formally in a house where he had reason to think that he would not be welcomed by his host, but his appearance and even his manners did not seem of a kind to endear him to the old-fashioned butler. However, she supposed that the servant hoped for some little romance to brighten the house and bring a little pleasurable excitement to the servants' hall, though of course nothing could have been further from the truth.

Nevertheless, she took the time to return to her room. Her gown of white cambric had seen better days and was limp with much washing, but there was no time to change it, so it would have to do, and it was at least clean and neat. Her hair she had arranged herself in a simple knot, and she smoothed it hastily, before dabbing her eyes and nose with cold water in an attempt to tone down their puffy appearance. She tried out several expressions in the glass, but the smile looked toothy and a little mad, while the severe look only made her look bad-tempered. She rubbed her cheeks and bit her lips, to get rid of some of the pallor he had complained of, and ran downstairs.

As she opened the door of the morning-room her

visitor was standing with his back to her, looking out into the garden. The room was very dark, for the ivy that grew over the back of the house had been allowed to encroach over the outside of the window, and no candles had been lit to counteract the greyness of the day. She could scarcely see more of him than a dark silhouette.

'Mr Smith! I did not think to see you today!'

He turned, and displayed, not the scarred and sardonic face of last night's visitor, but the handsome aquiline features of her betrothed. At once she wondered why she had not realised before. It was true that, with the grey light dimming the gold of his hair, his figure from the back did have a disturbing similarity to 'Lazarus's', perhaps in the set of the head, or even just the stance. Now, of course, she saw that he was shorter by several inches, dressed with his usual exquisite care, and could not have been more unlike him.

'Not see me today? How could you say such a thing, when you made me the happiest of men only yesterday!' He came forward and saluted her gracefully, bowing over her hand as he kissed it, then pressing his lips to her brow. If it was not the most passionate of embraces it was certainly performed with elegance and propriety, and since Hampton entered only a moment later with the Madeira she thought it fortunate that he had not attempted anything more lover-like. After all, she scolded herself, he could not possibly know how much she disliked to be kissed thus, nor that it reminded her unpleasantly of the rector.

Any further conversation was restricted to conventional inanities until the wine had been lovingly poured, the plate of biscuits and the more old-fashioned cake had been offered and partaken of. Mary saw, now,

why Hampton had displayed such avuncular approval
of her visitor, and she stifled a smile to see the older
man's pleasure that she had so personable and fashionable a gentleman calling on her. At last he withdrew,
closing the door with discreet firmness behind him, and
she felt quite sure that he would station himself near
by, far enough away that he could not be suspected of
eavesdropping, but near enough to be of use if needed,
and to prevent the entry of any less exalted servants
into their privacy.

'How clever of you to guess that it was I,' remarked
Jason Hadfield easily when they were alone. 'It was
not, I fear, an imaginative choice of name, but I
thought that to call myself even Hallfield might raise
some conjecture or suspicion among the servants.'

'Oh. . .yes, that was very wise,' she responded disjointedly. 'Of course, Smith is the name one always
thinks of, when disguising oneself. Not that I have ever
done so, naturally, but still. . .it is rather awkward for
you, coming here when Papa is so. . .but I am very
pleased to see you. Delighted,' she added, fearing that
her former phrase had sounded a little tepid.

'And I you.' He turned his glass slowly in his hand,
and the tawny liquid caught red sparks from the fire.
'You have not told your father of our intentions?'

'No. I should have done, of course, but I knew how
angry he would be.'

'It is a pity he is so set against my family. It is not my
fault, I think, that my father is his heir! And then,
surely our marriage is a very suitable one. After all,
you will be able to stay in your home, your money will
stay in the family—one would have expected him to be
delighted. And from your point of view you are better
off, for if your brother had married you might very

well have taken a dislike to his wife, or she to you! These things happen, you know.'

'Yes.' It all sounded very depressing, but true. She could not imagine feeling happy with any girl mercenary enough, or silly enough, to have married Giles.

'I hope you do not think,' she said in some discomfort, 'that I would marry you for such reasons? I could never marry someone I did not love, merely out of self-interest.'

'Of course, of course, it goes without saying.' He waved his hand dismissively. 'All I mean is that our match ought to please your father. Otherwise, what is to be done? Will he ever give his consent, or must we wait until he dies?'

'He will never give his consent.' She could not bring herself to mention the other choice. It seemed too much like wishing her father dead.

'Then what are we to do? If we may not marry, may not even let our engagement be known. . .'

'I do not know,' she said miserably. 'We must wait, I suppose. My father is not well, at present. The shock of my brother's death has been too much for him.'

'But he may well recover.'

'So I hope. That is what I meant—that he might be well enough to see things in a more reasonable light, or at least so that I need not fear that a second shock might kill him.'

'Of course, of course. But meanwhile, must we be condemned to use our youth in waiting? My dear Mary, another course is open to us. We are both of age, after all. You may marry without your parent's consent. A special licence is not so hard to procure.'

'You mean. . .elope?' Shocked, she stared at him.

'Do not be imagining anything too terrible! I do not

speak of a flight to Scotland through snow and hail,
with your outraged relatives in hot pursuit, so that we
may take part in some barbaric ritual over the anvil!
Merely, that I could procure a special licence in
London, and that we might be married there, quite
quietly and respectably. It is not so far away; after all,
you need only leave him for a few days, and say that
you need to see the dentist, or your modiste, or
something.'

'But my father! The shock would be even greater
than if I were to tell him we are engaged! I could not
do it.'

'You need not tell him.'

'Not tell him? Whatever can you mean? I cannot
disappear without leaving him word!'

He rose to his feet and came to her, kneeling
gracefully beside her and taking her hand into his own.
His handsome face was raised to hers, his hazel eyes
clear as water as they looked earnestly into her own.
The familiar glamour of his presence stole over her,
she was dazzled by him, her mind distracted from other
memories and thoughts. She could smell the delicate
scent of his pomade, and his handsome face was shaved
to such perfection that his skin looked as smooth and
soft as her own. Without knowing what she did she
raised her free hand to her lips, feeling the slight
soreness round them from the rougher skin that she
had felt the night before.

'I want to know that you are mine.' His voice was
low and impassioned. 'I want to be sure of you, and
what other way is there than this? I will not take you
away from your father: once we are safely wed, you
may return here and stay with him as if nothing has
happened. He need never know, you see. His last days

may be peaceful and happy with you at his side. And when he dies, then I will claim you for my own!'

'You mean we should not live together?' She blushed a little as she spoke.

'Oh, not all the time. But I could visit you, in secret! This is a huge place, and there seem to be very few servants. Surely we could find a way!'

'But if I should become. . .oh, it is not possible. Only think of the scandal! I should never be forgiven.'

'As the mistress of Hadfield Priory, I think you would find that much would be forgiven you that would not be allowable in lesser women,' he said, shrewdly cynical. 'But it would perhaps be better if we did not . . .stay together. But we must still be wed! You must be my own wife!'

'It seems very strange.' Mary looked at him dubiously, not knowing how to express what she felt. 'I mean, forgive me, but I hardly see the point of it! We should be husband and wife in name only, surely. What difference would it make? We could just as well wait, and then be married properly.'

He half turned from her, his handsome profile like a Roman coin against the dim light of the window. His voice was severe, wounded.

'Of course, I know that all girls want to have a lot of fuss at their wedding. Fine clothes, and a bevy of bridesmaids, and a breakfast. You must not think that I do not want that for you, also, but in the circumstances I had not thought that you would set so much store by such trumpery.'

'No, no!' she cried, stung by this unfairness. 'It is no such thing! That kind of display holds no pleasures for me, and I would willingly forgo them even if it were possible to have a big society wedding just now! You must not think it is that.'

'What else can I think?' he asked in wounded tones. 'You do not want a quiet, simple, private wedding. You just said that you could not see the point of it.'

'Oh, dear!' Mary put her hand tentatively on his arm but, feeling his lack of response, withdrew it again. 'Please, Jason, let us not quarrel over this! Of course I want to be married to you, as soon as possible! How can you doubt it? If you think it best that we should do as you suggest, then so be it. I am afraid that I sometimes worry too much about what others may think, but what does it matter, after all?'

She was rewarded with a brilliant smile, and he turned back to her once again.

'I knew you would see it my way, once you had thought about it! Dear Mary, it is only that I want to know that you are mine! An engagement that is known only to us two is after all scarcely binding.'

Mary was so relieved that all was well again between them that she did not allow herself to dwell on the fact that he did not appear to trust her. She did think fleetingly that she would have considered herself bound to him just as firmly by her word, once given, as if she had a diamond ring and a paragraph in the *Gazette*, but decided that it was really very flattering that her cousin was so eager to tie the knot between them.

'I cannot leave my father just at present,' she said. 'I have already sent for the doctor, and I do not think he will be well enough to be left for some days. You would not wish me, I am sure, to excite too much comment in the neighbourhood by taking myself on a shopping expedition when my father is ill! In any case, I suppose it will take some time to get the special licence, and make the arrangements. I am afraid I do not know much about such things.'

'Nor I—believe it or not! But I shall make it my business to find out. I shall do myself the honour of calling on you tomorrow morning, for I may not leave my hosts too abruptly, but when I have done that I shall go to London directly. I suppose I may write to you here? Send me word when you think you may safely leave the Priory, and I shall be waiting for you.'

Rather breathlessly Mary agreed, and her lover rose to take his leave. Once again he bowed over her hand, and this time Mary, blushing a little to find herself so forward, raised her face to his kiss. He seemed a little disconcerted, having expected to salute her brow again, to find her offering her lips, and there was a small, but perceptible hesitation before he touched his lips to hers. Scarcely had she felt their pressure than they were gone, but Mary would not allow herself to acknowledge any disappointment. His manners were most correct, and it was surely only uncouth men like Mr Smith who seized one in their arms and almost crushed one with the strength of their embrace.

Mary rang the bell, and when Hampton appeared she bade her caller farewell with great correctness under his beaming and avuncular regard, then took herself up to her apartments in the hope of finding a few moments of solitude in which to explore her feelings, and enjoy the happiness which she knew she should be experiencing, and which surely would well up in her when she had freedom to give it rein. Sarah, however, was waiting for her, and insisted on knowing the identity of the visitor.

'Mr Hallfield? That danced with you at the Fordcombes' ball? What ever did he want?'

'Why should he want anything? It was merely a visit of form,' prevaricated Mary.

'That's as may be. You want to be careful, Miss Mary. A girl like you, in your position, with no brother and her father too ill to protect her; it doesn't do to make talk.'

'Sarah! When you yourself brought Mr Smith up here, to my own private sitting-room, only last night! If that wouldn't make talk, I should like to know what would!' Mary was well aware of the relative merits of attack and defence, and knew also that she would need a good strategy to mislead someone who knew her, probably, better than anyone else in the world.

'That was different,' dismissed her maid loftily. 'You asked him to help you, didn't you? Besides, you know you can trust him, though he may go round the countryside calling himself Smith. I know a gentleman when I see one.'

'Merely because he happened to be handy when our coach overturned! Granted, I suppose he could have ridden off in the opposite direction, or stolen my jewels and ravished us both, but the fact that he helped us then does not turn him into an angel!'

'Did I say it did? I hope I should have more respect than to compare a mortal man to one of God's holy messengers,' responded Sarah sanctimoniously. 'All I say is, he's a good man.'

'But I didn't say he wasn't!' Not for the first time, Mary was finding her maid exasperating. 'Only why should you think Mr Hallfield is not?'

'Why should he come calling, and give his name as Smith?' asked Sarah suspiciously. 'You can't tell me that's the conduct of a gentleman.'

'He had an excellent reason for that, which I do not

propose to discuss with you,' Mary said with an attempt at firmness. 'You may take it from me that Mr Hallfield is a perfect gentleman, and I suggest that if you cannot find anything good to say about him you keep your own counsel. Better still, try to get accustomed to the idea of liking him.'

In her irritation she had said more than she had intended, and Sarah stared at her round-eyed.

'Oh, never say he's spoken! Never say that, my chick!'

'Well, I didn't say it,' Mary pointed out reasonably.

'Oh, my lamb! To think that there I was thinking. . . well, no more of that, though you did write him a letter! My dear, dear child! I'm sure I hope he's the finest gentleman in the kingdom, for you certainly deserve it!' Sarah gathered her nurseling to her bosom, and shed tears, while Mary resigned herself. 'But what do you know of him? Not that I mean to speak a word against him, and I'm sure any friend of the Fordcombes . . .but still, you've known him such a short time! What of his family? Is he rich?'

'I really do not know how rich he is, but I do know that he has. . .expectations.'

'Well, so I should hope. I'd not see you tied to a fortune-hunter, if I had any say in the matter.'

'I am not that rich, Sarah.'

'But not that poor either,' responded her maid shrewdly. 'And now you have poor dear Miss Martha's money as well, it's a tidy sum, when all's said and done. There's many a man would think himself lucky to line his pockets with that.'

'I think you may take it from me that Mr Hallfield is in a position that precludes any mercenary interest. Oh, Sarah, I wish you would stop carping! I have no one else in the world to tell, for my father is unwell and finds the thought of my marrying so distressing that I may not even tell him!'

'Ah, my poor little love! Of course I am happy for you, as happy as you are for yourself! And I ask your pardon if I seemed to say otherwise. Oh, what fun we'll have, planning your wedding! That'll brighten the house up, and no mistake! Surely Mr Hadfield will be better soon, and then he'll be happy too!'

Mary agreed, but her maid's speech banished any pleasure she might have been feeling and her doubts, which she had succeeded in banishing, returned. Her spirits were not raised by the doctor's visit, for after examining the patient he came out of the bedroom and shook his head at the waiting Mary.

'I can't say that I'm easy about him,' he said in low tones. 'There's no single condition that I can put my finger on. His pulse is moderately even and strong, his temperature normal, but I am not happy. There is a debility, a degree of depression, that worries me. I fear that he could think himself into death, if that does not sound too fanciful.'

Mary sighed.

'I know just what you mean. He has always been liable to periods of melancholy, but this is not the same. He is so quiet, so gentle! I do not wish to sound undutiful, but it is so unlike him! I do not know what to do.'

'I have left some stimulant cordial, but other than that we can only trust to time that he will become more cheerful. Try to see that he eats, of course, and takes a little exercise, if he will. I will call again tomorrow.'

He did so, and was encouraged to find his patient no worse, if no better. Mary listened to him half distracted, for Jason had not yet paid his promised visit, and she was listening all the time for his arrival. At last Hampton came to find her, but instead of announcing a caller he handed her a letter, offering it carefully on a silver salver.

'This has just arrived for you, miss,' he said.

The handwriting was unfamiliar, and once alone in her sitting-room Mary skimmed it quickly, her heart sinking as she did so. It was from Jason himself, informing her that news had reached him of his own father's illness. He wrote:

It may be that it is no more than a false alarm, for he has always been as strong as an ox, but I think it best to go and see. My dear Mary will, I know, understand and forgive my haste, for, the sooner I am gone, the sooner I may return to London and pursue the matter we spoke of. Therefore I will not do myself the honour of calling on you today, as I had intended, but will, by the time you read these words, be already on my way home.

He finished with protestations that were very gratifying to read, and seemed warmer than his behaviour the day before had been. Mary decided that in spite of his handsome face he was perhaps a little shy, and her heart warmed at the thought. She could not answer the letter, since he had omitted to give the address of his home and she knew only that it was in Yorkshire, but the loving words that she soon knew by heart cheered and comforted her through the days that followed, when her father was querulous, irritable and melancholic by turns, giving her tearful apologies and unmerited scoldings almost in the same breath. To her anxious eyes he was thinner than ever, and his colour so bad that at times when he slept she could hardly tell whether he still lived or not.

Nevertheless, he continued in life, and it was not he but his hated heir, the man as strong as an ox, who breathed his last barely a week later. Mary received a short letter informing her of the fact, and that her betrothed must therefore stay in Yorkshire to see to the obsequies. She went to her bed that night knowing that she would, indeed, be marrying the next master of Hadfield Priory. The thought, however, gave her little comfort or pleasure.

CHAPTER EIGHT

THE letter announcing the death of Jason's father was the culmination of a truly dismal week. Mary's worry over her father's health was exacerbated by loneliness, for Emily had a bad cold, and her prudent mother had confined her strictly to her bed lest it turn to a putrid throat or, worse, a congestion in her lungs. The late Mr McLaren had died of consumption, and his widow was in constant fear of the appearance of the dread disease in her only child. Mary longed for someone with whom to be able to discuss her doubts and fears, and never had the ills of her motherless state been so apparent to her.

With Jason so far away, and without the pleasure of his polished manners and handsome person, she found herself wondering whether she had not acted hastily in betrothing herself to a man she scarcely knew. That such doubts were normal in a prospective bride she knew, but it had to be admitted that even by the standards of a more formal age she had spent very little time in his company, and when she thought of their conversations it seemed to her that although she knew that he danced gracefully, and paid the most elegant compliments, his opinions and feelings about more serious and important subjects were a closed book to her.

Only one thing occurred to lighten the gloom of the passing days, but that was enough to afford her great pleasure. During the day after Jason's departure she

had a message from the stables that was mysterious
enough to send her hurrying there as soon as she was
at liberty to leave her father. The groom, an elderly
man with a face wrinkled like a walnut and just as
brown, led her in silence past a sad row of empty stalls
to one that was newly filled. A pretty chestnut mare
turned her head from the manger of hay she was
lipping, and regarded them with an expression of gentle
pleasure in her liquid eyes. A good horse blanket, quite
new, was draped over the partition of the stall, plain
but for the letter 'J' embroidered in one corner. Mary
stepped forward and stroked the glossy neck, smooth
and warm to the touch, and the mare nuzzled at her
hand, hoping for a titbit.

'There, now, my pretty, if I had known you were
here I should not have come empty-handed! She is
lovely, Studeley. Where has she come from? I did not
know my father had bought her.'

'No more he did, Miss Mary,' said the groom, his
wizened face scowling, which was his way of expressing
pleasure. 'Master don't know nothing of her. Brought
here this very morning early, she was, and all the man
would say was that she was a gift for the young lady,
from a friend, and that you was to be sure to take her
out every day, if the weather allowed.'

'A gift? But I cannot possibly accept anything so
valuable!'

'Don't know as how you can refuse, 'less you know
who give you her.'

'Of course I do not! At least. . .' She paused,
blushing slightly.

'Thought you might,' said Studeley laconically.
'Well, miss, you know the saying about gift horses. Not
that you'd need to look in her mouth, with this one,

for anyone with half an eye can see she's a prime one,
just what I'd have picked meself for you.'

'Yes, indeed, and so gentle. I know I ought not to,
but after all I do not really *know* who has given her to
me, so I cannot send her back, can I? I shall take her
out today, after my father has taken his luncheon. He
usually sleeps then for an hour or two.'

'I'll have her ready for you, miss.'

'I think, perhaps, I shall not mention to my father
that I have been given the mare. It might. . .worry
him.'

'That's right, Miss Mary. Time enough to tell him
when he's up and about again. I shan't say nothing.'

The mare proved to be as delightful to ride as she
was to behold, with easy paces, a soft mouth, yet with
a spark of fire in her that was often lacking in horses
considered to be a suitable ride for a lady. Mary
relished the freedom of being once more on horseback,
the more so when she rode to visit a newly recovered
Emily and found her and her mother busy with prep-
arations to go to the seaside.

'I am quite well now, but Mama is still not easy in
her mind, and I own I am excited at the prospect.'

'Brighton, at this time of year? You will die of
exposure, surely?'

'We are assured that the rooms are very warm, and
sea air has always agreed with me. It will be like a
holiday, only I shall be so sorry to be away from you.'

'And I! How I shall miss you! It is the greatest
misfortune, just when I have the means to visit you
more often!'

'The mare? She is very pretty, isn't she? A gift from
your father?'

'A gift, yes, but not from my father. No, do not

tease me! I may not tell you anything, and if you knew how I long to do so!'

Her friend contented herself with a speaking look, and a kiss. Now, as she cantered down a ride in the woods, Mary's thoughts were full of gratitude to the giver, whom she had longed to name to Emily. It was not, she thought, so difficult to guess who he was, for very few people knew of the state of the Priory stables. Mrs McLaren, though she had frequently mourned the loss of her young friend's mount, and regretted the lack of such healthful exercise, could never have afforded such a generous gift, nor would she have made it in so secretive a fashion. No, the mare must of course have come from Jason, whose initial was on the blanket, and her heart warmed with this evidence of his kindness and thoughtfulness. He had remembered what she had mentioned about the selling of the horses, and had sent her a betrothal gift that she valued ten times more than the more conventional jewels.

'And now I know what I shall call you,' she said aloud when she had slowed the mare to a walk. 'You shall be Jewel. Then you have your very own initial on the blanket. How do you like that, Jewel?' The mare twitched one ear back, and Mary gave the first spontaneous laugh that she had given for days.

Thereafter she rode every day, usually at the same time when her father had less need of her, and found that both her health and her spirits benefited from the exercise, and that she was better able to withstand the debilitating effects of long hours with her demanding father in the stuffy air of the sickroom.

The day after the arrival of Jason's letter she went out as usual. The day was fine and mild, and Mary went further than she generally did, through the new plantations and into the older, wilder part where last year's bracken, dry and brown, would soon be pushed aside by the tight-curled fronds of this year's growth. Her father had seemed a little stronger that morning, had eaten more breakfast than usual, and she had been emboldened to tell him the news of his heir's demise. Not much to her surprise, this had acted on him like a tonic, so that he had sat up in his bed with a brisk air, eyes sparkling with malicious pleasure, and talked with something as near cheerfulness as one of his disposition could achieve.

'So, he is dead! Older than I, of course, but I always heard he was a coarse, robust sort of fellow. Always the same, these tough yokel types! Think they're as strong as horses, then pouff! The slightest thing knocks them down. No resilience, do you see? No real fibre. All bluster and hot air. And there's an end of all his bragging and boasting! Saw himself as Hadfield of Hadfield Priory, but what is he now? Cold clay.'

'Now, Papa, you are unfair. I am sure he never expected to inherit, or gave it the slightest thought.'

'That's all you know, my girl. Wrote to me, he did, after your poor brother. . . Damned impudence. Cruel, heartless impudence.'

'He wrote? I did not know.'

'Not worth mentioning. Hypocritical stuff anyway, had the nerve to send his condolences! Said he was sorry to hear about Giles! Then, as if that wasn't enough, he had the audacity to suggest that since he would be inheriting the estate he should come and see it! Get to know the place! Coming to gloat, more like. I soon set him right, told him if he so much as set foot on my land before I was cold in my coffin I'd have him shot for trespass. Meant it, too!'

'But surely it would have been sensible, Papa? You could have taught him about the way you do things, introduced him to our people. I know it is hard to think of a stranger coming to make this his home, but then he would not have been so much of a stranger, would he? Still, as the poor man is dead now I suppose it would hardly have made any difference.'

'Now I think of it, it wasn't he who wrote, but the son. Not the first one—he was hanged or transported or something disgraceful; he's been dead for years. No, this was the next one. Had some fanciful name— Ulysses or something.'

'I fancy it is Jason that you mean, Papa. I have heard that is his name. Oh, then it is not too late! You might still write to him, and invite him to visit.'

Her father glared at her as though she were proposing to wrap a large and venomous snake round his neck as a cravat.

'Invite him! Have him sniffing round here, pricing everything up, snooping into matters that don't concern him? Never! Over my dead. . .yes, well, suffice it to say that I utterly forbid it. He shall never set foot on my land while I am here to prevent him!'

Mary thought guiltily that the feet to which her father objected had not only pressed his land, but actually trodden across his threshold, and been made welcome in the morning-room. Certainly, she thought with a little sigh, this was hardly the moment to broach the subject of her engagement.

Her father, at least, appeared highly refreshed by this passage, and announced his intention of getting up for a while, and sitting in a chair. He spent what was, for him, a pleasant morning musing on the fact that justice had, for once, removed her blindfold and given

his opponent what he deserved, and retired to bed
after his luncheon, spiritually refreshed if physically
tired. Once she was sure he was asleep Mary slipped to
her room to change into her habit, then ran down to
the stables where Studeley had Jewel saddled and ready
for her. He deplored her habit of riding out alone, but
since she had done so for many years he knew that
there was no point in offering to accompany her, so he
merely begged her not to go too far, and not to be
putting the mare at every gate she came to.

It was therefore with more than her usual relief that
Mary found herself alone in the forest. She should
not, she was guiltily aware, have been riding there, for
she was outside her father's land, but the chances of
meeting anyone were so slight that she did not scruple
to go against convention. She knew the paths and
tracks as well as she did her own garden, and had no
fear of losing her way, or of being troubled by footpads
or gypsies, who would be unlikely to venture so far
from roads or villages.

It was all the more of a shock, then, when a figure
on a large black horse, muffled in a cloak and with a
hat pulled well down over his face, stepped out into
her tracks and stood blocking the way. She was moving
at a brisk canter, so that she was obliged to rein in
sharply to avoid colliding with him, and there was no
time to pull up her mare short of him, while the path
was too narrow for her to be able to turn quickly. So
she made the best of a bad job, raised her chin, and
spoke as imperiously as she knew how.

'Who are you? What do you want? Kindly move
over, for my groom is behind me and will be here
directly, and you are in our way.'

At once he removed his hat, and the thin winter

sunshine glinted on his dark hair. He smiled approvingly, the thin line of scar creasing his cheek.

'Bravo! Bravely spoken!'

'I might have known it would be you,' she said
bitterly.

'Well, yes, you might. Surely you want to hear
whether I have learned anything, and what? I cannot
forever be creeping up to your boudoir.'

'It is not a boudoir, it is a sitting-room! You make it
sound as though it were full of yapping pugs and lace
cushions. And of course I do not want you in it. But
nor do I want to be frightened half out of my wits when
I take myself out for a solitary ride!'

'Solitary? What about your groom, or is he so far
beneath you that he does not count as company?
Where is he, by the way?'

'Nowhere, as you very well know. That was merely
a pretence, when I thought you were dangerous.'

'Not quite out of your wits, then. I should not care
to meet you when you are fully in them.'

'I hope I usually am. But you must stop this habit of
appearing so suddenly, when I least expect it. I could
have fainted, and broken my neck falling from my
horse! You should be thankful that I have not even
fallen into the vapours.'

'Oh, I am, I am, believe me. But you have done
neither, have you? Nor did you jab at your mare's
mouth, which would have been almost as bad. I
congratulate you; you are an excellent horsewoman.'

'A compliment! I thank you, sir.'

'Yes, and when you come to think of it, two compliments, for I took it for granted that you would behave
as you did, like a woman of sense.'

'I am overwhelmed.'

'So I see. Now, if we have finished this delightful exchange, shall we ride on? You would not want your new mount to take cold, would you?'

'By no means. She is lovely, isn't she? I am so delighted with her. Her name is Jewel.'

'An unexceptionable name. Why did you call her that?'

'Because she is a betrothal gift,' she said with pretty modesty. 'I had mentioned to—to Jason that my father had cleared the stables, and he must have remembered it, for the day after he left she arrived. Is that not delightful? So much more welcome than a pair of earrings, or a brooch, or even a ring, though I suppose I will have that by and by.'

He looked grimly amused.

'Very possibly. And what did he say when you thanked him?'

'Nothing, for I have not been able to do so. I have not seen him since he was called away, naturally, and I foolishly never thought to ask his address, so I was not able to write to him. Then, when I did write in reply to his letter, it seemed hardly appropriate to mention it, for he had sent me sad news. You will not be aware of it, but his father has died, only a few days ago.'

'I had heard.' His voice was blank, almost dismissive, but she sensed that he was not as unmoved as he appeared.

'How strange! I myself only received the letter yesterday, and I would not have thought he was sufficiently well known for his death to be common knowledge in London. How did you come to learn of it?'

'Need you ask?' He raised a sardonic eyebrow. 'Everything that concerns you, or your family, is of concern to me, since it might have some bearing on the matter you asked me to investigate. Naturally I have made it my business to find out as much as I could.'

'Oh, my goodness, I was so distracted that I had quite forgotten! Tell me, have you learned anything? About my brother's death, I mean?'

'Yes.' He looked down at her. They rode side by side, the narrowness of the path making it necessary that they should be almost touching, but his horse's height carried him far above her. His eyes were unreadable, fixed on her face. 'Are you sure you want to hear what I have learned?'

'Yes. Quite sure.' She wasted no time on protestations, but returned his look as steadily as she could, though her heart seemed to be beating in her throat. 'Was he murdered?'

'No. At least. . .not murdered, in the sense that someone forced a fatal draught down his throat. That he did indeed kill himself, I have come to be as certain as one may be. But you yourself said that he was not the type of young man to commit such a deed, and everything that I have learned from those who knew him confirms your statement.'

'Then what are you saying? He was not murdered, he was a suicide, but did not kill himself? I do not understand.'

'I am sorry. I am not making myself at all clear. I am afraid there are matters here that are not easy to speak of to one of your sex, and gentle upbringing. I should say that, though your brother poisoned himself with opium by his own hand, and even with the knowledge of what he was doing, he was driven to that desperate act by someone else, on whose head the guilt of the death lies as firmly, to my way of thinking, as if he had stabbed him with a stiletto.'

'But who? Who is this man?'

'That, I am afraid, I cannot tell you. I have not been able to learn his name, or anything about him.'

'But how can this be? Surely my brother's friends must have known him, seen him, met him?'

'It seems not.'

She reined in, and looked him earnestly in the face.

'Is this true? You are not saying it just to protect me? Or him?'

His eyes were unwontedly serious, devoid of their usual impudent twinkle.

'Quite true.'

'But you said it was something difficult to explain to me. I wish you would try. I am not stupid, you know, and I do have some knowledge of the ways of the world. Also, you know that I had no love for my brother, nor any respect for him. It pains me to say it, but I do not think that I would be surprised by anything that you could tell me about him, though I might be shocked.'

He continued to look at her, a questioning stare that she returned without flinching, then he sighed.

'Very well. But it is not a pretty tale, and I should have preferred not to sully your ears with it. I know that you had cause to dislike your brother, but still. . . I will tell you about it, as I learned it.'

He encouraged his horse into a walk, and she followed suit, all her senses concentrated on what he would say.

'First of all I went, naturally, to your brother's friends, and talked to them, asked them everything I

could think of. And then. . . I hunted for his lodgings,'
he said slowly.

'His lodgings? But surely Papa had opened the town
house for him? I thought he was living there?'

'He had been, but some months ago he moved out,
to all intents and purposes, returning to the house only
occasionally, holding a card party there, entertainments of that sort. At first he would be away only for
the night, and the servants thought little of it that a
young man of his wealth and tastes should be absent
once in a while. Then the disappearances became
longer, until at last he had his things moved to these
lodgings, the address of which he kept secret from your
father's servants. When he returned to the house, it
was on the day before he died, and it was the first time
he had visited it for weeks. He only came back, I think,
to die there. I do not suppose your father knew that he
had moved out.'

'No. He would surely have mentioned it. But I do
not think he would have minded very much. I suppose
he had a—a *chère amie*? And kept her there? Papa
would not have been worried about that. He would
probably have thought it a great joke.'

'Possibly. That was certainly what I assumed to have
been the case, but I was a little surprised when I found
that none of your brother's friends knew of the address
either, until I thought that perhaps the lady was not a
. . .not a professional, but some respectably married
woman whose identity had to be kept secret from her
husband and from society.'

'That would be just like Giles,' said Mary bitterly.
'He was never in the slightest bit interested in the kind
of girl who would have made a suitable wife for him,

though Papa was almost desperate to see him married,
with a nursery of his own.'

'Understandably. It is a pity the young man was not
more biddable, and there is not a little Giles to take
the place that his father has left vacant. However, all I
could then learn was that he would not be seen,
sometimes for as much as a week at a time, and then
only in gambling hells.'

'Gambling? I did not know he cared for that. What
of his poetry? Surely he was still writing?'

'It seems not. And during the last few months of his
life he seems to have been betting heavily. Drinking
heavily, too, and those of his friends who saw him said
he was almost frantic with excitement, laughing to
excess, but secretive. I am afraid——' he glanced
apologetically at her '—that none of them were sufficiently interested to find out what his secret was. He
was no longer good company, you see.'

'I knew some of those friends. Toadies, most of
them, flattering him because he was rich. He was never
any good at making friends, even at school.'

'More than that I could not learn. And yet I was sure
that if I could find the lodgings I must be able to
discover more. I asked among all my acquaintance—
some of them rather dubious, I am afraid——'

'I always said you were a smuggler!' Mary exclaimed
with satisfaction.

'Well, I do know some, as surely you do too, living
in Sussex! And one of them gave me the name of a
man he had heard of. A gentleman, as I suppose, but
one who makes it his business to seek out information.
He is known in all the best circles—you might meet
him any evening at Almack's, or even at Carlton
House—but he must have led a strange, chequered

life, for what he does not know about the affairs of the
underworld is nobody's business. He must have friends
and spies everywhere, I should think. An interesting
man; I liked him. Anyway, not to make too long a
story of it, this man Forester agreed to find out what
he could, for a fee, and I agreed.'

'For a fee? I thought you said he was a gentleman?'

He gave her an ironic look.

'Aye, so I did. But maybe I am not the best judge!
To my way of thinking he was. He is educated, speaks
well and with some wit, and I take him to be a man of
honour. If he is not rich, how many gentlemen cannot
say the same? He remedies it with the only skill he has,
and all credit to him, say I!'

'I beg your pardon! I did not mean to criticise this
paragon! And, I assume, he found the answer?'

'He did.' He fell silent, staring at the ground. Mary
waited in patience, aware that he did not want to
continue and that no urging of hers would make him
do so if he decided against it. 'It was not a pretty tale,'
he said at last, low and reluctant. 'Your brother had
become entangled with a man—no one could say where
they met, but it was almost certainly at the card tables
somewhere. He. . .fascinated Giles. Under his influence he gambled more and more recklessly, losing
money hand over fist, often to his new friend. He led
your brother to drink more heavily, and to experiment
with opium, not just in laudanum, but in other forms.
Giles left the London house to be with this man, and
took the lodgings, which I visited. The landlord was a
surly fellow, who cared for nothing so long as his rent
was paid regularly, but his wife had talked with your
brother's friend. She, it was plain, had adored him,
been fascinated by him almost as your brother was.

She did not know his name, or rather she referred to
him as "Mr Smith". . . yes, I know,' he added as she
gave him an expressive glance. 'There are altogether
too many Mr Smiths in our world, just at present.'

'More than you know,' she murmured, 'and I don't
believe any of them were born to the name.'

He disregarded this dig, and continued,

'Mr Smith, she said, was a fine young gentleman, a
very fine gentleman indeed. Friendly and pleasant, and
handsome as a god, as an angel, she said. That, of
course, did not surprise me.'

'Why?'

He looked down at her with exasperation tinged with
pity.

'You have not understood, have you? When I said
that your brother was obsessed with this man, that they
stayed at the lodgings together, I mean that your
original guess was not so far out. But it was not a *chère
amie*, nor a well-born wife of another man, that was
the secret he was hiding, but a more unnatural lover.
A catamite, in fact.'

'You mean that they. . .that he. . .? But how?' In
her shock she spoke without thinking, and a flood of
fiery red flowed over her face and body so that her very
fingertips prickled with embarrassment at his amused
glance. 'No, no, pray do not tell me! I was merely. . .
Good God, no wonder he kept it hidden! I did not
know that such things happened! The ancient Greeks,
of course, but that was then, not now, and I had always
thought it no more than a kind of extreme form of
friendship, not an actual. . .' The flood of words with
which she attempted to cover her feelings dried up,
and she turned her flaming face away from him.

'You see why I would have preferred not to tell you!

Forgive me, my dear girl, and do not be distressed. I can imagine only too well what your feelings must be, and how you must be wishing me a thousand miles away! But if there be shame in such things, it is not for you to feel it, and I can assure you that I am very hard to shock! Such things happen in most societies, and often far worse. Young ladies like you are brought up to be pure and virtuous in thought and deed, and that is right for young girls. But you are old enough to be aware that our bodies may not always be ruled by our minds, and that there are in all of us darker feelings and passions that cannot always be denied. Your own purity is not sullied by speaking of such things.'

The blood ebbed slowly from her face, and she drew a little hiccuping breath that was half a sob.

'Yes. I am afraid I am being missish. But it was a shock, you know. I could never have imagined that Giles. . . I mean, he never seemed at all. . .and then there were the housemaids!'

'It was not, probably, a settled inclination. Given time, no doubt he would have given up his illegal affair, and settled into a suitable marriage. From what I can learn of him, he was a seeker after novelty, after the pleasures of new sensations.'

'Yes. My father denied him nothing, and from an early age his every whim was gratified. He loved excitement, and danger. I can see how he could have been tempted by so new and titillating an experience. But I cannot understand how he could have continued with it, and why he should have killed himself.'

'As you say, such a young man would find it more and more difficult to satisfy his quest for a new pleasure. And this other man, with whom he became embroiled, obviously had the kind of charm that is almost irresistible to others. Your brother was certainly completely enthralled by him, and I imagine that if, later on, Giles had been rebuffed or taunted by him, it might have been enough to drive him to suicide. Such a thing, after all, had never happened to him before. And if, as I understand, he had been losing heavily at cards, it would be all the more reason.'

Mary shivered. She still could not imagine the Giles that she had always known desperate and miserable enough to do so fearful a thing as to take his own life.

'It is pitiful,' she said, low.

'Yes, it is. A weak character, led into darkness by one who appears to have been altogether callous and heartless.'

His final word recalled Mary to herself, and to her duties. She glanced up at the band of sky that showed between the trees on either side of them.

'Good heavens, it must be very late! It will soon be dark. I must hurry back, or they will be sending out search parties for me, and even alarming my father, if he should hear of it.' She turned her horse, and he did likewise.

'I will accompany you to the border of your land.' She did not answer, but kicked her horse to a canter, and heard the thud of hoofs as he rode after her. She reached the gate at a gallop and, knowing the ground well, put Jewel to it, exulting in the effortless surge as the mare responded and jumped, landing neatly. Glancing behind, she saw that he had not copied her, but sat like a statue on the further side, so that she was obliged to turn and trot back.

'I cannot stay! Will you not come back to the house?'

'No.' It was a flat refusal that brooked no argument. 'No, I will return to London.'

'To London?' She was dismayed. 'I thought you
would stay at the inn for a few days. I wanted to. . .
that is to say, surely I should reimburse you for the
money you have spent on my behalf.'

He grinned.

'Oh, I shall expect a full accounting, never fear. But
my task is not finished yet. Only half the tale is told. I
mean to find this man.'

'Oh. Of course. I suppose you must.'

'Do you not want to know who he is, why he did it,
call him to account?'

'Yes, I suppose I do. Yes. Yes, of course it must be
so. If he is guilty, he should not go unpunished. But
. . .shall I see you again?'

'Of course. Did I not just say there must be an
accounting between us?' He looked at her, the little
frown of perplexity between her brows, underlip caught
unthinkingly between her teeth. His voice was gentler.

'Do not distress yourself. Even if you had not wanted
me to continue, I should have done so. It is not in my
nature to leave such a thing half done. Go back to your
home, Mistress of Hadfield. Maybe—who knows?—it
may all be happily resolved. And if not, are we wrong
to try? Trust me.'

His hand stretched across the gate, and she leaned
forward and put her own into it. Even through the
leather of her glove she felt the warmth of his clasp,
and the firm strength of his fingers comforted her. She
smiled tremulously, withdrew her hand, and turned
towards the Priory.

CHAPTER NINE

IT WAS with a feeling of unreality that Mary sat with her father, later that same day. Refreshed by his sleep, he was unwontedly lively, almost cheerful. His eyes, which had been as lifeless as those of a fish, snapped and sparkled, his thin wrinkled face seemed already fuller, the glow of the fire casting a spurious lustre of health over the yellowed parchment skin. He spoke of Giles, recounted tales of his childhood and schooldays, as if he were not dead but away on some extended holiday, and Mary repressed a shudder. She tried to concentrate her mind on that little boy, but her memories of him at that time were so much at variance with those of her parent that she could think of nothing to say that would please him, and contented herself with smiles and nods.

This, however, was enough, and such was his flow of spirits that he ate a good dinner, taking a large portion of buttered crab and, when Mary was unwise enough to protest, demanding another spoonful.

'I do not know why you order such dishes, if I am not to be allowed to eat it! Since you know it is one of my favourites, I had assumed it to be a kind thought on your part, but I dare say that you had forgotten my partiality for crab! You will not grudge me so small a pleasure, I hope.'

Mary forbode to mention that the last time he had been offered crab he had refused it with disgust, saying that shellfish in any form was far too indigestible, and asking whether she was trying to poison him. The crab, one of her own favourites, had in fact been sent up by Cook as a small treat for her, as had been the dish of damson tarts that was to follow.

'I am so glad that you have a good appetite this evening, Papa, and that you are enjoying the crab. I was only worried that it might be too rich for you, especially at this time of day.'

'Nonsense,' he said through a mouthful, a dribble of butter slipping down his chin in an unlovely manner. 'I do not know why you must treat me like a baby. You will be feeding me pap out of a boat, if I am not careful.' Another forkful went into his mouth, the pink-white shreds gleaming richly and fragrant with nutmeg. 'Besides, the doctor said I was to eat anything that I could fancy.'

There was no point in mentioning that the doctor had also prescribed a light, nourishing diet. Nor, later on, did Mary have any more success in preventing her father from taking his port.

'A good wine never hurt anyone,' he pronounced, 'and port is particularly strengthening. My father drank a bottle a day, as I have always done, and he lived to a ripe old age.'

An attempt to dissuade him made him almost incoherent with rage, and Mary soon abandoned it, contenting herself with staying with him rather than withdrawing, as she usually did, to keep up the illusion of a formal dinner although he was eating it in bed. Over the wine he was increasingly loquacious, with a kind of frantic energy that began to frighten her. His words grew more and more wild, until it seemed that he was moving into some kind of fantasy landscape, woven out of his wishes and longings and desperation, a world where his son, still living, was dutiful and fond, where a golden future stretched ahead for all of them. Mary, lost in a blend of pity and distress, did all she could to calm him, and at length, to her relief, his wild speech became slower, and slurred, finally ceasing altogether as he sank into sleep.

She stood at his bedside, waiting to be sure that he would not jerk himself awake as he sometimes did. A snail track of spittle wound its way from the corner of his mouth, even in his sleep his face twitched, the lips moving convulsively round half-formed words, his breath moaning a little in his throat. With a kind of horror she thought of what she had learned, only a few hours before, about the last weeks and months of his adored son's life, and she prayed with a fervour she had not felt since Martha's final illness that the old man before her would never learn of it. Better, she now realised, that he should believe his son foully murdered than that he should know that the heir from whom he had hoped so much had died for love of a male whore.

Longing for solitude, she sent an unwilling Sarah to bed, saying that she would sit and read for a while. Alone, she laid down the book she had been sightlessly looking at, and pressed her fingers to throbbing temples. She wished, fleetingly, that she had not asked her unlikely acquaintance to make his enquiries. If only, she thought, she had been sensible and delayed her journey at East Grinstead, she would never have met him at all, and there would have been no one to ask. Or, which might have been worse, she would perhaps have asked Jason Hadfield, and then it would have been he, not Lazarus, who would have made the discoveries and reported them to her. Even alone, she felt her whole body flame with embarrassed horror at

the thought of discussing such matters with the elegant
beau who was her betrothed.

Exhausted, she dozed, waking with a start to find
that the fire had died down and she was cold in her
dress of fine white muslin. Sighing, she bent to untie
the ribbons of her kid slippers, feeling the ache of
tension in the muscles of shoulder and neck. As quickly
as tired limbs and mind would allow she slipped off
gown, petticoats, chemise and stockings, and pulled on
the lace-trimmed nightgown that Sarah had left warm-
ing by the fender. The bed was cold, but soft and
welcoming, and Mary was just tying the strings of her
nightcap before blowing out her candle when she heard
rapid footsteps coming to her door, and a low, insistent
rapping.

Huddling a shawl round her shoulders, she climbed
wearily out of bed, calling an answer as she did so. The
round, florid face of the housekeeper appeared in the
opening, incongruously framed in voluminous goffered
frills. Her habitual placid calm was overlaid with
concern.

'Oh, miss, Johnson sent me to tell you he doesn't
like the look of Master. He thinks Doctor should be
sent for. Will you come and see?'

'Yes, of course.' Her tiredness forgotten, Mary
quickly put a warm robe over her nightgown, and
thrust her feet into slippers. 'But let us waste no time!
Send someone for the doctor at once. If Johnson thinks
it is necessary, then I am sure he is right, and every
moment may be precious.'

'Very good, Miss Mary.'

'Don't wait for me. I have my candle already lit. Oh,
I knew I should never have let him eat the crab, and
take all that port!'

'Nobody could blame you for that, miss,' retorted the housekeeper robustly. 'Nobody that knew the master, that is.'

'Thank you, but please do go and send one of the grooms for the doctor!' Mary kept her voice equable, but she could have screamed at the sight of the large figure in its ballooning night attire still hovering in the doorway.

'Yes, miss. At once, Miss Mary.'

Johnson did not open the door to her hurried knock, and when she did so herself she could see why. He lifted worried eyes to her in mute appeal, and continued to hold down the writhing, thrashing figure of his master. With an exclamation of horror Mary ran forward and pulled the bell for help, then went swiftly to his side and added her own strength to his.

She would not have believed that her father's frail limbs could have so much strength. He fought to be free, mumbling incoherently, the only distinguishable words being 'No, no', uttered in tones of such anguished pleading that Mary felt her throat tighten.

'Papa! Papa!' she cried out, and his eyes turned to her, but there was no recognition in their depths, and when a moment later his arm slipped from her grasp she received a buffet on the side of her head that made her skull seem to ring like a bell.

'Don't take on, miss.' Johnson was breathless with exertion, but soothing. 'He's dreaming, miss. I've seen him like this before, when he got over-excited or ate too much rich food. It's like a bad dream that he can't come out of.'

'That crab!' she exclaimed in remorse. 'I knew I should have stopped him.'

'That, and the other news. But you've sent for the

doctor, Miss Mary? He's never been as bad as this before. I feared he'd do himself some hurt, and when he does wake he'll be exhausted, as like as not.'

'Can we do nothing to waken him? Cold water, perhaps, or smelling salts?'

'I daren't let go to fetch them, miss. When Mrs Turvey comes back. . .ah, here she is.' For all his attempt at calm, his voice betrayed relief at the sight of the housekeeper. 'The smelling salts on the table there, if you please, ma'am, and then a towel dipped in cold water. Yes, hold them under his nose. That's the way. Now then, sir! Master! Mr Hadfield!'

The ammonia salts were waved before the head that tossed feverishly from side to side. Mary could feel the fumes making her eyes water, and watched in hope to see her father come back to himself. The breath caught in his throat, and he coughed convulsively. Mary feared that he would choke.

'Mercy on us! He was never this bad when you first called me, Mr Johnson!'

'No, or I should have asked you to stay. Now, the wet towel to his brow, and I hope that will calm him.'

Certainly the body was quieter now, and Mary dared to relinquish her hold and take the towel from the housekeeper. Her father lay still, his eyes closed, with only the occasional shudder to show how his body had been racked before.

Then his hand came up, and weakly pushed at the cold towel that was dabbing his face. Mary dropped the towel on the floor, and took the hand in her own.

'Papa! Are you awake, Papa?'

His eyes opened slowly, looking at her first blankly, and then with recognition.

'Mary.' His voice was fine as a thread.

'Yes, Papa, here I am. How do you feel, Papa? You have had a bad dream, I am afraid, and frightened us all.'

'I am very ill, Mary. I am afraid I shall not be with you long.'

'Come now, Papa!' Mary spoke in rallying tones, as she had so often done in the past when he had spoken these self-same words, but her heart misgave her at the look on his face. He turned away from her look.

'I am sorry, my child. Forgive me.'

Now indeed a pang of terror shot through her.

'There is nothing to forgive, Papa,' she said gently. He shook his head, but did not speak again, only sighing a few times. His hand was cold and still within hers, so cold and still that when the shallow breaths slowed and then ceased she could feel no difference, and she was still holding it when the doctor came into the room, interpreting at a glance the stricken faces of the servants, and the still form on the bed that Mary still watched in anxiety, though no ill could come to it now.

Later, in her room, Mary lay sleepless in her bed. Sarah had fussed over her, had brought warm drinks, and cold, a hot brick for the bed, sympathy, even tears. Now, to Mary's relief, she had gone, driven away by her charge's silence and her determined pretence of sleep. After the door closed behind her Mary let her eyes open, the effort of keeping them closed having been as great as the reverse effort required to keep open eyes that wanted to sleep.

She should, she knew, feel something. A dutiful daughter should feel, or at the very least show some semblance of, grief. Tears should be shed, quiet, broken words uttered. Poor Papa. So sudden. Such a shock. Not strong, of course. And then the distress of poor Giles. . . The morning would come, and in the days to follow such phrases would be murmured, by her and others, as they moved through the prescribed patterns. But for now she need not pretend a grief she could not feel, and could even admit, guiltily, that her strongest emotion was simple relief.

Not that she would have wished her father dead. On the contrary, she would have gone to any lengths, braved any discomfort, if any effort of hers could have prolonged his life. But since it was not to be, how simple things now appeared! All her difficulties seemed to be melting like snow. Free of her father's prejudices, she might announce her betrothal to her cousin, knowing that her friends would be no more than pleased by so suitable a marriage. They must postpone the wedding, of course, for some months, but surely she would be able to continue living here, at the Priory, as she had always done? Even the revelations about her brother seemed less terrible than before. Her father could no longer be hurt by them, and if Lazarus did discover the name of the guilty man he would surely be able to devise some form of justice that would not involve them in scandal.

The following week was just as bad as she had known it would be. In hushed-voiced, mourning-clad huddles her relatives arrived. The only mitigating circumstance was the presence of Georgina and her new son, only a few weeks old but proclaiming his health lustily to all within earshot. His voice was loud, his utterances prolonged, but not so prolonged as those of his uncle the rector, who rendered the hours hideous with his pious platitudes and endless prayers, so that Mary was driven to hiding in her bedchamber and feigning indisposition. Once again the funeral cortège set out, with even more pomp than before and with slightly more sincerity among the mourners. Once again Mary insisted on being present, though her sisters stayed obediently at home, and was treated with offended forbearance by her priestly relative, who had a profound disapproval of any of the women connected with him behaving in so outlandish a fashion.

It seemed to Mary that the interval between Giles's funeral and her father's had shrunk to no more than moments when, as before, she slipped away from the rest of the party to lay her posy of flowers on Martha's grave. She could not help glancing at the churchyard wall, and it was without much surprise that she saw a dark figure waiting there. With so many people present, and feeling the rector's eyes fixed on her, she did not dare to approach him, but bent to rearrange, quite needlessly, the flowers she had brought.

He made her a slight, formal bow which she answered with an inclination of her head. He made no attempt to draw nearer, or to speak to her, but made a gesture of greeting and farewell, and turned to stride away. It was not much, but she felt both warmed and comforted that he had come. It would have been quite improper, of course, for Jason to have been present, as well as shockingly ill bred, but at least she felt that she had one friend to support her.

On her return to the Priory, she was drawn aside by an agitated Hampton. Refreshments were being served, and already a hum of the kind of relieved conversation that invariably followed a funeral was issuing from the saloon. Mary, bracing herself for some domestic crisis, like a burned cake or insufficient quantities of Madeira, found that her presence was requested by her father's man of business.

'Mr Camden? Now? But surely that sort of thing is for later, when the guests have gone? I cannot leave them now.'

'He was very insistent, miss. He says it is important that he should speak to you now, alone.'

'Well, I suppose I could see him for a few minutes. My sisters are with the guests; I will not be missed. Where is he, in the library?'

'Begging your pardon, miss, but I have taken him up to your sitting-room. He said he must be quite private with you.' Mary raised her eyebrows. Mr Camden must indeed have been insistent if he had induced Hampton to take him to her private room, where only one other male visitor had ever set foot.

Upstairs, Mr Camden greeted her with grave courtesy. She had known him all her life, though never well, and was surprised by his attitude of avuncular anxiety. Although he had been eager to speak to her, now that she was there he seemed to be at a loss to know what to say. Restraining her wish to be gone, Mary sat down with as much serenity as she could muster, and asked him to do likewise. He did so, but continued to utter platitudes.

'Mr Camden, I understood that you had something very particular to say to me? If I am absent for too long my family and our guests will be offended. Pray tell me what it is you wish to say.'

'You are in the right of it, Miss Hadfield. I am wrong to prevaricate, and yet. . .how hard it is to speak! I cannot hide from you that I have news to impart of the utmost seriousness. Indeed, I fear you must prepare yourself to hear something that I fear can only cause you distress! Miss Hadfield, are you aware of your brother's activities in the last months of his life?'

'Am I aware of——? Yes, Mr Camden. I am sorry to say that I am.' Mary stared at him in horror. Surely this dry, precise man, old enough to be her father, and with whom she had never exchanged more than the most formal of civilities, was not about to discuss with her Giles's unfortunate love-affair? If so, she could only be relieved that she knew of it already, and would be able to cut him short before his explanations went beyond the bounds of supportable embarrassment. She saw that he looked relieved.

'Then you will know, I suppose, that he had lost considerable sums at the gambling tables. Very considerable sums indeed! I do not know what led him to this——' Mary, at this point, relaxed a little '—for he had become so very secretive, and I learned only the other day that he had no longer been living in the London house, but had taken lodgings somewhere!'

'So I had heard,' murmured Mary. Obviously the disclosures she had feared were not to be made.

'Then it seems that you know as much as, or more than I. But were you aware, Miss Hadfield, that his debts of honour were such that I was no longer able to find the money to cover them? That he came to your father for help?'

'No.' Mary was puzzled now. 'It must have been while I was staying with my sister, Lady Tarrant. I have not seen Giles for months.'

He sprang to his feet as if unable to remain still, and commenced pacing up and down, his eyes on the floor. With an air of violent distress he said,

'Miss Hadfield—Miss Mary, the debts to which I allude were monstrous! What he could have been

thinking of. . . But there is no good speaking this way.
I must tell you, Miss Hadfield, that in order to meet
them your father was forced to raise every penny he
could muster. All the available funds, everything that
was not strictly part of the entail, even a parcel of land
that had been bought some years since—all disposed
of. I was not, I need hardly say, a party to it. I was not
consulted, though, in fairness, if I had been, it is
difficult to know what I could have done.'

'Good heavens! No wonder my father was in such
distress, and behaved so oddly, after Giles died! I had
no idea why he should sell all the horses, and be so
quibbling about the household accounts. If only he had
told me, I should not have minded his economies. I
could have helped him, perhaps.'

'If he did not mention it to you, it was because he
was ashamed.'

'Ashamed? Papa? Why should he be ashamed? His
was not the fault, though I know he hated to think any
ill of Giles. Was that why?'

The man of business gave a little groan, and ceased
his pacing, coming to stand before her.

'You have not understood me, my poor dear child!
When I said that everything went that was not entailed,
I meant absolutely everything. Including, of course,
the money your mother left. The money that should
have come to you. There is nothing left. . .nothing!
You are—God help me that must say it to you—you
are penniless. And, unless the heir consents to help
you, homeless as well.'

There were actually tears in his eyes, and so strong
was her urge to comfort him that Mary could scarcely
take in what he had told her.

'You are kind to be so concerned for me, but please

do not distress yourself! I am sure I shall be all right. There are my mother's jewels, after all. I should be loath to sell them, but they are of great value, and if need be. . .' Her voice tailed off as she saw that he was shaking his head sadly. 'You mean. . .my father sold those, as well?' She was silent for a moment at this final blow, which hurt her more than the loss of the actual money. 'No wonder he asked me to forgive him,' she said bitterly.

'I begged him to warn you, when I came before, but he refused to speak to you of it, or to allow me to do so. My dear Miss Hadfield, you must believe that if I had known of his intentions I would have done everything in my power to prevent him. Everything!'

'I know. You are very kind. Dear Mr Camden, your kindness induces me to confide in you that I am not quite friendless. Oh, I have my sisters, of course, and I know that they would offer me a home, reluctant though I would be to subsist on their charity. But I have hopes in another direction. Nothing has been announced, and I had not even mentioned it to my father, but there is a gentleman who has asked me to marry him. So you see I shall be well provided for, and you need have no fears for me.'

He looked at her sadly, then seated himself at her side and took her hand in his.

'I would be only too glad to know it, but my dear child—forgive me—you are young and perhaps not as wise in the ways of the world as you might be. It pains me to say it, but a man, and his family, may not view marriage to a young woman in your position in quite the same light as a connection formed with a young lady in possession of thirty thousand pounds. I hope, for your sake, that the gentleman is above such mercenary considerations, or at least that he is a man of honour who will stand by his word.'

'I should not dream of holding him to it, should he be reluctant,' said Mary proudly.

'I know you would not. And if, as you say, nothing has been announced and nobody knows of this betrothal, it would scarcely be possible for you to do so. Ah, you think me cynical, but such things are not unknown.'

Mary was not as worried as he. It did not seem to her that the heir to Hadfield Priory would need to marry money. However, she was as yet reluctant to let the name of her suitor be known, and she contented herself with vague and soothing protestations. He appeared somewhat comforted, and at last left her alone with her thoughts.

'I expect you will prefer to be by yourself for a while. I must, of course, go down and read the will—not that it is of any moment now, since there is no money to fulfil any of the bequests. I shall explain matters, with your permission, to Sir Anthony, and the rector.'

The thought of the result of such an explanation made her shudder.

'Oh, yes, please do. And perhaps you would tell them that I would like to be alone, for a while? I shall stay up here, if they will make my apologies.'

He assured her that, if he could do nothing else for her, he would see that she was left in peace. After he had gone Mary allowed herself the luxury of a few tears, not so much for the sake of what she had lost as for her father's betrayal. When the door opened a few moments later she said, with an averted head,

'I should like to be alone, if you please. I thought I had made that clear.'

'Well, not to me. But I will go away if you want.'

She whirled round, handkerchief still to the nose which she had been blowing.

'Mr Smith! What on earth. . .? How did you get up here?'

'There are so many people around, it was not very difficult. And of course I knew the way already. I've been here for some time, waiting for you, but when I heard someone coming up, wheezing like a grampus, my needle-sharp mind told me it was not you, so I took myself off.'

'Where were you?'

He had the grace to look abashed.

'In your bedchamber, as a matter of fact. No need to look so shocked! I can assure you I have seen far more shocking things in my time. I would, naturally, have waited in the dressing-room, but I found that the voices carried too clearly. I am not,' he declared virtuously, 'an eavesdropper, so I removed myself beyond another door. And now, the grampus having departed, I am here. Do you want me to leave you alone?'

'Yes! No. Oh, I don't know.' She gave her nose a final scrub and raised her eyes to his, knowing that they were red-rimmed and puffy, and that her face was blotched and shiny with tears.

'Forgive me.' His voice was gentle. 'This is a sad day for you. I had not thought you would mourn your father so deeply. I will leave.'

'No, no, it is not that. At least, of course I am sorry for him, but I am afraid I would be more likely to weep for his shortcomings than for his death. The truth is, I have just been told some distressing news, and it has overset me for the moment. I shall be quite all right presently.'

'The grampus?' She nodded mutely, her eyes filling once again so that she rubbed them crossly with the damp handkerchief. 'What did he say to make you unhappy?'

He looked so angry that she was driven to protest.

'It is not his fault! Indeed, he was in the greatest distress himself. But it seems that my brother's gambling debts were far greater than we had realised, and my father has sold everything to pay them. My mother's money, that should have come to me. And her jewels. Everything. And I wouldn't mind so much, only he didn't tell me.' Her voice wobbled, and she firmed her lips, blinking hard and sniffing.

For about three seconds he successfully subdued the urge to take her in his arms, then he pulled her towards him and held her in an embrace that he told himself was no more than brotherly, while she leant thankfully against him and wept comfortably into his chest. His hands were warm and strong as he stroked her back, his voice tender as he murmured the little, loving words that he had not heard since his early childhood. When her sobs had subsided to the occasional hiccup he took out his handkerchief, and tactfully withdrew his arms while she mopped and blew again.

'Better now?' he enquired, as to a three-year-old.

'Yes, thank you.' Her smile was tremulous, but unforced. 'You are very kind. I am afraid you must think me very weak, and silly.'

'It is bound to be a shock, learning that you are penniless. And then, of course, there is your betrothed to consider, and his feelings on the matter. Will he mind, do you suppose?'

'Of course not,' she said stoutly, but her eyes did not meet his.

'Well, if he does, you had better marry me instead.' His voice was so prosaic that she hardly knew whether she had heard him aright.

'Marry you? Are you proposing to me?'

'Oh, only as second-best, of course. I could not hope to compete with the handsome Mr Jason Hadfield. But you did say, early in our acquaintance, that you would like to have adventures.'

'And to be married to you would be an adventure?'

'I think so,' he said with becoming modesty. 'Of course, I would not dream of putting any pressure on you, but I would not like you to think you had no other alternative than living with your sisters, or being a governess, or some such nonsense.'

'You are sorry for me.' It was an accusation.

'No, no. At least, yes, but that is not why I asked you.'

'Then why did you?' Her face, raised to his, was the reverse of flirtatious. She looked suspicious, even worried, and the little frown was back.

'I do not think I am going to tell you, just now,' he said. Then he bent and kissed, not her lips, but the furrow between her brows, and was gone.

CHAPTER TEN

MARY managed to avoid seeing any of her relatives that night, but she could not hide from them for ever. The following morning she steeled herself to go down to breakfast, where she found her two brothers-in-law and her sister Caroline. Georgina, of course, was still upstairs with her baby. There was a short, charged pause in the conversation when she entered, and, though both the rector and Sir Anthony rose to their feet and set her chair, neither of them met her glance, or looked at the other. Caroline busied herself feverishly at the urn.

'My dear Mary——' began the rector.

'Mary, my dear——' said Sir Anthony at the same moment. They glared at one another and Mary stifled a giggle. Both of them, obviously, felt the right and the need to settle her future for her, and neither would agree to give the other precedence. In most things, Sir Anthony would have given way to the claims of the Church, but his wife had not made the journey to Sussex with a new baby, she had informed him in the course of the night, so that poor Mary should be made into some kind of unpaid female curate in Caroline's chilly house.

Mary decided to follow both her inclination and the forms of precedence.

'I must thank you all for your support and assistance yesterday. Your address was most—most comforting,

Rector. Sir Anthony, I hope you slept well? You wished to say something to me?'

'Yes, I did. As to sleep, I should have been all right if it were not for the confounded. . .that is to say, I do not know why Georgie must keep the little fellow in the dressing-room, and not in the nursery! However, that is by the way. I need hardly tell you how very shocked I was, Mary, by what Camden told us last evening. It is altogether disgraceful, and what my father-in-law was thinking of. . .however, *de mortuis* and all that. Anyway, I feel, and Georgie with me, of course, that it is up to the family to make some kind of reparation to you. I can't promise to make you as rich as you should have been, but a few thousand, at least, would give you some security.' He blew his nose violently. 'So there it is, and I don't know that we need speak of it again.'

'Or at all! My dear brother,' replied Mary in moved tones, 'you are too good, too generous, but it is not to be thought of. That you, with all your dear family to bring up and establish in the world, should make such a sacrifice! No, it is not to be borne.'

'I am bound to say,' put in the rector, 'that I think this offer, generous and Christian as it undoubtedly is, has been made too hastily, and without proper fore-thought. No one, my dear Mary, could esteem you more highly than I. My home is always open to you. . .' He paused, and Mary murmured her gratification. 'And nothing could please me more than to see you find a refuge beneath my roof. But as to money. . .it is all very well, Sir Anthony, to speak of finding a few thousand, as if it were no more than a handful of sovereigns. You have your estates, your revenues. . .'

'As you have your tithes,' put in Sir Anthony with a show of belligerence.

'Indeed I do, but I have expenses, my dear sir, expenses! A man in my position must uphold the honour of the Church, and the tithes I receive are for that purpose, not for me to give away to a relative, however deserving! If Mary came to us, she would want for nothing, as I hope she knows, and she would have the satisfaction of using her hands and her time in the service of her Creator. No godly household could do less, or, I think, more.'

'If you can't spare her any money, fair enough, but what's to stop me doing it? And offering her a home, too, of course. I'll take another cup of coffee if you please, sister.'

'Oh! Oh, yes!' Caroline had been watching the menfolk with an expression of avid horror, and since she regarded herself as no more than a spectator it was alarming to be addressed directly. However, since she had been noticed, she ventured to remark,

'If my brother Tarrant wishes to do this, Rector, and we in our turn give Mary a home, does that not make everything right?'

Sir Anthony gave a snort of derision or amusement, and Mary, who had continued calmly to eat her bread and butter, lifted her napkin to her lips to hide a smile. Though her sister might not see it, the world in general would certainly have something to say about so uneven a providing. While the rector was reluctant to part with money, he was equally reluctant to have it seen to be so.

'Really, my dear, you speak of things you do not understand.' Caroline flushed, and shrank beneath the rector's look.

'It would be acceptable to me,' interrupted Sir Anthony, 'if it pleased Mary. But I should be still happier if she would make her home with us.'

'You are both very kind.' Mary thought it time that she brought their bickering to an end. 'But I will say once and for all that I will not accept any money from either of you. As for where I am to live, it is too soon to make any such decision. We do not yet know the intentions of the heir.'

Three faces were turned to her in silent amazement.

'The heir?' boomed the rector. 'What has the heir to do with it? You can scarcely expect him to give you a home. Of course, if there had been a dower house. . . but there is not, and, as for staying here with him, it is not to be thought of! Most improper! I know that you have always thought of the Priory as your home, but you must learn to see that its doors must forever be closed to you now.'

'Nevertheless——' began Mary, but she was interrupted by Hampton, who trod to her side with a note on a salver.

'This has just arrived for you, miss. The boy is waiting, but I am to tell you that it is not necessary for you to reply.'

'Thank you, Hampton.' Mary perused the few short lines, and passed it to the rector, whose hand was already outstretched to receive it.

'Mr Jason Hadfield! Presenting his compliments, and trusting that it will be convenient. . .hm. . .eleven o'clock this morning! He certainly does not mean to waste any time. Strange that he should address it to you, but perhaps he does not know we are here. Well, he is within his rights, and this is a perfectly proper message. I suppose we should be glad to be given any

warning at all, rather than thrown out of doors. I
imagine you will scarcely wish to receive the fellow,
Mary. You may safely leave it to me. And Sir
Anthony,' he added.

'On the contrary,' said Mary gently, holding out her
cup to Caroline for more tea, 'I certainly wish to be
present. I am still the mistress of this house, for the
moment at least. If you would like to be there, I shall
be happy to have your company. And, of course,' she
gave a warm smile, 'that of my brother Anthony.'

'Your bereaved state makes it impossible for me to
remonstrate with you,' said the rector heavily, 'but I
have a copy, which I shall lend you, of a sermon that I
once gave on the sin of pride. I say no more, at this
time. But you may rest assured that I shall certainly
not permit a young and inexperienced lady to meet
with this man, of whom we know nothing, alone and
unsupported by the male members of her family. If you
have finished, Caroline?'

He rose and his wife, who was still eating, hurriedly
swallowed and set down the cup she had been about to
lift to her lips.

'Oh, yes! Quite finished, thank you, Rector!'

The door closed behind him with what, in a lesser
man, might have been called a bang, and Mary met Sir
Anthony's eyes in a moment of shared amusement.

'I am afraid the rector is vexed,' said Mary
remorsefully.

'No more than I am,' he said, with mock anger.
'How can you be so stiff-necked, my dear girl? It would
be no hardship to me to settle some money on you,
and, as for living with that skinflint, just you dare! I
own I never cared for him so greatly, but I respected

his position, of course. Now, however, I find I want to do nothing so much as to kick him downstairs!'

'Then I had better keep you out of his way,' said Mary. 'Come, Anthony, don't tease me to take your money. If I should be homeless, you may be sure that I shall fly to you for aid, and eat you out of house and home if it will make you feel any happier. Now take me to see Georgie, and that delicious nephew of mine! I did not see him all yesterday and feel severely deprived.'

It was not difficult to distract him, and keep him talking of this and his other children. Georgina was more difficult to evade, but fortunately the baby set up a loud wailing and Mary had an excuse to leave them. In her room she inspected herself from head to foot. The funeral over, she had not felt obliged to wear black, but her morning gown of white muslin was very plain, adorned only with a small ruffle at the hem that was embroidered with a design of ivy leaves in black, with a similar band of embroidery on the little frill that encircled her neck. Her chestnut hair was arranged in a simple knot, from which a few soft wisps had escaped to frame her face, which looked pale and anxious. Hastily, with her ears straining for the bustle of an arrival, she rubbed her cheeks to bring a little colour to them, and pinched her pale lips. Then, with her heart beating so hard that she thought it should have been visible through the white muslin bodice of her gown, she went downstairs.

Her timing was perfect. As she reached the foot of the stairs Hampton was opening the door, and holding out his hand for the visitor's hat and gloves. At the sight of the unforgettable golden head and handsome face he paused, and opened his mouth to speak. Mary stepped forward.

'Thank you, Hampton,' she said firmly, fixing him with her eye. He looked at her, read the unmistakable message in her glance, and turned impassively back to Jason.

'It is Hampton, is it?' he enquired with easy charm.

'Yes, sir.'

'And you have been here many years?'

'Oh, yes, sir. Very many years.'

'Then I hope you will stay for many more. Perhaps you would be kind enough to inform the staff that, while I may need to make a few changes, I should like to know that as many of them as feel able to stay will do so.'

'Thank you, Mr Hadfield. That is very gratifying news.'

Mary had remained at the foot of the stairs while this interchange took place. Now, Jason came towards her, his face expressing just the right blend of polite concern and pleasure. Even in the dim light of the panelled hall he seemed to glow with a kind of radiance, and as always in his presence she felt the pull of his attraction, the glamour of his presence fall over her like a spell.

'Miss Hadfield! Cousin Mary! I am very pleased to see you.' He bowed punctiliously over her hand.

'I must speak to you in private,' she whispered, adding more loudly, 'Welcome to the Priory, Cousin. My brothers-in-law are waiting in the library to greet you.'

'They do me much honour. You must allow me, Cousin, to express my regret at the loss of your esteemed father. I wish that it had been possible for me to have met him. It is dreadful to think that I do not even know what he looked like.'

Mary looked at him with approval.

'There is a portrait of him in his study, which was thought to be a very good likeness. Should you like to see it?' She led the way as she spoke, moving quickly, and closing the study door firmly behind them as soon as she might, in case the rector took it upon himself to follow.

'There is something I must tell you,' she said baldly. 'I have heard some bad news, which may affect our plans. The plans for our marriage, that is.'

His eyes had been roaming round the room, passing indifferently over the portrait that hung above the fireplace, taking in the fine panelling, the buhl table against the wall, the air of luxury throughout. Now his gaze sharpened and he fixed it on her.

'Bad news? Concerning what? Your brother?'

'Yes, in a way.' An expression of anger crossed his face, instantly banished. 'Only indirectly, however. It seems that he lost so much money, gambling, that all my fortune is gone.'

'Gone? The thirty thousand, gone?'

'Yes. I had to tell you. If you no longer wish. . .if it is not now possible for us to marry, you have only to speak. I would never hold you to your word, now that I am penniless.'

'Your family would, however.'

'They do not know. I have not spoken of it. That was why I wanted to speak to you, first, so that you should be warned.'

His expression was unreadable; he was as aloof and beautiful as the statue of an ancient god.

'Do you wish to withdraw from our engagement?'
He was neither hopeful, nor angry.

'I? No. But I will not tie you to me. I should tell you
that there may be—are—some unpleasant and even
scandalous circumstances surrounding my brother's
death, which it may not be possible to hide.'

'How do you know?' His voice was light, cool.

'Someone—a friend—told me. I had heard something from my father, you see, that worried me, and I
asked him to find out what he could.'

'You should have asked me.' His tone was silken
now, a caress. 'In fact, you may leave it all to me.
After all, I shall be your husband, shall I not?'

Something within her relaxed.

'You still want. . .?'

'Of course I do! How could you doubt me, my dear
Mary? Surely you did not think me a fortune-hunter,
did you?'

'Of course not. But the estate has been so impover-
ished. My father has sold off everything that he could,
to pay the debts. I do not know anything of your own
circumstances. It might have been necessary for you to
marry a rich wife, so that things might be put to rights.'

He gave an odd little laugh.

'I have plenty of money, my dear. I can take care of
you, and the estate, in every respect. And who is this
friend who has been helping you? Somebody I know?
Should I, perhaps, be jealous?'

'No, no, not at all!' Was her reply perhaps a little
too hasty? She tried to speak calmly, to dismiss from
her mind that strange proposal—surely not meant?—
and, above all, those kisses. 'An acquaintance, merely,
someone quite chance-met, a gentleman fallen on hard
times who will undertake, for a fee, to solve other

people's problems.' Impossible to explain about Lazarus—or John—whose true surname name she did not even know!

'A strange occupation for a gentleman. Now, of course, you will tell him that you have no further need of his services? If he is working for his hire, I do not suppose he will mind, so long as he is paid. You must allow me to give you the money for that. It shall be my first gift to you, but not the last, I hope.'

'And not the first, surely? You are forgetting the lovely mare you sent me! So generous a gift, to forget so lightly, and one above all others that I am grateful for.'

'The mare?'

'Yes, that you sent me just after you left. I wrote to thank you, of course, after you sent me the news of your father's death!'

'Of course, the mare! You must think me quite about in the head! I have been so preoccupied, since my father's death, that it had quite slipped my mind. And you are pleased with her? I am delighted to hear it. Now, I think I have paid my respects to the old gentleman for long enough, don't you? We had better rejoin your brothers-in-law.'

Rather shyly she drew nearer to him, laying one hand on his chest and raising her face to his. His hesitation was infinitesimal, then he bent and touched his lips to her own. The touch was so light and fleeting that she had no time to respond, but the sight of his hazel eyes looking so warmly down into hers was enough to quell any disappointment she might feel.

'Come, my dear. We must tell your family our happy news! Will they be pleased, do you think?'

'Oh, undoubtedly! But very surprised. You must not mind if the rector breaks out into a prayer.'

'Will he be *that* pleased? I shall have to take care not to please him too often.' His light, bantering tone carried just the right nuance of cheerful amusement, but Mary had the feeling that his thoughts were elsewhere. But then, she thought, he must have a great deal on his mind.

Neither Caroline nor Georgina had felt equal to supporting this encounter with the young man who was to deprive them of their ancestral home, so it was to an audience of only two that Jason and Mary confided their secret. Sir Anthony, in his kindly way, at once expressed his pleasure, kissing Mary warmly and shaking Jason by the hand with his firm, sportsman's grip, and never thinking to ask how it was that the couple had so swiftly learned to love one another. The rector, frowning a little, was not so blinkered.

'It is a sudden start! Am I to take it, sir, that you have just this instant proposed to Mary, at your very first meeting? And she has accepted you, a stranger—though a cousin? And are you aware, sir, that she will have nothing, nothing at all, coming to her?'

'I am aware of it, sir.' Jason spoke with the modest look of one who had done something worthy of praise. 'Mary has told me so herself. That fact alone, Rector, would have been enough to have induced me to offer her such protection as a cousin might give—had I not already offered her my heart.'

'Very prettily spoken! Charming, indeed!' Sir Anthony was delighted with this fairy-tale ending. 'Love at first sight, I suppose?'

'Yes, sir. The very first time I set eyes on Mary—not knowing, then, that she was my cousin—I knew that she was the one woman in the world who could make me happy.'

Sir Anthony beamed, but the rector was looking dour.

'Am I to understand,' he asked in an offended tone, 'that you were acquainted with my sister before today? That you have, in fact, known one another for some time?'

'Of course! I had the pleasure of meeting my cousin at a ball given by the Fordcombes, when I was staying with friends in the neighbourhood some months ago.'

'And you have been carrying on this clandestine courtship since then? For I suppose I need hardly enquire whether my father-in-law was aware of it, Mary?'

'Yes, I have,' she answered boldly. 'And knowing my father's unreasonable prejudices as you do, Rector, I do not think it is anything to wonder at! Surely, as a man of God, you cannot object to the healing of so unnecessary a breach within the family?'

He huffed a little, but could find little to say beyond,

'Naturally, my dear child, nothing could be more of a Christian duty than to make peace between members of our family! Indeed, when poor Giles was taken from us so untimely, I suggested that very possibility to your father, but I am afraid that he was unwilling to listen to me. But what is proper in a man, my dear Mary, is not quite to be equated with what is proper, and dutiful, in a daughter.'

'Well, I am afraid that I was always a source of dissatisfaction to my father. But you must agree, Rector, that, left as I have been, such a marriage is both desirable and appropriate.'

He saw that she was not to be put down, and,

knowing the strength of her character, sighed, but said
no more, merely offering with ponderous goodwill to
perform the actual ceremony.

'Of course, it cannot take place for six months, at
the very least. Anything sooner would be most
improper. Most.'

Mary was glad to be able to agree with him, for,
irritating though she found the rector, she had no wish
for a falling out between them. Jason, she thought,
looked less than satisfied, and she felt a little glow of
pleasure in knowing that he was so eager to make her
his bride.

'In the meantime, my dear Mary, where are you to
live?' queried Sir Anthony. 'Surely you will come to
us, now? We will be going to London soon, for the
start of the season, and only think what fun you and
Georgie might have, choosing your bride clothes! And
I dare say Mr Hadfield will come and visit us, as often
as he can!'

Mary was about to accept this invitation, when Jason
stepped in.

'I confess that I had hoped, Sir Anthony, that Mary
would stay here, at least for the next month or two.
You are aware, of course, that my own father died not
more than two weeks before hers, and as his eldest son
I am naturally very occupied with his affairs, as well as
those of the Priory. Much of my time must be taken up
by the lawyers, and it will be impossible for me to
spend any time here, other than for occasional visits,
for a long while. A house like this needs a mistress,
you know, and who more fitted to care for it on my
behalf than its past and future one? She knows the
people, the routines, the neighbours. In her hands,
Hadfield Priory must be safe.'

'Stay here, alone? Most improper.' The rector was in his most contentious mood, and unable to see any of the advantages.

'I had thought of proposing my mother as a suitable companion,' countered Jason. 'She is, of course, much distressed by the loss of my father, and a visit to Hadfield would be of great benefit both to her health, and her spirits.'

'That would, of course, be perfectly proper,' conceded the rector. 'A new mother for one, a daughter for the other, uniting in their grief and in their joy. I could see no possible objection to such an arrangement.'

Sir Anthony, however, was indignant.

'Could you not? And what of Mary, who has just passed so many anxious weeks shut up in this dismal place—forgive me, my dear, but it is a little gloomy, you know!—with one sad old parent, and must now endure the same again? Does she not deserve a little gaiety, a little pleasure? Mrs Turvey does not need help in running the house, and the estate steward has always seemed perfectly competent.'

'Of course,' said Jason gracefully. 'I would not dream of depriving Mary of pleasure, merely to be of assistance to me.'

At this, Mary was driven to exclamation.

'As if I should not wish to be here! This is my home, and will be in the future. Where else should I be but here, and if Mrs Hadfield will give me her company I should be more than happy.' She sternly repressed a slight pang at the loss of some of the pleasures of London, and shopping with Georgina. 'Maybe, later on, we could both come to London? But truly, Anthony, though I do thank you for your kindness, I should not be able to go to parties or anything, so soon after Papa's death, and I should be no more than a nuisance to you and Georgie.'

Sir Anthony was far from happy, but there seemed to be little more that he could say. The rector plainly considered the whole matter to be satisfactorily settled, and, since Mary looked both pleased and determined, he gave in.

Hampton arrived with wine and cake, and after a quick interrogative glance at Jason Mary quietly told him of the engagement. His delight was plain to see, and there were actually tears in his eyes when he offered his congratulations, and begged leave to inform the rest of the staff.

'No question of any of them leaving *now*, it seems,' Jason remarked cheerfully when he had gone. 'I can see that you are a treasure beyond price, my dear.' Mary blushed at the compliment, and it was a pleasantly cheerful group that finally made its farewells, since Jason said that he must return to London almost at once.

After a nudge from Sir Anthony, the rector reluctantly agreed to withdraw so that the young couple might say goodbye in private. The stern glance that he fixed on them before going through the door was quite unnecessary, however, since the gentleman showed no sign of giving way to his baser passions, and their conversation was more practical than lover-like.

'I shall write to my mother at once, of course. I hope she will be able to join you here within a week.'

'That will be very nice. Naturally I will write to her, too. Will she like me, do you think?' Her voice was wistful, but he seemed not to notice her need of reassurance.

'I am sure she will like anyone I have chosen,' he said. 'And you will be pleased to have the company, I imagine.' Mary banished the thought that company was only a pleasure if it was congenial. Surely Jason's mother must be that, after all. 'And you will write to your—acquaintance?' he continued.

'My acquaintance? Oh, you mean the one who was finding out about my brother?'

'Yes, the very same. Let me know what he charges you; I will sent a draft on my bank.'

'And you will try to find out the truth yourself? I am afraid that my brother was under the influence of a. . . of a person of unpleasant character and habits. Oh, dear, it is very difficult. I wanted to find out this person's name, for I believe that he is, to a large extent, responsible for my brother's death. It is not a pleasant story.'

'Then do not soil your lips with it, or bother your head with such thoughts. I shall see to it all.'

'But how can you, if I have not told you what we have already learned?'

'My dear, I have a large circle of friends in London. I am known everywhere, I believe. You may be quite sure that I can discover whatever you need to know. The best thing you can do is to forget all about it.'

In all her life, Mary had invariably taken much of the responsibility for the running of her day-to-day affairs. Her father, of course, had housed her, clothed and fed her, given her pin-money, and required her services as the mistress of the house. While he had governed her movements, he had never shown any interest in her thoughts and feelings, or even appeared aware that she might have any. The choice of her friends, her books, and within certain bounds her

occupations, was hers alone. Her problems, when she
had any, she solved for herself, and it would never
have occurred to her to take them to him. It seemed
strange, just at first, to have someone not only able,
but willing, to take on these responsibilities. In time,
she was sure, she would come to appreciate it, but just
at first it did seem a tiny bit irksome.

'Thank you, Jason,' she said with tolerable
meekness.

'And you will write tonight?'

He was very insistent, and there seemed no reason
why she should not humour him.

'I shall write tonight,' she agreed, and they parted
amicably, with another of his graceful compliments and
an equally graceful embrace.

Her letter, when she wrote it, was carefully worded.

> My fiancé, Mr Hadfield, wishes you to cease your
> enquiries on my behalf, and I have promised to write
> to you accordingly.

She finished with thanks and good wishes, but
nowhere did she say that she, Mary, also wished him
to stop. Knowing, of course, that he would not do so
anyway.

CHAPTER ELEVEN

THE rest of the day passed in a glow of congratulations. If the rector was inclined to be shocked by Mary's behaviour in engaging herself to the son of her father's most hated rival, only his wife seemed to support him, and even she took the opportunity, when he was not by, of whispering her pleasure at this happy outcome. Georgina, of course, was almost wild with excitement, and loud in her lamentations that Mary was not to come to London with her.

'You are not saying no because you have no money to buy your bride clothes, are you?' she asked the next day, suddenly struck by this awful possibility. 'Because, if you are, you must not give it another thought, but let us give them to you as a wedding gift. No, really! You know Anthony would gladly have done much more than that, and I shall be quite offended if you refuse me now.'

'I am so lost to shame that I will not do so, for I own that my last quarter's allowance is all but gone! I shall not buy a great deal, however, for I may just as well buy things after I am married, when I suppose Jason will give me pin-money. I know he is generous—look at my lovely mare!—and he says he has plenty of money.'

'How fortunate. And strange, too, for I had always heard that they were not wealthy, but scarcely more than farmers.'

'That was probably Papa talking, and you know how

he always exaggerated. He could not bear to think that the other branch of the family might be successful, or happy, and so he determined that they were not.'

'Oh, dear, yes, poor Papa! Perhaps we had better not speak of him any more.'

'No, I would much rather talk of dear little Giles. I have not seen him yet this morning, but I hear that he is in fine form.' The baby, named with what Mary considered an excess of family feeling, had rendered the early part of the morning hideous with his yells.

'Yes, I am sorry. He does make such a noise, one can hardly call it crying, for he is not unhappy, only cross! He hates to be undressed and dressed, you see. I had him in here with me, but he is such an active little fellow, he is only happy if he is moving about, so I have wrapped him up and sent him outside. Nurse is walking him around the garden, as the day is so mild.'

'Yes, spring is definitely here. The daffodils are quite out in the orchard, and in the old field. I thought of riding out to see them, later on, and perhaps going on into the forest. I love it when the buds are about to break on the trees.'

'I do not care to ride just yet, but you should go. I am afraid you will go quite distracted if you have to spend the whole day with the rector and poor Caroline. Anthony has ridden off to look at the farms, and doesn't mean to return before nightfall. Thank heaven the rector's church duties require him to return tomorrow!'

'But if I go out you will be left to listen to him on your own. It seems hardly fair.'

'Ah, but I have an infallible method of getting rid of him. I have only to send for Nurse to bring little Giles, and he is out of the door the next instant!'

In the end Mary decided against riding, which the
rector seemed to consider indecorous so soon after the
funeral, but she was determined on having some exercise, so arrayed herself in a warm pelisse and a pair of
stout boots, and set off to see the daffodils on foot.
The field was not much more than a mile beyond the
immediate confines of the garden, and she strode
briskly out, not heeding or minding that the path was
very muddy, or that a few ominous clouds had gathered
to spoil the clear blue skies of the morning.

The air was honey-sweet with the smell of the poplars
in the hedgerow, knots of primroses decked the bank
beneath the vivid green of the new hawthorn leaves.
Mary, a child of the country, gathered and nibbled at
the hawthorn buds as she went, and promised herself
that she would bring back a posy of the primroses for
Georgina, as well as the armful of daffodils for which
she had brought a basket. Alone, like this, she could
admit that a shadow had lifted from her life, and that
her future shone ahead of her almost as brightly as the
spring day.

The daffodils grew thickly in one corner of the field.
Mary had always marvelled at them, for the place had
been ploughed up, to her certain knowledge, at least
twice. The second time had been by a whim of her
brother's, and she had pleaded with him not to have it
done, until she saw that he was all the more wishful to
destroy the place because she cared for it. Then she
feigned indifference, but it was too late, and the plough
had come, furrowing the soil and cutting up bulbs and
roots. The following year only a few poor clumps had
shown, but now, three years later, the leaves and
flowers were as thick as ever they had been, giving

Mary the promise that spite and malice could not, in the end, have their way.

The flowers were double, their hearts frilly and crisp, the outer petals thin, fine and pale. She was carefully picking buds, hunting for those that showed a good gleam of gold through the protective green that would burst open when put in water. Her gloves she had long since discarded, since there was no point in soaking them with sticky sap, and she was humming contentedly, sliding cold wet fingers down the satin-smooth stems to snap them crisply at the base. She thought herself alone, and when a shadow fell across her where she crouched in the grass she jumped, and would have fallen inelegantly backwards if he had not put a supporting hand on her arm, and held her up.

'Proserpina, I suppose?' He held out his own offering, a fistful of fully opened flowers picked rather short. 'Mine are prettier than yours.'

'Not tomorrow they won't be, but thank you. I hope you are not "gloomie Dis"?'

'Come to ravish you away to the underworld? Well, I will if you like; in fact it was rather on my mind. But perhaps I am Orpheus, though. It accords better with my other name, don't you think? Returning from the realms of death, and all that?' Lazarus smiled at her, and she felt herself responding with genuine pleasure.

'I thought you had gone straight back to London, but perhaps it is as well you did not. Why are you still here?'

'Because you have not given me an answer, of course.'

'An answer?' She continued to pick, and did not look up at him.

'Yes, to my proposal.'

'But. . .surely that was a joke? You know that I am engaged to my cousin.'

'Perhaps I thought that was a joke too?'

'If it is, not many people will laugh at it. I can assure you it is quite serious. He called yesterday, and I told him that I would have no money at all. And it made not a scrap of difference! In fact, we have told my family, and the servants, so you see it is all quite official.'

'Ah. He can afford to marry you, in spite of the great losses to the estate? I had not thought his family so rich.'

Mary was puzzled.

'Surely you do not know anything about them? He told me himself that he has a good deal of money, and will be able to restore things as they should be, so I suppose his father must have left him well off.'

'I had heard otherwise, but no matter. What about your answer?'

'But I have just told you, I am engaged to Jason Hadfield! What other answer is necessary?'

'You are quite sure about this, Mary? It is not just that he will inherit the Priory? No, don't take offence at my question! I put it badly. I know you are not mercenary, that you would not tie yourself to anyone merely for worldly gain. But this is your home, and you love it. It offers a strong temptation, the chance to stay here for ever, which might be enough to blind you to other things. Are you sure that you truly love him?'

His voice was unwontedly serious. Mary stood, idly moving the daffodils in her basket so that each stem lay neatly ranged side by side, separating those fat buds that still pointed guardsman-straight from those that had already turned to the horizontal, and laying these last carefully so that they all faced in the same direction. She hardly knew how to answer.

'I do. I am sure I do.' She could not put her feelings into words, describe the sensation that came over her when in Jason's presence, how her eyes were drawn irresistibly to him, how he seemed more brightly coloured, more shining than anyone else in the room, how her skin tingled at his nearness, and the breath caught in her throat. He had never kissed her roughly, with passion, as this man before her had done, but that also seemed right to her. It seemed all of a part with his finesse, his perfection of behaviour.

Lazarus, whose mother had called him John, studied her downbent profile and cursed himself, and fate, and his brother. She had loosened the strings of her bonnet and let it fall back, wanting the feel of soft spring air on head and neck, and the chestnut of her hair caught fire from the sun as it lay in a soft curve against the smooth cusp of cheek, and fell in coiling wisps against the white skin of her neck. Any trace of coquetry was completely absent as she gnawed at the fullness of her lower lip with two white teeth, and he knew that the little frown would be between her brows that always made him want to snatch her in his arms, and protect her from the world and its dragons.

Now he was riven with anguish for her, wanting desperately that she should be happy, and fearing that she would not. It was true that his brother had been no more than a child when he had known him, with the cruelty and selfishness of an over-indulged infancy. That it had been Jason who had revealed his love-affair and his subsequent plans to his father he had never really doubted, but he was sadly aware that even without such interference his father would soon have found some reason for anger with him. It was inevitable, he thought, that he and his father would have crossed swords sooner or later, and the final outcome would doubtless have been the same. Though saddened to think that his father was now beyond any hope of making peace with his eldest son, he did not really regret that he had left home, and would almost have been grateful to Jason for making it happen.

Where Mary was concerned, however, it was not so easy. He wanted to doubt that she really loved his brother, and he could not believe that Jason loved her, though he had been shaken by the news that he was still prepared not only to hold to a secret engagement, but to announce it publicly, knowing that the marriage would bring in no money. The Jason he had known would not have behaved thus. Nor had the family circumstances, in the past, been such as would permit Jason to marry a penniless girl, however much he might love her. His own mother's fortune, he knew, had been swallowed up by debts. Still, he himself had made his own fortune, and perhaps his brother had been able to do the same.

How easy it would be simply to declare himself! That would be a test indeed, for both of them. But if he did so, he must inevitably take on the rights and duties of primogeniture, and deny his brother the Priory. And she, of course, would be deprived also. For if Jason had stood by his engagement when he had learned that his betrothed would have no portion, how much more would she stand by hers, though it should take her away from her home?

Becoming aware of his scrutiny, she blushed, and turned away to crouch once again among the clumps of daffodils. She picked slowly, choosing each stem with exaggerated care. He waited long enough to show her that he would not pester her with more questions, and to let her embarrassment subside. When she spoke, it was in a friendly, conversational tone, and only one who knew every nuance of her voice could have detected, as he did, the reserve beneath it.

'Have you received my letter? I sent it to the inn, yesterday. I suppose that is where you have been staying?'

'Yes. That is another reason why I came to meet you. It grieves me to say it, but I am afraid I have no intention of leaving this investigation until I am in full possession of the facts.'

At once she abandoned her picking and rose to face him.

'But you must! You must stop, if I ask you. You only began it at my behest, after all. You do not have to continue now.'

'I am acting of my own free will,' he pointed out gently. 'I am not a servant, or an employee, that you may hire and dismiss at will.'

It was unfair, and he knew it.

'I never said you were! I am asking, not demanding!'

'Yes. I am sorry. But I have my reasons for wanting to find out, reasons that concern you, and others that do not. If you like, I will keep my findings to myself and not tell you, if they distress you.'

'It is not that! Only Jason has said that he will do it himself. He was. . .a little displeased to hear that I have asked somebody else.'

'Did you tell him who you had asked?' He kept his voice casual.

'How could I? I do not know your name! Lazarus is, after all, rather fanciful, and I could hardly say, merely, "thou shalt call his name John", as if he were Zacharias in the Temple. It was very foolish of me to ask you in the first place, I see that now. Of course, I did not know that I would be marrying him, then, but now I do not want to hurt his feelings, by letting him think I turned to another, and not to him.'

'Jealous, was he? So what did you tell him?'

'Well, I remembered that other person, who helped you. The gentleman, who finds things out. I said that I was paying him to help me, and he offered to pay his fee, so that he would not have to do it any more. And of course he would expect him to stop, because that kind of man would, wouldn't he?'

Effortlessly disentangling this confused speech, he smiled reassuringly.

'I quite understand, and I think you did exactly the right thing. After all, when you are married, you will be able to tell him the whole story, won't you?'

'Yes,' she replied dubiously. 'But you do see why you must stop?'

'I do. Don't worry about it any more.' She looked relieved, and did not notice that he had not, in fact, agreed to anything. That a newly betrothed man might be jealous of his bride's friendship with another was understandable, but he was not quite clear why Jason should be so very insistent that no one but himself should continue the investigation. Knowing Jason as he did, it gave him the best reason in the world to wish to carry on.

Now that her mind was relieved of that worry, Mary had time to remember something else that had bothered her.

'You said that you came to meet me. How did you know that I would be here?'

He grinned, no whit abashed.

'Aha, I have my sources, you know.'

'It is from Sarah, I suppose. She certainly knew I was intending to come here, for I spoke of it to her this morning. You have certainly charmed her, anyway! I do not know how she can be so indiscreet!'

'She is a woman of great intelligence, and since you have turned me down I shall probably console myself with marrying her instead.'

'An excellent idea,' she responded at once. 'I shall find you a little cottage. Or are you proposing to carry her off to the wilds of—where was it? Australia? If that is the case, I warn you I shall put a spoke in your wheel if I can. I could not bear to part with her.'

A puff of air blew across the field, sending a ripple of silver over the new grass and shivering the daffodils. As they talked the clouds to the west had built up, and now they were perceptibly moving to cover the sky. The breeze came again, more strongly, and Mary shivered, putting down her basket to lift her bonnet back on to her head.

'You must hurry back. It looks as though there is rain coming, and you have a fair distance to walk back. What a pity you came on foot, instead of on horseback. Is Juno well?'

'Juno? You mean Jewel, surely?'

'Of course. I had mistaken her name. She is not lame, is she? I expected you to ride.'

'My brother-in-law the rector thought it wrong, and I did not care to upset him, since he is already displeased with me for carrying on what he calls a clandestine courtship. But the mare is very well, and I hope to be riding soon. The rector goes home tomorrow.'

The sun was gone, and with it the illusion of arriving summer. Suddenly the air that had been fresh was now cold and damp. The clouds were boiling up, the wind gusting more strongly. He made up his mind.

'Wait, I have my own horse tethered near by. You will never reach home in time, and will be soaked to the skin.' Before Mary could protest he was gone, and she knew him well enough to know that any protest she might make would be ignored. She contented herself, therefore, with tying a large handkerchief, from the pocket of her pelisse, across the basket, to keep the daffodils in place. The primroses, she knew, must wait for another day.

She saw Lazarus lead his horse along the side of the hedge, and made her way down the field to the stile, beyond which was the narrow lane, more of a track than a road, by which she had come. By the time she reached him he was mounted, and bending to reach for her. Gripping the basket in one hand, and climbing on the topmost step of the stile, she allowed him to lift her up before him so that she was seated, not very comfortably, across the pommel of his saddle in front of him.

'I suppose you must bring the flowers with you? Very well, then. At least you are awake, this time.'

He kicked the horse to a trot, which was rather painful, since she had no way to rise to the movement, but could only cling round his waist with her free arm and hope that his firm grasp of her would keep her from slipping. After a few jolts the horse was cantering, and with the easier stride she slackened her grip though he, she noticed, did not. Plashy mud flew out from the horse's hoofs as they hurried along, and if it had not been so uncomfortable Mary would have found it rather exhilarating. Her bonnet, insecurely tied, had slipped back again, and she lifted her face to the rush of cold air and laughed, hearing and feeling that he was laughing too.

There was a little gate set in the wall of the park, which led into a small plantation and thence, by a gravel path, to the house. At this gate he reined in. Mary raised her eyebrows.

'You know your way around very well, sir! Not many people are aware of this gate.'

'No time to bandy words now, girl! You must run to the house!' In spite of his words he did not relax his hold round her waist, and though she would have let go her hold of him she was unable, without pushing at him, to bring her own arm back, so she left it where it was.

'This is one of the things I must not make a habit of, I suppose, like visiting you in your sitting-room! Still, third time pays for all, they say, so I shall not promise not to do it at least once more! Stay there; I'll lift you down.'

His arm was gone, and suddenly the cold was biting again, and she was shivering. He dismounted, took and laid aside her basket, then held up his hands to catch her as she slid inelegantly down into his receiving arms.

'Thank you,' she said, breathless. 'I suppose. . .now that my father is dead, there is nothing to prevent you from coming up to the house, is there?'

'But the new owner may object to me just as strongly. In fact, I am quite sure he would! Not just yet, and maybe not at all. But you may be sure that I shall see you again. Now, run!'

He opened the gate, turned her round with his hands on her shoulders, and sent her on her way with a gentle slap as if, she thought indignantly, she had been a

horse, or a small child. However, a few heavy drops of
rain were already falling, so she did not wait to upbraid
him, but snatched up her basket and ran towards the
house, reaching it just as the full cloudburst started.
Glancing back, there was nothing to be seen through
the driving rain, but she had a sudden complete certainty that he had followed her to the edge of the
plantation, and watched her safely home. Glowing with
the warmth of exertion, and perhaps another inner
warmth that she did not care to examine, she took off
her muddy boots and pelisse and ran upstairs in her
stockinged feet, greatly scandalising Caroline, who met
her on the stairs, and upbraided her as a hoyden. Mary
only laughed, and gave her a handful of daffodils.

It was no hardship to say goodbye to the rector and
her eldest sister the following day, and for almost a
week Mary and Georgina lived a carefree life. Sir
Anthony, an active man, was happy looking over his
father-in-law's coverts, and discussing new farming
methods with the tenants, so Mary and her sister were
left in full enjoyment of the baby and one another,
taking little strolling walks in the garden when the sun
shone, and discussing the latest fashions, a subject on
which Lady Tarrant could talk for hours. Jason did not
visit, but wrote a charming letter saying that he would
be bringing his mother down quite soon, and Mrs
Hadfield also wrote in reply to Mary's letter, expressing
herself delighted with her son's matrimonial plans, and
equally pleased to be coming to the Priory.

The Tarrants had intended to remain until her
arrival, but the news that the governess, in whose
charge the older children had been left, had slipped on
the stairs and broken her leg put Georgina into a fever
of anxiety. Convinced that without Miss Elstead's firm

hand her children would be running amok and putting
themselves into all kinds of danger, she packed in
haste, kissed her sister a hasty but affectionate goodbye, and was gone the following morning. The house
seemed empty after she had left, and Mary was pleased
when she heard from Jason that he and his mother
would be arriving the day after next.

Mary dressed with especial care that morning. She
would, naturally, have done so for her betrothed in
any case, but his mother, being a woman, might be
expected to have a still sharper and more critical eye
for the niceties of female adornment. Though her gown
was of necessity one from the previous year, it was still
in the first style of elegance, and of fine silk rather than
her usual white muslin. Promptly at eleven the carriage
drove up to the door, and Mary went out to meet her
future Mama as Jason stepped down and turned to
hand his companion down the steps. She stooped a
little, as was natural, to come through the carriage
door, but when she reached the ground and stood
straight Mary found herself looking down, for Jason's
mother was scarcely bigger than a child, with the
slender proportions and build of a young girl. The hair
beneath her decidedly fashionable bonnet was the same
gold as her son's, her eyes a clear, pale blue, very
widely opened and with dark lashes that Mary instantly
decided were artificially blackened.

She held out a hand, tiny in its kid glove.

'So this is Mary! You may kiss me, my dear, but
gently, for travelling always gives me the headache. I
am afraid I am ridiculously delicate!'

She tilted a porcelain cheek towards Mary, who bent
and brushed it carefully with her lips, feeling suddenly
like a lumbering giant against this doll-like creature. It

seemed that she had not been careful enough, for Mrs Hadfield closed her eyes for a moment with an air of exquisite anguish, then smiled bravely.

'How do you do, ma'am?' Mary began, moderating her voice almost to a whisper when she saw her guest flinch delicately. 'I am sorry you are unwell. Should you like to lie down? I will take you up directly, and Mrs Turvey will send you up some tea.'

'No tea, thank you. I find it too stimulating to my nerves, after a journey. My woman will make me up a tisane, and I dare say that if I lie down for an hour, in a darkened room, I might be able to sleep a little, and then I could bring myself to take a little dry toast. Jason, my dear, where is my travelling case?'

'Your maid has it, Mama.' His voice held a trace of impatience, and he greeted Mary absently. 'I regret that I shall not be able to stay beyond one night. The lawyers are damned exiguous, and I must leave in the morning.'

Mary, used as she was to hear her father and Giles, did not blink at his speech, though she was glad that the rector was not there to hear it. She began to express her disappointment, but was interrupted by the sweetly plaintive voice of her visitor.

'I am afraid that the air is a little cold out here. I am so susceptible to chills!'

Mary apologised, and took her diminutive guest indoors, where the staff had collected to greet their new master and his mother. Mrs Hadfield smiled wanly at them all, and drifted to the stairs with Mary in attendance. She commented favourably on the proportions of hall and staircase, ran a finger absently along the carved balustrade and gave a disapproving look at the resultant dust, and in her room kept both Mary and her maid busy hunting for her vinaigrette, her handkerchief, her pastilles, her tisane mixture, and her lavender drops, before commencing the dispiriting regime that she had outlined earlier, leaving Mary to creep from the room while the maid dabbed her brow and chafed her hands.

The sleep, the tisane, and the dry toast seemed to revive her, however, and when she came down to dinner later she was vivacious, complimenting Mary on her toilette, her cook, and her great good fortune in making so excellent a match. When they left Jason to his solitary wine-drinking, she treated Mary to a minute description of her late husband's last days, and the splendours of his funeral, delicately touching a lace-trimmed handkerchief to her eyes from time to time, blotting away any moisture before it had time to form, and avoiding her lashes. Her gown was of purple silk trimmed with quantities of black lace, and she wore some very fine amethysts. Mary, in her white tarlatan, began to feel dowdy as well as elephantine, and she was glad when the tea-tray arrived, and Jason rejoined them.

He left straight after breakfast the following day, long before his mother had left her room, and Mary was glad she had come down early, for that meal was their only chance of exchanging a few words in private. There was a subtle pleasure in pouring his coffee, and learning that he liked rolls, not toast or bread, and cut all the fat off his ham before eating it. He seemed preoccupied, and when he replied in monosyllables to her tentative attempts at conversation she decided that he was a man who preferred silence at his breakfast table. Since her father had been the same she was neither surprised nor distressed, but sipped her tea and took pleasure in watching him surreptitiously, admiring the perfection of his travelling clothes and the way that his hair, even at this hour, fell into place with careful naturalness.

'Did you dismiss that fellow?' His question was so abrupt that she jumped, and had to think what he was talking about.

'Dismiss. . .? Oh, yes, Jason. I told him that he need not continue.'

'And you paid him? How much?'

'Oh, nothing. That is, he did not require payment, I suppose because he had not finished the work.'

He frowned.

'Strange, if that's how he's paying his way. And you are quite sure that he is not still prying into your brother's affairs?'

Mary hid her misgivings.

'Yes, Jason. I certainly told him he must not carry on.' He seemed satisfied, and lapsed back into silence. Afterwards, as if recollecting himself, he began to express his sorrow at having to leave her.

'Yes, it is a shame. I am so looking forward to showing you the estate, and the house, and everything! But of course your business must be attended to. Still, we shall both be busy, I suppose, and the months of waiting will soon pass.'

'Yes. Though I should prefer. . .never mind. I must be gone. I shall hope to visit soon, and then. . .we shall see.' He kissed her brow and, when she offered them, her lips, and was gone.

Mary did her best to amuse Mrs Hadfield. She did not care for riding, but was fond of driving out in the carriage. Not, unfortunately, the open curricle, which she found too draughty, so Mary found herself spending afternoons shut in the stuffy coach, being driven very slowly round the countryside, without even the distraction of paying calls, since it was too soon for any but their nearest neighbours to have visited. As the days passed she learned that Jason's mother's fragile appearance concealed a will of iron, and that she was adept at gaining her own way with the use of sighs, little frowns, sweet little disclaimers and, if necessary, the big guns of headache, palpitations and moments of faintness.

It began to seem to Mary that she had exchanged one domestic tyrant for another, though she had to admit that so long as she was never disagreed with, or refused anything, her guest was perfectly cheerful, amiable and conversible. Nevertheless, she was pleased to learn that Mrs Hadfield was not intending to make her permanent home at the Priory.

'No, no, my dear. Nothing would please me more than to be here with you, to help you with your little duties and give you my company, but I fear that, in my delicate state of health, I would not be able to bear the discomforts of the country. The air in Sussex is not what I am used to—I fancy it is a trifle heavy—and now that I have found a doctor who so exactly understands my constitution I think that I could not do better than to make my home in Bath. I went several times, you know, with Mr Hadfield, in the hope that a course of hot baths might help him, and never have I felt so well!'

The joys of Bath—its shops, its assemblies, its concerts and the delightful company to be found there—occupied her conversation for some time, and Mary found it a useful distraction whenever other matters palled, and on the whole she thought that the visit could be counted a moderate success.

It was three weeks before Jason visited, though he wrote as regularly and delightfully as before. When he did come, it was without warning. Mary and Mrs Hadfield were sitting after dinner, Mary reading aloud and her companion knotting a fringe, when the sound of wheels on the drive made them look up in surprise. As Mary laid aside her book they heard Hampton's voice in the hall, and a few moments later Jason walked in, laughing at their amazed pleasure.

'Well, my dear Mary! And Mama, how do you do? I need not ask; I can see that you have been enjoying yourselves together, not heeding my absence!'

They both cried out at this, and Mary protested that she wanted nothing more than to be with him every day.

'In that case, I have something that will make you happy, I hope!' He patted his pocket. 'I am as weary as you, my love, of our enforced separation, and I have determined that it is no longer to be borne. I have a special licence in my pocket, and propose that we should be married at once. What do you have to say to that?'

CHAPTER TWELVE

MARY stood where she was, as unable to move as if she had been sheathed in ice.

'Married at once?' she heard herself repeating stupidly.

Mrs Hadfield had also risen, or rather jumped, to her feet, and now danced across the room, her little hands uplifted and the fine French lace on her cap fluttering like butterflies' wings in the breeze of her movement.

'How charming! How delightful! How romantic!' She darted between one and the other, bestowing little scented kisses as if they had been bonbons. 'It is so exciting, I declare I am quite about in my head! To think that I should live to see this happy day!' As far as Mary could tell, there was no reason why she should not have lived to see it even had it taken place six months or six years hence, but her mind was numb with shock.

'But. . .the arrangements?' Her lips felt dead and cold, and she had to frame the words carefully to be understood.

'Now, my dear daughter—I may call you that now, mayn't I?—you are surely not going to make a great fuss about a wedding gown, and bride clothes, and such like? Of course I know most girls like to have such things, but I had thought you above such mundane considerations. Besides, you have no money, you know, and once you are married you will be able to shop, and have everything nice!'

'My dear Mary looks beautiful to me in whatever she chooses to wear.' Jason was beside her, lifting her hand to his lips. Mary gazed at him, almost hypnotised. As she watched him he put his other hand inside his coat, and drew something out of his waistcoat pocket. It was a ring, a large ruby set with diamonds. It glowed against the white of his fingers like a hot ember, and when he slid it on her unresisting finger it was warm from the heat of his body.

'Oh, what a fortunate girl! Such a beautiful ruby! And so very big! You will be the envy of all, my dear Mary.'

The ring was heavy on her finger, the shank a little loose so that she had to crook her finger to keep it from sliding over her knuckle. The stone was cabochon cut, smooth and round, and reminded her rather horribly of a large drop of blood.

'I didn't mean clothes,' she said, feeling the need to explain herself more clearly. 'Of course I don't mind about them, though my brother and sister Tarrant were going to give them to me. I meant—oh, I don't know. The vicar. And telling our friends and family. That sort of thing.'

'My dear, you might trust me to have thought of all that. Impatient though I am to call you mine, I am not quite so lost to the proprieties as that! Merely, I had been thinking that even by waiting six months we will still only be able to have a quiet sort of wedding, since we have recently been bereaved not only of your father, but of your brother, and my father also. It must have been a sad, dismal sort of affair, the kind of thing that is quite repugnant to me. Not worthy of my Mary!

What I should have liked for you is a wedding that
would be talked of for years to come! Bonfires! Fire-
works! A feast for the village and the tenants! The
world and his wife here, the church overflowing! But
that would mean waiting so long, and neither of us
wants that, do we? So I thought something quite
sudden, private and dignified, with no guests but my
mother, who is with us anyway, and then we might slip
away to the Continent! Boney's posturings need not
bother us, I am sure, with the Duke taking command
of the allied forces, and all ready to take him on.
Brussels, they say, is very gay just now. We might go
there, what do you think? We may travel around for
six months or so, and when we come back we can plan
a proper celebration. Who knows but there might not
be another, still more auspicious event to celebrate in
a certain number of months from now!' He gave her a
burning look, which made Mary blush and drop her
eyes. He had never spoken to her in such warm terms
before, and she did not know how to respond to him.

'My dear! To visit the Continent! You could not then
complain of missing your bride clothes, for you might
buy them in Brussels, which is as good as to say Paris!
I do not know how you can stand there so calmly,
Mary!' Mrs Hadfield made a playful tap at Mary's hand
with her furled fan. It caught Mary across the knuckles
quite painfully.

'I am sorry. You must think me very stupid. It is just
that it is so sudden.'

'Missish, my dear? Or perhaps——' Jason's tone
dropped to one of earnest melancholy '—perhaps you
doubt your love for me? You cannot doubt mine for
you, for I believe I have given ample enough proof of
it, but maybe you cannot do without all the frills and

furbelows of a fashionable wedding? Does it mean so much to you, my dear Mary? If it is so, I shall naturally wait. God forbid that I should cause you a moment's pain.'

'Ah, cruel girl! You would not play with my poor boy's heart, would you, Mary?'

'No, no!' Mary turned from one to the other, the hazel eyes and the blue eyes of mother and son seeming, at that moment, equally sharp and yet, at the same time, equally reflective betraying nothing of the mind beneath. 'You are quite misunderstanding me! I doubt neither you, nor myself, and, as for clothes, I would be married in rags and not give it another thought! But you must be aware of the problems that would arise! Even with a special licence, the vicar will think it very strange, and I think he would be quite hurt to think that he was not able to read the banns for us! And then my sisters! They must be offended, to say the least, to feel that I did not want them to be with me. The neighbours, too! We should be universally vilified and in the country, you know, that will not do! I do not see how it may be done, without causing a scandal.'

'What a clever little girl she is!' exclaimed Mrs Hadfield, looking up at Mary who seemed in that moment to tower over her petite figure. 'She thinks of everything! I do wonder, Jason, whether she may not be right. Six months is not so very long, after all, and then you might have a very pretty wedding, and go abroad after that. Might it not be better?'

Her son gave her no more than a look, his face turned away from Mary, and Mrs Hadfield paled. When he spoke, however, his voice was gentle, smooth as silk.

'No, Mother. On the whole, I think it would not be.'

'Then, of course, there is no more to be said.' She fluttered to Mary's side, putting a cozening arm round her waist, and leaning against her like a confiding child. 'It must be for the best, my dear, if Jason thinks so.'

Jason Hadfield drew them both back towards the fire, and obliged them to sit.

'I have been too sudden, I perceive! In the impatience of my love, my longing to be with you, I have been too precipitate. But I am not blind to the problems you, with your quick mind, have perceived, my dear. Do not think that I wish to upset your sisters, or the neighbours among whom we shall live. Nor, of course, the good vicar. For that reason I propose that we go at once to London, and have the actual ceremony performed there. No one there will wonder at us, or be surprised. We could almost invite your sister Lady Tarrant, since she and Sir Anthony are in town, but I suppose we had better not, or we shall upset the rector and his wife. So, a quick, quiet, private ceremony, and then straight to Dover! I have our passages booked already!'

'Already? But when——?'

'We leave at first light tomorrow morning. You would not wish, I know, to stay at a common hotel, so we shall drive straight to the Church, and then set off for Dover. I have arranged for us to sleep on board, and we sail with the tide the following morning. In two days' time, we shall be in Belgium, as man and wife!'

It was all settled, all decided. Mary could think of nothing to say, no protest that she could make without bringing down the reproaches of Mrs Hadfield, or the more subtly expressed plaints of her betrothed, upon her head. She smiled, with stiff lips and cheeks that felt as though they might crack.

'It is hard to believe! Almost like an elopement, in fact!'

'Did I not say it was the most romantic thing I have ever heard? Quite a fairy-tale, you might say!' Mrs Hadfield, obviously, saw nothing improper in the proposal, and Mary thought that perhaps she was being old-fashioned, even a little priggish, in finding it shocking.

She turned back towards the tea-tray, automatically seeking a refuge in the safe normality of everyday forms.

'You dined on your way, I suppose? Will you have a cup of tea? There is plenty of hot water, and I can soon make some fresh for you.'

'Something a little stronger, perhaps?' He glanced towards the tantalus. Mrs Hadfield gave a little titter.

'My dear Mary, now that you are to be a married woman you must learn that a man who has just driven fifty miles should be offered something more stimulating than tea!'

'Of course. I beg your pardon.' Mary rose in a flurry, but Jason forestalled her and took out the decanter.

'Brandy, I think. Your father kept an excellent cellar, my dear. Smuggled, I suppose?'

'Probably. He never said.'

'I must find out his source, and see that we are kept as well supplied as he was. Will you join me in a glass, ladies?'

Mary, who disliked the taste of brandy, would have refused, but before she could do so Mrs Hadfield clapped her hands with childlike delight.

'Oh, yes! A toast! We must drink a toast to the bride and groom!'

Smiling, he turned back to the table and poured more, making a little ceremony of it and taking several moments, so that when he brought her a brimming glass it seemed easier to Mary to accept gracefully. His eyes gleamed as he raised his glass to her, and once again the familiar magic stole about her, so that she lifted the glass to her lips as if in a trance, and sipped.

It tasted so unpleasant that it seemed better to be rid of the drink as quickly as possible, as if it had been medicine, so she schooled her expression to one of happiness and drank as fast as she could without choking on the fumes. To her dismay, when she set the glass down, Jason refilled it almost at once, without giving her a chance to refuse. She made an incoherent protest, but he smiled.

'It will do you good,' he said. 'We have a tiring day tomorrow, and you must be sure to get a good night's sleep.' Gently and kindly he insisted that she must finish it, and by the time she had done so her head was buzzing, and when she rose to her feet they seemed unimaginably far away, so that she was not sure that she could control them.

'I must go upstairs,' she enunciated carefully with a tongue that felt as though it were made of shoe leather. 'I must tell Sarah to pack. Get things ready. For the morning.'

'There is no need for you to worry about anything,' he said soothingly, as to a fractious child. 'I have already had instructions sent up to your woman to pack for you. We need not take a great deal, in any case, for as my mother has pointed out we may buy newer and better in Brussels. Just travelling clothes, for a few days, will suffice. I have told her that we are going to London—no need to say more. As you yourself so wisely said, there is no point in setting the neighbourhood by its ears, by announcing our intentions. And servants gossip, you know! If one should hear of it, I dare say it would be all round Sussex by tomorrow!'

'But. . .I must take Sarah with me! I cannot go without my maid!'

Mary could hear the note of rising panic in her voice, so it was certain that Jason did too.

'My dearest girl, she shall come, if you like! I had thought to engage you a French maid, but after all a bride must be humoured! Only, I beg of you, say nothing to her of our plans, until we are on our way tomorrow!'

He led her to the foot of the stairs, and stood watching her as she made her slow way up. Reaching her room, she was not greatly surprised to find that Sarah was on her knees before a trunk, while gowns, pelisses, spencers and bonnets were laid round the room.

'Well, here's a start!' she exclaimed. 'Off to London in the morning, without a moment's warning! What maggot has he taken into his head, may I ask?'

Mary removed a pile of neatly folded chemises, and three pairs of kid gloves, and sat carefully in the chair she had emptied. Her head felt heavy, and it seemed unfair that she should have to deal with Sarah's crossness on top of everything else.

'It is Mr Hadfield's wish. Mr Hadfield who is, I should remind you, the owner of this house, and my future husband.' She leaned her head back and closed her eyes, but at once the room seemed to sway and whirl around her, so she opened them again. 'I should like to go to bed,' she enunciated with careful dignity.

Sarah, frowning suspiciously, laid aside the gown she was folding and came to her charge.

'Have you been drinking, Miss Mary?' she asked with incredulity. She could smell the brandy on her breath, but she still found it hard to believe.

Mary put up clammy hands and rubbed her forehead.

'I couldn't help it, Sarah,' she said. 'Didn't want to, but it was a toast, you see. You have to drink a toast, and then he gave me more, and I had to drink that. Celebrating. But I can't tell you the toast, not until tomorrow, and you're to come with me, come with us instead of a French maid.'

'So I should think! A French maid! The very idea!' Sarah clucked soothingly as she bent to undo the ribbons of Mary's soft kid evening slippers, then helped her to undress and get into bed. There was a moment when she thought the girl might be sick, but it passed, and she stayed by the bedside until the alcohol-laden breath was steady and slow, and she was sure that Mary was asleep. Her eyes rested, thoughtfully, on the ruby that gleamed balefully on Mary's finger, which even in sleep was bent to restrain it. Then, frowning, she abandoned the packing and went to sit for a while in the chair that Mary had cleared. Whatever her thoughts, they did not please her, and presently she left the room and was gone for half an hour on an errand that she would have denied, had anyone seen her. They did not, however, any more than they heard the sound of galloping hoofs as one of the grooms rode away down the drive. Listening to the retreating sound, and somewhat reassured, she finished the packing, and went to her own bed.

In the cold dark of early morning Mary dragged herself, shivering and miserable, from her bed. Her stomach was queasy, she had a vile taste in her mouth, and her temples throbbed so fiercely that she thought that the sound of them must be audible to others, like jungle drums. Sarah was brusquely sympathetic and gave her a disgusting mixture that she had concocted expressly, which made Mary feel well enough to enter into an argument about what she should wear. Since she was not permitted to say that she was on her way to her wedding she could give no satisfactory reason why she should wish to wear her best silk dress to sit in a coach and travel, but she won by a mixture of tenacity and, had she known it, her pallid looks and slightly haunted expression.

The coach was crowded, since Mrs Hadfield naturally wished to bring her own maid, and Jason wisely elected to ride alongside. Mary and her future mother-in-law sat side by side, rather silent, with the two equally silent servants facing them. There were hot bricks for their feet, and with warm wraps they were cosy enough, but the chill air, smelling of dust, of the worn leather of the seats, and of Mrs Hadfield's cologne-scented handkerchief, was charged with unspoken questions and words. Mary watched the familiar landmarks, faintly illuminated by a pallid dawn, recede, then fell into an uneasy slumber, in which she was once more in the schoolroom, and facing a barrage of questions to which she did not know the answer.

They halted only once, at Croydon, where a cup of coffee revived her spirits and settled her insides, which were more upset than usual by the motion of the carriage. Mrs Hadfield had been unwontedly silent since they had left the Priory, and for this Mary had been thankful. After Croydon Mary stayed awake, but her companion kept her eyes resolutely closed, only the occasional lifting of the scented handkerchief to her face betraying that she was not, in fact, asleep.

They went not to the London house where Mary had expected to make a halt, but to a hotel. It was a small, quiet, genteel place that Mary had never heard of, where they were greeted with the utmost deference, and shown up to a private sitting-room.

'Just a few minutes, my dear,' said Jason, smiling at them meaningfully, 'and then we must be off.'

Mary tried to return the smile, but her legs were cramped and her headache had returned with new violence, and the prospect of another journey dismayed her. All she longed for was to climb into a warmed bed and hide her face in a pillow. Mrs Hadfield, however, seemed to have a new energy, and bustled round, dismissing both the maids.

'There, you may go, we shall do very well without you! The girl will show you your rooms, and you may have a little rest. Have you my bandbox? Ah, good. We shall be going out in about an hour, with Mr Hadfield.'

'Shan't I stay with you, Miss Mary?' Sarah ignored the older woman, looking like a large sheep being harried by a small and yappy dog.

Mary found that she wanted to cling to Sarah, to beg her not to go away, not to leave her. She was tired, of course. She summoned what she hoped was a bright smile.

'No, Sarah. I shall be all right. I will call you if I need you.'

Mrs Hadfield removed Mary's bonnet with her own hands.

'Shall I send for some wine? You are rather pale, my dear. Of course, you must be feeling very excited.'

'Yes,' said Mary vaguely. 'But a little tired, and the motion of the carriage. . . I should prefer some tea, if you please.'

'I am sure Jason would wish you to take a glass of wine! It would make you feel much better, and you do not want to be fainting at the altar, do you?'

With some difficulty Mary managed to insist that she wanted only tea, and when it came she drank two cups, and felt a little better. The whole morning, however, had so unreal an air that she could scarcely tell how she felt. Not, certainly, like a bride on her wedding morning. Unless all brides felt like this? She called up an image of Jason's face, and like a lucky talisman it banished, for a while, the wreathing fogs of uncertainty and carried her back into the magic, fairy-tale world where he was her handsome prince.

Lost in this dream, she allowed Mrs Hadfield to fuss over her, sitting unresisting as a lay figure while her hair was taken down, brushed, and rearranged. Obediently she washed her face and hands, submitted to having her gown tweaked and shaken into more becoming folds, her cheeks pinched to bring some colour into them.

'A bonnet veil, I think,' said Mrs Hadfield. 'I have one in my bandbox, especially. You should go veiled to your bridal, my dear, and, besides, you would not want to have nasty, vulgar men staring at you, would you? The Church is near by, we are to walk there, and I should not care for you to experience any unpleasantness.'

Mary could not imagine why any nasty, vulgar man should wish to stare at her, for even in her best gown and Russian pelisse she was aware that she cut an

uninteresting figure. Nevertheless she submitted to
having the black lace arranged over her bonnet, finding
that the resultant restriction of her vision accorded well
with her own feeling of unreality.

A knock at the door heralded Jason's arrival.

'Are you quite ready, my dear?' he asked. He, too,
was in travelling clothes, and she felt a little pang of
disappointment, quickly suppressed. 'We must leave at
once. The parson will be waiting for us. It is not far.'

'Where is Sarah? I must ring for her.'

'Sarah? Who is Sarah?'

'My maid, of course! You said I must not tell her of
our plans, and I have not, but there can be no harm in
her knowing now.'

'Your maid! How very strange, my dear! You have
me to attend you!'

'Yes, and of course I am very grateful, Mrs Hadfield,
but Sarah has been with me for so long, she is almost
like a mother to me. I should so like her to be there.'

'A servant, as a wedding guest! Still, you may please
yourself, I suppose.'

Mary rang, but no Sarah came. Jason was growing
impatient, consulting his watch, his lips thinning. Mary
rang again, anxiously, and this time Mrs Hadfield's
maid came running to the summons, with the news that
Sarah was nowhere to be found.

'The young person went out, madam,' she said,
confining her lofty remarks to her mistress, 'as soon as
she had been dismissed. I thought it strange, but then
she is no more than a farmer's daughter, after all! I
supposed she had gone out to look at the sights.'

'Sarah has been to London many times!' Mary
snapped. 'She has no need to look at sights she has
seen time without number. Oh, where can she be?'

'Well, wherever she is, we cannot wait for her. As it is we are almost too late. After all, she does not know what she is missing! Ten to one she has run off to buy something, and doesn't realise how long she has been.'

Mary realised that to insist on waiting for her maid would do no more than annoy her companions; nevertheless she could not help glancing behind her several times as they walked briskly down the narrow back streets. It was not an area of London that she knew; indeed it was not the kind of place she would have expected to be married in. The houses were poor, leaning against one another like drunks in need of support, and the narrow streets were dirty, so that they were forced to pick their way. Jason had her on his right arm, and his mother on his left, and his long legs made no concessions to their shorter strides, so that Mary was forced to increase her pace and his mother, at times, was almost running.

The Church, when they reached it, was dark, dank and cheerless. Though doubtless very old, its age was conveyed by worn dips in the dirty flagstones, by the greenish tinge of the glass in the windows, which made the light within dim, and by the smell of mice and dust, rather than by ancient monuments, carvings, or the delicate tracery of vaulting. Their footsteps sounded loud in the gloomy hush, as if they were the first people to venture inside for several centuries. A bent, black-clad figure materialised from the shadows, so silently that Mary jumped.

'Mr Hadfield?' His voice was hoarse and shaking, nearly as unsteady as the bony hand that came out and received the shining coin that Jason slipped into it. 'Thank you, sir. Thank you. Just wait here. Vicar'll be just a moment, just a moment.'

He shuffled off in a miasma of dirty clothes and old, unwashed body. Mary felt her skin shiver, as if it had a life of its own.

'My dears, I am so happy, I am quite overcome!' Mrs Hadfield was hanging on her arm, peering up into her face. Through the gloom and the dismal shadow of her black veil Mary looked down at her, seeing a white, disembodied face that seemed to float free of its surrounding black clothes. Unable to speak, she looked at her in silence, and the older woman hurried on, seeking to distract her. 'Flowers! We should have had some flowers, Jason! At least a posy for the bride! I believe I saw a woman with a basket of violets, as we were on our way here. It was not far; I can run back for some! No, no, it is no trouble! Nothing is too much trouble, today!'

'It is too late for that now, Mother. The parson is coming, look. We must go up to the rail.'

'Yes, yes, never mind about the flowers. Afterwards, my dear. Afterwards you shall have flowers, but now . . .let me straighten your veil—it is slipping a little. There. . .and your pelisse. . .' She tweaked at Mary again, but Jason brushed her aside as if she had been an importunate insect.

'Not now, Mother. Come, Mary, my dear.' He took Mary's arm in a firm grip, which steadied her a little, and led her up the aisle. Something scuttled away from their approach, in the dirty darkness within the pews, but Mary scarcely noticed, though Mrs Hadfield drew aside her skirts with a squeak of dismay. Then they were at the altar rail, and it was a little lighter. The priest stood waiting for them, and at first Mary thought her own eyes were at fault, until she saw that he was swaying gently. He breathed out a powerful waft of spirits, and eyed them blearily with little, bloodshot eyes. His linen was decidedly grubby, and there were unidentifiable stains down the front of his waistcoat and coat.

'Dearly b'loved brethren,' he mumbled, 'the Scripture moveth us in sundry places——'

'Not that, you fool,' muttered Jason. 'The marriage service, not Matins.'

'Yes, yes, all right,' he replied testily. 'It was just habit, you know. Just habit. Now. Dearly b'loved we are gathered together here in the sight of God and in the face of this congregation. . .'

What am I doing? wondered Mary. What am I doing in this horrid old Church, with a drunken parson who cannot even remember what he is doing, and who gabbles out the words without any stop or sense? Seeking the comfort that she had always found before, in the sight of him, she lifted her eyes to Jason's face.

Aware of her movement, he looked down. His hand was still holding her arm, as if to support her, but now he released it and took her hand instead. His clasp was warm, but her fingers lay still and icy within his. He smiled at her, and Mary stared up at him, her eyes fixed on his face. With a shock that went through her like a bolt of lightning she realised that she felt nothing, nothing at all. What, before, had been enough to cast a glamour over her mind and her spirit was now just a face. A handsome face, to be sure, even beautiful, but bereft of its magic it was no more than eyes, nose, mouth, put together by the exact rules of beauty but moving her to no more than a faint pleasure, as at a well-executed picture. It was as though she had slept and dreamed, and was only now wakened to everyday reality.

'No,' she whispered. 'No. I can't do it.'

In front of them the parson, either unaware or simply not caring that they were paying him no attention at all, continued to drone out words that issued like a stream of dribble from his lips.

'Thirdly It was ordained for the mutual society help and comfort that the one ought to have——'

'You must. It is too late.' Jason's voice was cold and hard. He made no attempt to lower it, nor did its sound interrupt the droning words of the service. Society, help and comfort? thought Mary. This man is a stranger to me!

She saw, now, that she had allowed herself to be blinded by a handsome face, and perhaps also by the knowledge of this man's position as her father's heir. Not that she had coveted his future possessions, even after her brother's death, but that she had always believed that her father's dislike of his cousins was unreasonable. There was an insidious pleasure in the idea of reconciling the feud, of being, perhaps, a Juliet to his Romeo. And it had brought her to this, that she was marrying a man she did not love, because she did not know him, and whose love for her she now found suspect.

'No! You cannot make me do it, Jason!' She struggled to free her hand from his, but he gripped it.

'Can I not? You would be ruined, my dear Mary. You have come to London with me, after all, of your own free will. If you will not marry me, you shall be my mistress. It is all one to me.'

'You cannot do that! There are people! I can shout, or scream!'

'And have the truth about your brother known to all? Oh, yes, my dear cousin. Think what such a piece

of gossip would do to your family name! The saintly
rector, and dear Sir Anthony!'

'You could not! You would not!' Her voice was
rising, but the priest paid no attention, merely raising
his own monotone to be heard.

'. . .why they may not lawfully be joined together let
him now speak or else hereafter forever——'

'Stop! I say there is an impediment!'

The voice, from the back of the Church, rang out as
clear as a trumpet, so that the cobwebs in the rafters
seemed to shiver. Startled, Jason's grip loosened, and
Mary snatched her hand away from him, turning and
already running to the large figure that stood waiting,
outlined against the light streaming in through the
opened west door. Mrs Hadfield gave a little cry, but
Jason stood frozen as Mary ran straight into the other
arms that were already held out to receive her.

'. . .when the secrets of all hearts shall be disclosed
that if either of you know any impediment——'

'Shut up, you drunken old fool,' snarled Jason,
knocking the book from the parson's hand with a blow.
Like a musical box running down, the man continued
for a few more words, until he finally ground to a halt.

'. . .ye do now confess it. . . Confess it. . . The
lady's gone? Is there to be no marriage?'

'No marriage.' Again the voice came. 'Not to you,
at any rate, Brother.'

Mrs Hadfield gave one small scream, and collapsed
in the ungainly huddle of a genuine faint. Her son paid
her no attention, but stepped over her and down the
aisle.

'John? Damn it all, it can't be. You're dead!'

'Don't you wish I were?' said John Hadfield.

CHAPTER THIRTEEN

'IT IS a trick. I do not believe it.' Jason Hadfield
continued to walk towards them, lithe as a cat, his
hands poised but empty. John Hadfield tightened his
arms round Mary's trembling figure and turned her,
slowly, so that his own body was between her and his
brother. He did not take his eyes off the other, and
spoke without withdrawing that steady, watchful gaze.

'Sarah,' he said, pitching his voice to carry. Behind
him another person, obedient to his call, slipped
through the open door and waited. 'Shut the door, I
think. Is there a key?'

'Yes, sir. It's there, in the lock.' At the sound of her
maid's voice Mary lifted her head a little, and opened
her eyes.

'Sarah? Is that you? Oh, thank goodness. Where did
you go?'

'To fetch him, what else? Seeing as you hadn't the
sense to send for him yourself.' The rejoinder was tart:
Sarah had been frightened, badly frightened, for her
nurseling, and the relief of tension made her edgy. The
key scraped in the lock as she turned it, and at the
sound the ancient verger came hobbling from whatever
dark retreat he had hidden in.

''Ere! You can't do that!'

'Just see if I can't,' said Sarah, pulling the key from
its hole and placing it in John Hadfield's waiting hand.
He slipped it into his pocket.

'But the marriage? What of the marriage?' The

222

parson had retrieved his book, and was dithering by the altar rail. No one paid any heed to him, and his voice rose. 'My money! I've not been paid my money! I demand that I be paid!'

Incongruously, he was climbing over the rail, bending to grip it with shaking hands so that he might lift one foot after the other over without falling flat. He scuttled after Jason, tripping over the outstretched foot of Mrs Hadfield without giving her a second glance, and clutching at Jason's arm. The other shook him off without looking at him, so that the parson fell heavily against a pew and struck it with his head. The verger came to his assistance, and together they hurried away. A little trickle of blood stained the wispy hair where the pew edge had caught. Somewhere in the gloom a door opened and was slammed shut.

Jason ignored them as he walked, stopping when he was a few feet short of his brother. His eyes were flat, unreadable. Slowly the other man released his hold on Mary, and unwound the arms that clung to him. Without moving his gaze he pushed her gently away from him.

'Sarah! Take your mistress. Go to Sarah, my love.'

Mary was unwilling to leave the safety of that warm embrace, but she could see that he did not wish to be encumbered by her, so she moved obediently to one side, and felt the pull of familiar hands on her arm. She let Sarah pull her close, but her eyes were fixed on the two men, now within a few feet of each other. Seeing them together, now, Mary wondered why she had not realised that they were brothers. Though they could not have been more different in their colouring or in their dress, still there was something from their shared blood—the shape of the skull, of the ears, of their general physical appearance. She remembered, fleetingly, the day when she had seen Jason silhouetted against the window; she had seen it for a moment and discounted it.

Looking at the two men, she also wondered how she could have fancied herself in love with Jason. It was as if he had been some kind of sickness, some disease of the mind or the blood, of which she was now cured, so that she could look into her heart and perceive what had always been there, since their first meeting. Lazarus Smith or John Hadfield, it did not matter. He was her lover, and her friend.

'It is really you. I would never have believed it.' Jason spoke conversationally, even affably. 'When you no longer wrote, I felt sure you were dead.'

'You knew that I had written, then? From my father?' A considering look crossed Jason's face. 'No point in lying to me now. Whether he knew or not can make no difference now. And yet I find it hard to believe that he would not have replied, if only to tell me never to write again. You kept the letters from him?'

'Yes.' The admission of truth seemed to surprise him for a moment, then he gave a shrug. 'Yes, I thought it best. It would have made no difference, in any case. He would not have forgiven you lightly, you must know that. After all, he never cared for you, did he?'

'No. No more than I cared for him. But we owed a duty, each to the other. My father—our father—would not have shirked a duty.'

'Then you should both be grateful to me. He, because I saved him from the unpleasantness of having to deal with you, and you because you did not suffer the pain of his rejection.'

'I am. . .obliged.'

'So, you see, you would do very much better to take yourself off again. There is nothing for you here. Not a penny from my father, of course, and as for Hadfield—a great millstone of a house, cumbered by debts? You cannot wish for that.'

'And. . . Mary? You would give me her as well?'

'Willingly, so you take her abroad, and stay there. She has no money, of course, and her appearance is no more than passable, but then I suppose you have not been used to anything better, living as you must have been.'

Once, Mary would have been cut to the quick at hearing herself described by Jason in such terms, but now they passed her by, though she felt Sarah's stir of anger. Her only thought was for John's reaction. It was true that his hands curled slowly into fists, but his expression did not change. His eyes were steady, fixed on his brother.

'So, we are to leave you in possession? And in exchange?'

'In exchange, my dear brother, your Mary and the rest of them may be assured that no word of scandal concerning her brother will ever sully the family name.'

'Your name as well, surely?'

'Ah, but a different branch of the family, after all! No scandal attaches to me, do you see?'

John Hadfield did not turn his face to Mary as he spoke, and there was no emotion in his manner.

'Well, Mary, my dear, what do you say? Will you come with me? As my wife, of course. You said that you wanted a life of adventure.'

'I will go with you wherever you choose.' Her voice was low, but steady.

'And. . . Hadfield? You will never see it again, you know, if we accept my brother's offer.'

'I do not care. But you—what of you? You are the eldest son. The entail falls on you. Why should you give up this great inheritance, to protect my sisters? They can mean nothing to you. I cannot expect you to make so great a sacrifice and nor, I believe, would they.'

He was smiling, and for the first time Jason's assurance seemed to waver as he saw that smile.

'There need be no sacrifices, my darling. Neither yours, nor mine. Forgive me for testing you as I did, but I had to know what you really felt, what you really wanted. For myself, I have no need of great houses, of land and estates. But I will take my inheritance, not for my sake or yours, but because no man should gain by his own evil deeds. My brother shall never have Hadfield.'

Jason took one more step forward and stopped again, folding his arms.

'You speak very confidently, Johnnie. Big brother Johnnie, poor Johnnie, he never joined our games. Didn't care for them, did you, Johnnie?'

'No. Not your childish games, with their small torments, small tricks, small evils. Nor your adult games, Jason. You were always good at them, weren't you? Always encouraging others to play, leading them, teaching them. . . And you had an apt pupil, in Giles. Eager. Already part way along the road, perhaps.'

Mary bit her lip to keep back a wordless cry. Jason's face was ivory-white, now, gleaming in the dusky Church. A sheen of sweat stood on his brow. He licked his lips.

'You speak in riddles, Brother John.'

'You wish me to speak more plainly? Very well. I am talking about a man befriending a spoiled, impressionable boy. Encouraging him to gamble, more and more heavily, and lining his pockets with the boy's money and, later, his promises of money. Bad enough, you might think, even if the boy had not been his own cousin, and possessor of all that he coveted.'

'You can prove nothing.' Jason spoke through thinned lips, his voice sharp and high. 'It is not a crime to gamble. It is certainly not a crime to win. And if he were my cousin, what of it? He did not care. He could have stopped betting any time he wanted.'

'But he did not want, did he? He was already drugging himself, after all. I imagine he scarcely knew what he was doing, much of the time. But you did, Jason. You did.'

'You can accuse me of nothing. None of this is of any consequence. He was my friend, we gambled together, and I won. Such things happen every day of the week, every week of the year.'

'His friend?' John's voice was heavy and cold. It filled the musty dankness of the Church, coloured the dark shadows. Nearer the altar, there was stirring movement. Unnoticed by any of them, Mrs Hadfield pushed her shoulders from the icy stones of the ground, holding herself painfully on forearms, then on braced hands as she raised herself up. She gave little, whimpering moans that were as little regarded as the rustling of the mice among the hassocks.

'His friend?' repeated John. 'Say, rather, his seducer. His whore. His catamite. Brought by you to the gateway of hell, and then discarded. It was the betrayal of your love, your abandoning of him when he had no more to give, that led him to his death.' The words fell from his lips like stones. Mary found that she had lost the power to feel surprise. Even disgust and anger were lost in a kind of aching numbness.

'And yet. . .you would have married me?' The words came without her conscious volition. Jason spared a quick glance in her direction, no more.

'Why not?' His tone told her that he was answering her to give himself time, no more. 'I had to marry at some time, after all. And you would have brought me money, I then supposed. It was so easy, after all, to dazzle you—a little country mouse. Even easier than your brother. So romantic, was it not? Quite a modern Romeo and Juliet.'

So, after all, she had seen it, then. And it had seemed good to her, to heal the breach in the two sides of the family. She remembered the coldness of his caresses, and shuddered.

'You came to me. . .straight from him? From Giles?'

'He was becoming such a bore. Always demanding, always complaining. It was quite a relief to be done with him.'

'But then, when you learned I would have no money? Why not be done with me, also?'

'So I should have done. But then I had learned that someone was sniffing around, asking about the wretched Giles. If, by any mischance, there should be a scandal, then I would need you beside me. You, after all, were the only person who might have a claim against me. If there should be any trouble, where should my wife be, but at my side?'

'And afterwards? What was to become of me then? A wife, in name alone? While you pursued your other interests?'

'By no means. Although it is true that I prefer the

company of my own sex, I am not averse, upon occasion, to the more usual pleasures. And I should need an heir, of course: several sons, to make my position secure. A child a year, and you would have been well occupied at the Priory, and only too happy to see me leave for more sociable climes. You would not have been unhappy.'

'As a brood mare? I think I have deserved better than that. And Giles, too.'

'Words! Words! It is all words, no more! There is no proof!'

'But it is true, none the less.' John had stood silently by, while Mary questioned her erstwhile lover. Now his voice was tight with anger on her behalf.

'True. False. They are but words, also.'

'I can bring proof. You were less clever than you thought, Jason. There were several who saw you together, who would not hesitate to condemn you. And Giles himself. . .he left a letter, did he not? A letter to you? And sent on to you by the landlord's wife.' The hazel eyes flickered. 'You destroyed it, of course. But you knew Giles, surely. The would-be poet, the writer. Even at such a time, particularly at such a time, he would be bound to weigh every word, to polish each sentence. There would be earlier drafts, half-written attempts, a rough copy made before the fair copy was penned. You had not thought of that?'

Jason's lip lifted a little, like a dog's, showing the tips of his white teeth.

'You lie. You whoreson bastard, you lie!'

John put his hand, slowly, inside his coat, drawing out a sheet of paper. Jason put out a hand and snatched at it, casting his eyes swiftly down the few lines of writing it contained.

'Maudlin rubbish. My name is not on it. It could be to anyone.' He screwed the paper contemptuously into a ball, and flung it to one side. His arms returned to their folded position.

'Did you really think,' John's voice was almost amused, 'that it was the only piece? Or that I would carry them all with me, knowing you as I do now? There are plenty more and, yes, some of them have your name on them. Pieced together, they do not tell a story that you would like to be made known, I think. Nor, of course, would we. But which of us has more to lose?'

'So, why tell me all this? What do you want from me?'

'Surely that is obvious. Your absence. Now, at once, and never to return. You may go where you will, and I will even forgo any claim to the money you obtained from Giles. But, you may be very sure, I shall know where you are. I have many friends, in many countries, and your doings will be known.'

'And this is your revenge, I suppose? Because you were sent away, you will do the same to me?'

'It *was* at your doing? I cannot say that I care, any longer. Nor that it is any surprise to me, for I have always suspected it. No, this is merely to protect Mary, and the rest of her family.'

'And leave you to take the Priory?'

'I shall take it, though unwillingly, and do my utmost to break the entail, whatever it should cost. It has done damage enough.'

'I will not do it! You shall not make me! I do no man's bidding, least of all yours, Brother!'

So quickly that Mary scarcely had time to see the movement, his arms left their twined position and he sprang forward, both hands upraised. Such light as there was gleamed dully on the blade that had appeared, as if by magic, in his right hand. Mary's hands came up to cover her lips, and at the same moment she felt Sarah's arms come up to support and restrain her. John, who had faced death in many forms and in many countries, had not missed the warning flicker of his brother's eyes, and had leaped back, his fist coming out to grasp the striking hand as it came.

There was a patter of feet, and a waft of air that lifted the dust in eddies from the floor and stirred the cobwebs, as Mrs Hadfield ran forward. While the rest had talked, she had risen to her knees, and then to her feet. Unnoticed, she had listened to all that they said, her mouth twisting in tearless anguish as her son condemned himself by his own words. Now, still without speaking, she darted to his side and hung with her full weight on his other arm. She was not heavy and he was a strong man, but she took him by surprise. In an instinctive reaction against her pull, he jerked his arm to free it. Her strength was so little that she could not hold him, and the force of his movement carried his uplifted arm across his body, and then down to the rigid arm which John held stretched high and straight.

For a moment they stood, the three of them, frozen as in a tableau. Then Jason's left arm moved as of its own volition away from himself, with his mother still clutching it to her breast until he shook her off, as if she had been a puppy. The hand opened, its fingers splaying outward like the limbs of a starfish, and on the upturned palm a small penknife, scarcely longer or thicker than a bodkin, lay for a moment. The fingers curved away from it as if it were a red-hot ember, and then with a convulsive jerk the knife was sent clinking to the floor. Jason looked not at that hand, but at the other, which was still upheld by his brother, the cuff of shirt and sleeve falling away from the upraised wrist.

A thin cut, just beaded with starting blood and no greater than a line ruled with a pen, bisected the fleshy pad at the base of the thumb, and ran down to where the tendons of the wrist stood out taut. Jason gave a high, shrill whine, and the larger knife slipped from suddenly limp fingers. Frowning, John released his grip, though careful as he did so to kick the weapon out of reach, but his brother showed no sign of wishing to retrieve it. He brought the injured hand up to his face, staring at it, the breath whistling through wide-stretched nostrils. He shook his head, whimpering, then put the cut to his mouth and sucked, hard. The cords of his neck stood out like ropes of steel, his cheeks hollowed until the lines of his teeth could clearly be seen. He stopped, spat, then looked again at the mark.

A few more drops of blood flowed sluggishly from the cut, which looked swollen and angry. He stood hunched over it, then raised his head and cast about like a dog, ignoring the people who watched him with surprise and disquiet.

'The knife! Where is the knife? Give me the knife, damn you!' His voice rose to a breathless scream, he wheezed slightly as he breathed, and his left hand came up to wrench his neckcloth off. Mrs Hadfield, who had been staring up at him in incomprehension, crouched to the floor and scrabbled at it obediently, finding and retrieving the penknife. It had slipped into a crack between two of the stone slabs, and her hands in their fine kid gloves picked at it, until with a little exclamation of satisfaction the handle came up between her fingers.

'Here, dearest! Here you are!' She held it up to him, and he started back. His foot came up, hard, and kicked her hand so that she fell back with a cry, and the penknife flew through the air and landed, unseen, with a tiny, deadly clink. John's face showed the dawning of suspicion and horror.

'What have you done? For God's sake, Jason, what was it?' His brother ignored him. He was scrabbling at the cut, dragging at it and spitting out a froth of saliva and blood. His once handsome face was livid, the bones of the skull showing in highlights on the sweaty skin. His lips were slate-grey, drawn back from his teeth in a rictus that was the parody of a smile.

'What it it? Oh, what is happening?' Mrs Hadfield, nursing the hand he had kicked to her breast, crouched at her son's feet and stared up into his face. 'What is the matter with you, Jason? Surely it was only a scratch!'

With an exclamation John turned away, and ran to where the larger knife still lay. It took him a few moments to find it, then he snatched it up and straightened to hurry back. Jason turned on his mother, his eyes so wide that the whites could be seen gleaming round the irises.

'Poisoned, you stupid bitch! You have poisoned me!' He thrust the hand towards her, and she recoiled from it and from the ghastly face that he turned to her. John reached his brother's side, the knife in his hand, and Jason cowered from him with a shriek that ended in a fit of gasping coughs.

'Don't be a fool, man,' said John roughly, snatching Jason's right wrist in his hand and pulling his arm out straight. 'I'll do what I can. What in heaven's name did you have on that blade?'

The other was shaking now, his teeth rattling together, his legs buckling. Tears ran down his face, ignored. On his knees now, he pawed at John with his free hand, clutching at his coat, dragging at his sleeve.

'Cut it, cut it,' he snivelled. 'It burns like fire. I can't breathe. Oh, God, I never meant. . . I'm sorry, I'm sorry, I didn't know. . .oh, cut it out, cut it deep, it's . . .help me. . .'

'Come and hold him still.' John flung the order over his shoulder. Mary and Sarah started forward together. Jason's body was trembling so violently, now, that it took their combined strength to keep him still, while John drew the knife blade in a slashing cut along the line of the first. Mary watched in fascinated horror, unable to withdraw her eyes. Blood welled where the blade had gone, wobbled over, fell with a splash, but slowly, heavily.

'What are you doing? You are hurting him! Look how he bleeds! Jason! Jason! What are they doing to you?' Mrs Hadfield cried.

He ignored her, and so did the rest. Jason was on his knees now, supported by Sarah behind him, while Mary held the top of his arm and John the forearm, just above the wrist. Mary could feel the weight of it dragging at her hands, and she heard Sarah gasp with the effort of holding him.

'Let his arm down, Mary,' said John in a low voice. 'It will bleed better if it is lower.' She did so, not releasing her grip until the arm hung down by Jason's side. Another gout of blood splashed down, spattering the already dirty silk of her gown. The gown that would, she had thought, have been her wedding dress.

'Is it enough?' she whispered. 'Will he. . .?'

'I do not know,' John answered wearily. He looked down, becoming aware that he still held the bloody knife in his hand, and he laid it carefully by. 'I am afraid it was too late, if indeed it would ever had done any good. Whatever the poison, it is obviously quick, and deadly. I have seen such things before, in India, but I never thought to see them here, in London, in the hands of my own brother.'

'He meant it for you,' she said, answering his tone of voice rather than his words.

'Yes, and he would have done it, if his mother had not interfered. I should have realised something was wrong, when first he drew the knife. Let him down, Sarah. You cannot hold him like that.' Between them they eased the dying man to the ground. John pulled off his caped greatcoat, and spread it over the dank stones. Sarah, behind him, supported Jason's shoulders and head. Mrs Hadfield looked from one face to the other, uncomprehending still, seeking reassurance that could not be given.

'You did not think he would attack you?' Mary had been puzzling over his last remark.

'Yes, I feared that he would. I knew what an unwelcome shock my return would be to him, particularly when he discovered that I was in possession of information that would be enough to send him to gaol, if not hang him. No, I meant that he was fighting with his right hand. I had been away too long, and forgotten that he was left-handed. That, you see, was where the real weapon was.'

'It would have been you.' Mary looked at him, seeing him lying on the ground as his brother now lay.

'But it is not. His mother saved me, all unknowing.

And I fear that she has killed her son. Poor unhappy
woman, what use will my gratitude be to her? She has
never seen his faults; he has always been the epitome
of perfection to her.'

Mrs Hadfield ignored them. She had taken a handkerchief from her reticule, and was attempting to bind
up the wound that gaped on the hand that was now so
swollen. Jason's other hand came across his body to
clutch at her.

'Make it better, Mother,' he whined. 'Make it
better.'

'Yes, yes, my dear. The naughty man has hurt you,
and shall be punished. You will be better presently. It
is a nasty cut, but Mama will tie it up for you, and soon
the bleeding will stop.'

He seemed satisfied, and lay still. The breath rasped
in his throat, his chest heaved as he gulped for air. Mrs
Hadfield finished tying the handkerchief and sat back,
keeping the injured hand in both her own. Already the
white linen and lace were stained with blood.

'There!' she said brightly. His head was twisting from
side to side, his mouth grinning wide. A terrible
grunting sound issued from it and his lips moved, but
he seemed incapable of speech. 'Jason! Jason, what is
it? Speak to me, Jason!' Her voice rose shrill as a knife
on glass, and Mary gritted her teeth, then bent to put
her arms round the other woman.

'Mrs Hadfield! Madam, you should come away. Let
me take you away; you should not be seeing this.'

'Nor you, my dear,' added John in a low voice. But
Mrs Hadfield would not leave go of her son's hand.
She looked up at her stepson, and John wondered
whether she would attack him again as the author of
Jason's illness, but after a wordless moment she looked

down again, her face suddenly sagging and falling into
the lines of age.

'It was not true,' she said, but her looks and voice
belied her words. John, watching, prayed silently that
the end would be soon. The eyes of the man on the
ground were closed now, and he thought it likely that
consciousness had already fled. He hoped that it was
so.

As they watched, the body suddenly arched into
convulsion so that Sarah was unable to hold it, and
John moved swiftly round to add his own weight and
strength to hers. The limbs threshed, jerking violently
so that Mrs Hadfield, clinging desperately to the hand
she had been tending, was thrown from side to side,
the feet drumming on the floor. Then, as suddenly as it
had begun, the paroxysm ended and Jason lay still,
limp and flaccid, the only movement the slow, dragging
rise of his ribs as he sucked air into his lungs with as
much difficulty as if it had been treacle.

His eyes opened, and against all expectation there
was consciousness there. They moved from face to
face. There was neither hatred, nor fear, nor apology
in his look, only surprise and annoyance. He frowned
a little, then his chest lifted in one long, easy breath.
For a moment Mary almost thought that the crisis had
passed, and he would recover, so smoothly did the air
slip down his throat. His mouth and nostrils returned
to their usual shape, and there was even a little smile
on the well-shaped lips. Then, as she looked at him,
she realised that no second breath had followed, that
the eyes were fixed and blank, the chest motionless.
Sarah moved, so that he was lying on the ground, as
still as the stones around him. A long moan came from
Mrs Hadfield. For her, looking with the anxious eyes

of love, there was no moment of blindness. She fell forward across her son's body, sobbing and wailing. Mary would have lifted her up, but John stopped her, reaching across the body to take her arm in his hand.

'Leave her. It will do no harm now. Poor woman, she has lost the very centre of her existence.'

'What will become of her? Where will she go?'

'Not to Hadfield, at any rate. Do not forget she has her own home yet, and another son still living. She is not your responsibility. But you are mine, and you cannot stay here.'

'But. . . I cannot leave you here! What will happen? His death must be explained, somehow. You will not be blamed for it, will you?'

'I certainly hope not. You and Sarah may speak on my behalf, if necessary, but I hope it will not be. Never fear for me. I will sent for Mr Forester. I feel sure he will know what to do, and how this may best be resolved without scandal. It can be done, I think, but not while you are here! The presence of a young woman would be hard to keep quiet.'

'I suppose so, though I do not know how we are to escape with no scandal at all. That, however, seems so unimportant to me now that I do not really care.'

'But I do, for you, and for your family. Trust me, Mary, to know what is best.'

'Yes, I do. But what shall I do?'

'You must go home. Sarah will go with you. Your own carriage and coachman are at the inn, it is still early enough in the day. If you leave at once, you should be home by nightfall, or soon after. Listen! I hear footsteps. The drunken parson, most likely. It is better that he should not see you again. He is drunk enough to remember nothing of what passed earlier, and we must hope that the verger has put himself into the same state. Come, now, be off with you!'

She rose and stepped back, pulling the skirts of her pelisse round the blood-stained hem of her gown. Sarah rose and came to her, taking the key of the door that John Hadfield held out. Putting her arm round her mistress, she urged her to the door, and Mary put out her hand. He looked at both his own, which were blood-stained, and shook his head.

'Go home, my dear. This is no place for you. I shall come to you, as soon as I may.'

His eyes followed her as she went to the door, watching her as she stood for a moment, silhouetted against the daylight outside, looking back. He raised his hand in farewell, and she was gone.

CHAPTER FOURTEEN

OUTSIDE the Church, its door firmly closed behind her, Mary paused and looked about her. She was vaguely surprised to see that the world had not changed. The day was still grey and dank, the street dirty and crowded, the people were. . .people. Tall, short, thin, rich, poor, ragged, neat, old, young, healthy, or sick. People in all the thronging guises that a city street could offer, each with their hopes and fears, joys and worries, sins and virtues, each as liable as the other to sickness, to cold, to misfortune, or to death.

It came to her, as she stood unregarded by the passers-by, that this, in the end, was what had made Jason different from the rest. Not so much that he had been greedy, cruel, or depraved, for there were few people who had not at least the seeds of evil within them, but that to him other people had no reality. Titled or common, rich or poor made no difference to him. They were ciphers, puppets, tools to be used when necessary and then set aside.

She wondered whether, unconsciously, she had always known this, and it had been part of his attraction. The spell he had cast over others, the enchantment he had laid on those who had thought to love him, had been in part the feeling of being able to get beyond that beautiful shell which isolated him from the rest of the world. To find the centre of the labyrinth, the heart of the maze, to be the only one to unlock the inner door of his being. And the centre of the enchant-

ment was, of course, that it was empty. There was no
inner door, no heart, no centre to find that was not
purely and wholly concerned with himself.

It should have been a discovery to chill her soul, but
instead she felt, deep within her, a glow of relief, of
freedom. She looked into her heart, and found it not
echoing and bereft, but filled with love that had grown,
unsown and untended, until its roots had twined deeply
through her, and it stood poised in its springtime,
needing only the sun of one man's presence to burgeon
into blossom, and ripen into fruitfulness.

It seemed to her that she had stood there for half a
lifetime, but Sarah was still turning from closing the
door behind them, and now her touch on Mary's arm
brought her back with a start. Like one awaking from
a dream, she looked round, her smile bemused but so
full of joy that the servant, for all her worry, could do
nothing but smile back. Suddenly the drops of damp
that fringed every surface took fire, and shone like
diamonds. A gleam of sun had come through the cloud,
and even the beggar that crouched in the doorway
across the street raised his face to its faint warmth, and
stretched like a cat.

Without speaking, Sarah took her mistress's arm,
and hurried her down the street and back to the hotel.
A few swift words were all that was necessary, and in
the time it took to order a post-chaise, and have the
horses put to, they could be ready. Upstairs in the
chamber Mary submitted, like a child, to having her
blood-stained gown removed, and being washed and
dressed in fresh clothes that Sarah hastily pulled from
the still packed trunk.

The tea Sarah had ordered arrived while Mary was
still in her clean petticoats and a wrap, and sitting by

the fire as Sarah brushed out her hair. With no words
spoken, it had seemed to both of them that Mary must
be completely dressed afresh, as if she had just risen
from her bed. Sarah swiftly pinned the hair into a
simple chignon, then took a small bottle from her
pocket and measured some drops into a glass.

'Here, now, Miss Mary. I think you should take
this.'

'Oh, Sarah, I need no physic. I am perfectly well.'

Sarah, looking down at the pale face and the eyes
with pupils still dilated, thought that her mistress was
still under the effect of the terrible events of the
morning, and that once the first numbing of shock had
worn off she was liable to feel very ill indeed.

'I'm glad to hear that, my dear. But do take it, won't
you, just to please me?'

'If you ask like that, how can I refuse? I owe you
everything, Sarah. If it had not been for you, I might
have married him. . .' Her lips trembled, and her eyes
swam with sudden tears. The hand she put up for the
glass shook so that it rattled against her teeth until the
maid put her own warm hand over the cold one, and
steadied it.

'There, there, my dear. You're safe now. Safe with
your Sarah. There, now, there. That's better, then.'
The old familiar words of comfort dropped murmuring
from Sarah's lips as they had done for as long as Mary
could recall, as she held the sobbing girl in her arms
and let her weep out some of the pent-up terror and
relief. When the first paroxysm had subsided into slow,
shuddering sighs, she withdrew her arms with a brisk,
consoling pat, and proceeded to wipe Mary's face with
a cold sponge, and help her into her gown and a warm

travelling cloak, less fashionable than her pelisse but far more comfortable.

They were soon in the coach and rattling through the streets. With good horses and a certain amount of luck, Sarah thought they would be home before the end of the lengthening day. Mary's eyes were heavy, her head nodded with the motion of the coach. Two or three times she jerked awake again, but soon Sarah was able to prop her comfortably into the corner with cushions, the cloak wrapped warmly around her, and had the satisfaction of knowing that her sleeping draught would keep her charge asleep for most, if not all, of the journey.

They drove up to the Priory just as the last light of sunset shone, jade and primrose, in the western sky. The house was dark and silent, with only a glimmer of light to show that the servants had taken the opportunity of their master's absence to enjoy an evening in their hall. The sound of their approach had been heard, however, and Sarah had not long to wait before her knock at the door was answered by a startled Hampton.

'What is amiss? Have you returned alone, Sarah? Where is my mistress?'

'Miss Mary is in the chaise. Oh, Mr Hampton, such goings on as I have to tell you! But first I must get my young lady upstairs and into her bed. She's asleep now, and I hope she'll stay that way, poor dear.'

One of the footmen appeared, hurriedly pulling on his gloves and tugging at his waistcoat. Hampton told him to carry Miss Mary indoors—carefully, mind!— and sent a housemaid running to light the bedroom fire, and another to fetch a warming-pan with hot coals from the range. Mary never stirred as she was carried upstairs, nor while Sarah and Mrs Turvey undressed

her and put her into the warmed bed. Unwilling to
leave her alone, Sarah withdrew into the little sitting-
room, leaving the connecting doors ajar, and there
regaled Mrs Turvey and Hampton with a suitably
expurgated version of events, leaving out the scandalous nature of the relationship between Giles and Jason
Hadfield, but telling the rest and trusting to their own
loyalty and judgement how much they would pass on
to the rest of the servants.

'Well, whoever would have believed that handsome
young man could be so wicked?' Hampton was truly
shocked. He had enjoyed his minor role in what he saw
as a romantic love-affair, and was bitterly disillusioned
to learn that his young mistress had been so misled.
'And this other gentleman, you say, is the rightful heir?
The true Mr Hadfield?'

'Yes, and a better gentleman never breathed. Saved
her twice over, he did, our Miss Mary. Right from the
start, I took to him, and now they'll be wed, sure as
eggs is eggs, and in our own proper Church, too. None
of this running off to London and special licences this
time. Come Easter, or maybe Whitsuntide, our young
lady'll be a bride for all the world to see!'

Mary slept the night through, and the following day
did not wake until midday. Her body felt stiff and
bruised as if she had been on the rack, or beaten all
over, and every joint seemed to creak when she moved.
It was an effort to leave her bed, and she was not sorry
when Sarah forbade her to dress, and set her in a chair
by the fire to eat the food that Cook sent up. She knew
her household well enough, however, to gauge their
feelings. When she saw the logs on her hearth were
from the lime tree, scenting her room like incense; that
her tray held every delicacy, in or out of season, that

the kitchen could muster; and that the choicest blooms from the hothouse were bunched in profligate profusion on every available surface, her eyes filled again with the easy tears of an invalid.

A second night's sleep, however, restored her to her usual resilient state. This time she overruled her maid when Sarah tried to keep her from dressing, and insisted on going downstairs. In the empty house everything was so normal, the quiet ticking of the clock and the rustle of logs in grates almost the only sound, that she went from room to room, seeing the familiar furnishings with new eyes as a setting for her own future happiness. John Hadfield did not come to take possession of his house, however, and though she hovered all day within reach of the front windows, her ears straining for the sound of hoofs, no one came.

She went to bed early, as soon as she knew that she could no longer expect him that day, and as a result she woke before sunrise. For a few minutes she lay still, courting sleep with closed eyes, but they would not stay shut. Her whole body felt light and strong, and she could feel the blood coursing in her veins, and she could no longer stay in bed, or even indoors. Quietly she slipped from beneath the covers, and, stripping off her nightgown, washed with the cold water in her ewer, her bare flesh quivering at the icy touch of the cold sponge but rejoicing in the sensation. Tingling, she dressed in an old riding habit, and tied up her hair with a piece of ribbon. Boots in her hand, she crept down the back stairs and out to the door that would take her to the stable yard.

The empty stalls no longer saddened her; soon they would be full again. Jewel whickered a welcome as her mistress slipped into her stall, dropping her head into

Mary's outstretched hands to lip up the apple pieces she had brought her. By the time the first light of dawn was dimming the stars and greening the sky, Mary had saddled her up and led her out to the mounting block in the yard.

She rode down the drive, where the tree shadows were bottomless pools of inky black, and out of the gates, turning towards the paths that would take her to the heights of the forest. It was still dark beneath the trees, and she kept her horse to a walk, finding her way by instinct rather than by sight. Higher up the trees were fewer, and the ride went between patches of gorse and birch that were still grey in the dawn light. Now she could urge Jewel to a canter, her hoofs thudding softly on the short, rabbit-nibbled turf. If Mary heard the echo of hoofbeats behind her she did not turn, but rode on to where a group of Scotch pines stood crowning the mound of a small hill, dark against the sky.

As she reached them the sun came over the horizon, and in the instant their trunks came to life in a glow of gold and red, the bark gleaming like amber. She slowed the mare to a walk, and they climbed the sloping hillside until they stood among the trunks that surrounded them like the pillars of some ancient Byzantine church. A clamour of birdsong rose from the surrounding woodland, and the air was sweet with the smell of new grass crushed beneath the horse's feet.

Mary lifted up her head to watch the sky, as the last star paled and faded in the light of the new day. The man behind her did not speak, but she was so aware of his presence that he might as well have announced himself with a fanfare of trumpets. Jewel, feeling her inattention, dropped her head to snuff at the grass. The silence between them stretched to an eternity.

'Mary,' he said at last, very low. 'Mary.' She thought she had never liked her name so well. He had dismounted and looped his horse's reins over a branch; now he stood at her side, looking up at her. The warm light cast a glow over his face, making him look suddenly young and almost vulnerable. He held up his arms, and without a moment's hesitation she let herself slide down into them, making no attempt to dismount but trusting in him to catch her safely.

He held her to him, and without any false modesty she raised her face for his kisses, returning them with an ardour that shook him to the core. He felt healed of an old hurt that he had not even noticed until now, her love filling an echoing gap within him that must always have been there, so familiar as to be unperceived. When his hands caressed her, feeling the soft contours of her body through the covering of her clothes, she did not shrink from his touch with maiden coyness, but smiled with lips reddened by his kisses and heavy-lidded eyes with pupils black and dilated with pleasure. He buried his face in the warm hollow of neck and shoulder, breathing in the faint flower scent that hung about her, stilling his wandering hands and willing the clamour in his blood to subside.

'Mary,' he whispered again, his voice hoarse. 'Oh, Mary.'

'You say my name,' she murmured back to him, kissing the scar that crossed his cheek, 'yet I hardly know what to call you. I cannot, yet, think of you as John.'

'You may call me what you will, so long as you kiss me between words.'

'Lazarus, then. Oh, Lazarus, what if we had never met? What would have become of us then?'

He felt her shiver, and held her close. He had put on a heavy riding cloak, and now he wrapped its voluminous folds round them both and led her to where the trunk of a fallen tree made a convenient seat. The sun was higher now, its strengthening beams appreciably warm on their backs as they sat pressed together.

'No need to think of that. We did meet, and as soon as I set eyes on you I knew. . .'

'You knew! And I did not. Yet you did not speak. What a deal of time we have wasted.'

'How could I, when you as good as told me you were in love with someone else? And that someone else my brother!'

'But you knew him! You knew what he was like, and said nothing.'

'I knew what he had been like, as a child. But children grow, and change. When we were younger I was jealous of him, because he had all my father's love. As a man, absent for so many years, how could I be sure that the faults I remembered were not coloured by that jealousy? I did not really even know why I had returned to England, after so long a time. Certainly I had no intention of presenting myself to my family. I thought I would get news of them, and see that all was well, but I did not want to make myself known to them. All the more so when I heard that your brother was dead, and my father must inherit. To turn up then, like the proverbial bad penny, just in time to make my claim on the inheritance—unthinkable! Particularly if, in so doing, I must deprive you of your home. I knew you too well, even at the very first, to think that you would abandon your love, and ally yourself to me, merely to gain the Priory.'

'But you did not go away.'

'I knew that I should do so, but it was already too late. I could not rid myself of the hope that you might come to need me, perhaps even learn to love me!'

'I did, oh, I did! Only I did not realise it!'

'If I had found that my brother had grown up a good and an honest man, one who would love you as you deserve to be loved, then I would have gone at once, and never have crossed your path again. But from what I learned it seemed very clear that my letters had never reached my father, and that it had been Jason who intercepted them. I spoke to an old servant, who had known me as a child, and she confirmed what I had already suspected. Knowing that, I could not leave you to marry him. But I never expected to discover what I did!'

'About poor Giles? I never thought that I would come to pity him, but now I do. My father was much at fault, in giving way to his every whim. But I felt the fascination that Jason could exert. What I felt was not love—I see that now. But for my brother. . .'

'We shall never know, perhaps. So powerful an influence could have worked for good, if it had chosen, instead of for evil. For Giles's sake, and for what he tried to do to you, I regret nothing. My brother carried the seed of his own destruction within him, and he has rightly perished by his own hand. I could not have killed him, even then, but perhaps death was the kindest end for him.'

'Was it all planned, do you think? Giles, I mean, and me?'

'Possibly. Probably. Certainly he meant to have as

much money as he could get from Giles, even if he did not intend his death. Though I think he would have hoped for that, as well, and that is why he encouraged him to take the opium. Then, of course, you were a tempting prize. Not only for your riches, though he would have wanted that, but because with you as his wife his position would be unassailable. That is why, when he learned you would have no fortune, he still wished to rush you into marriage. He feared what you might learn of his influence over Giles, and what better way to protect himself than to bind you to him as his wife?'

'What will happen now? You will not be accused of his death, will you?'

He soothed her with a caress.

'No, no, I shall be quite safe. My friend Forester has seen to everything. He will be found to have died in a street brawl, and nobody will be greatly surprised.'

'And his mother? Will she agree to that?'

'Poor woman, she is quite broken by his death. In spite of everything he was, of all that she heard him admit with his own tongue, she is heartbroken. To protect his memory she will say nothing, and we must hope that the company of her younger son will comfort her, at last. I remember him as a quiet child, not overly intelligent, but with no malice in him. He will farm the acres my father left, and do it well, I believe.'

There was a little silence. Mary sat held close and warm in his arms, at peace as she had never been since Martha's death. At that moment she would have gone with him, without a second thought or a glance behind her, have joined her life to his and travelled to any quarter of the globe that he might choose, so long as he would love her. She could almost have wished that the earth might swallow up the Priory for ever, so that they might be free of it.

'I am afraid your legacy is not much to your taste,' she said. 'It brings you nothing but debts.'

'They do not matter. I told you before, I am a wealthy man, though I do not choose to display it. As for my inheritance, I cannot turn it down, but I meant what I said about the entail. The Priory shall be yours, your very own, as is only right, since you have cared for it all these years, and your own money has gone into helping it.'

'I do not want it. I would rather be free from all such responsibilities.'

'You say that now, but I do not think you will always feel this way. Where else, after all, should we raise our children? It shall be a home, now, for us and our family. The shadows of the past will be cast out. One need not travel the world, my dearest, to find adventure.'

She sighed.

'I suppose you are right. But we shall travel a little, shall we not?'

'Certainly, if you wish it! But the Priory will always be there for us. It is waiting for us now. Do you think they will send out search parties for you?'

'I hope not! How scandalised Sarah would be if she could see me now! And yet she always liked you. She was wiser than I, I think, and saw that you were the right one for me long before I knew it.'

'Intelligent woman. And to think that you offered her to me as my bride!'

'That offer is rescinded. You will have to make do with me.'

'Well, I hope I shall be able to make the best of it.'

He kissed her again, a lingering kiss that left her
breathless. There was a snuffling sound, and something
cool, hairy and damp tickled their two faces. The mare
Jewel, who neither of them had remembered to tether,
had abandoned her grass and come to find them.
Unheard on the soft, short grass, she had ambled up
and was standing right behind them, her head lowered
to breathe lovingly down their necks. Mary laughed, and
put up a hand to caress the velvet-soft nose and lip.

'That wretched creature!' exclaimed John Hadfield.
'I should never have sent her to you if I had known she
would be so good a chaperon. Worse than any dowa-
ger, I declare!'

'You sent her to me! But I thought. . .oh, of course!
And her name was Juno, was it not?'

'Yes, it was. I was afraid I had betrayed myself,
when I said that, but of course you merely thought I
had misheard her name.'

'I should have realised,' she said with remorse. 'And
he let me thank him for her, and never said a word! He
must have wondered where she had really come from!
How did you know I was in want of a horse?'

'I saw the stables, the first time I came to visit you,
and could see there was nothing there that was fit for
you to ride. I was worried about you—you looked so
pale—and thought it would do you good to ride.'

'How very good you were! And without a word of
thanks!'

'Well, you may thank me now, if you wish.'

She did so, but with the mare still breathing over her
and tickling her neck it was impossible not to laugh.
'She is quite right, you know! We must go back. Will
you come with me? It is time you saw your house, I
think.'

'I will come, but only for a few hours. I cannot stay there alone with you.'

'Then I shall do as I had wanted, and go to London with my sister Georgina. You, I think, should get to know the Priory. I think you will find a welcome there, particularly if you mean to put right some of my poor father's desperate little economies.'

'I shall do my best. I know little about the management of such a place.'

'Then do not be afraid to say so. No one will think any the worse of you, if you are honest, and they will be so pleased to teach you.'

They stood up, still clasped together beneath the cloak, knowing that they should return, but lingering, reluctant to leave this island of joy and go back to the everyday cares of the world. At last, however, he lifted her up into the saddle and then mounted his own horse. They rode side by side, but how different was this ride from the last they had taken together! Now their talk was in low, confidential murmurs, much interrupted by halts when they paused to kiss. When they reached the gates of the drive he did not, as before, turn back. Together they rode up to the front door, and as the watchful Hampton opened it for them John Hadfield lifted Mary once more down into his arms, and under the butler's astonished gaze proceeded to kiss her once again.

Flushed and laughing, Mary led him to the door.

'Here is your master, Hampton,' she said. 'He is come home at last.'

Together they walked in, and the house folded its walls around them, as a mother held her child in her arms.

SCANDAL IN THE SUN
Yvonne Purves

Ramona Dominic and Gerard Fontaine had every reason to dislike each other – his mother and her father had eloped together, creating the most enormous scandal. Having never set eyes on Gerard since she was twelve years old, Ramona was unsure what to make of his reappearance. She had enough troubles now that both her parents were dead, and she had discovered that her villa was to be sold from under her.

Gerard came with an offer of help, but it seemed two-edged – and Ramona knew she had no option but to accept...

Look out for the two intriguing

$\boxed{\text{MASQUERADE } Historical}$

Romances coming next month

A ROYAL SUMMER
Sally Blake

Although it was exciting to be invited by Lady Greville and
her son to London for the pageantry leading up to Queen
Victoria's Coronation, Rosalind Cranbourne knew that her
father hoped for a marriage proposal from Sir George
Greville.

So it was both a relief and a shock to discover on arrival that
Sir George had transferred his interest elsewhere; to make
amends Lady Greville blithely assumed Rosalind would
accept her nephew instead! That the good-looking and
charming Captain Felix Holden seemed to approve his aunt's
matchmaking infuriated Rosalind—until she discovered Felix
was at odds with his father. This led to a situation that
seemed impossible to resolve. . .

TANGLED REINS
Stephanie Laurens

Miss Dorothea Darent was quite content to remain on the
shelf, but for her younger sister's sake she was happy to have
a Season in town with their fashionable grandmother. The
Marquis of Hazelmere had other ideas. One look at
Dorothea's vibrant expressive face was enough, but their first
meeting had put him at a disadvantage.

Careful planning was required if he was to win her to wife,
but the Marquis found Dorothea couldn't be manipulated
quite so easily, once she understood what he was about!

Available in July